THE INH...

Praise for *The Hunted*

'An original and high-octane read, it makes *Deliverance* look like *Picnic at Hanging Rock*.' *The Times/Sunday Times* Crime Club

'This slice of outback noir is . . . at once exhilarating, gleefully vicious and totally, race-to-the-finish-line unputdownable.' *Observer*

'An audacious walk on the wildest side of outback noir . . . a vivid thriller.' *Sydney Morning Herald*

'A perfectly paced, thrilling read with an unrelenting sense of dread and menace . . . building suspense at every turn of the page. Crime and thriller readers will love this savage Rottweiler of a novel that will clamp its jaws around their throat and shake them to the end.' *Books+Publishing*

'Tough, violent, suspenseful and peopled with great characters, *The Hunted* could well be the Australian thriller of the year. This is Jack Reacher for adults.' *Canberra Weekly*

by the same author
The Hunted

THE INHERITANCE

GABRIEL BERGMOSER

faber

First published in the UK in 2021
by Faber & Faber Ltd
Bloomsbury House
74–77 Great Russell Street
London WC1B 3DA

First published in Australia in 2021
by HarperCollinsPublishers Australia Pty Limited
harpercollins.com.au

Printed and bound by CPI Group (UK), Croydon CR0 4YY

A CIP record for this book
is available from the British Library

ISBN 978–0–571–37236–2

2 4 6 8 10 9 7 5 3 1

PROLOGUE

She waited across the road from the house she grew up in until the lights went out and her breathing steadied enough for her to cross. She paused in the front yard, looked up at her father's window, then decided to go around the back.

The door was unlocked. The familiar smell of stale booze almost made her turn around. She didn't. She moved down the hall to the ajar door of his office. Stepping around overflowing boxes and strewn bottles, she bypassed the paper-piled desk, making for the corner of the room. She ran her fingers along where the stained carpet met the wall and when she found the loose part, she pulled.

Beneath the carpet was a safe, set into the floor. Her father had never seen her watching him from the doorway as he drunkenly jabbed at the numbers. It had taken her a long time to be confident of the code and even now, when she was sure, doubt slowed her hand. But she keyed it in anyway. No tell-tale beep or sudden alarm. The door clicked open.

The money, bulky in calico bags, was the only thing in there. She piled it all into her backpack, then ran her hand around the metal interior of the safe. Her heart was louder now, even more so than outside.

Then the voice, a scrape of whisky-soaked spite, came from behind her.

'This is how you ended up then.'

She stood slowly. Turned. Her father leaned in the doorway, little more than a spindly figure in the dark, raising the bottle to swig then wiping his mouth with the back of his hand. 'You won't find her.'

She asked him, trying to keep the tremor from her voice, where the maps were. She had seen him going over them. Seen him cross-referencing town names with what had to be witness reports, part of his never-ending hunt for the woman who walked out on them.

'You gonna take the money, too?' He was drunk, too drunk to be angry. He laughed and she would have hated him less if he tried to hit her. She pushed past him, catching his horrible, sour smell as she made for the stairs. He staggered after her, slipping and falling. 'You thieving, ungrateful bitch?'

She walked up the stairs.

She had just reached the top when his taunts stopped. She heard the footfalls, heavy and fast. She turned as he reached the landing, and his snarling face was in hers, hand around her throat. He slammed her against the wall, then let go.

'I should have killed you,' he said.

2

She felt it then. The swirling blaze that filled every inch of her, that hardened her voice as she looked him in the eye and said, 'Yeah. You should have.'

She shoved him. He yelled, swiped for her, then was falling. She heard the crack of the first impact, the crunch of bone bent in ways it wasn't supposed to, the tiny, almost shy pop as his neck broke and he hit the bottom of the stairs.

The fire was gone, as quickly as it had come. Some shrieking instinct told her to run to him, to call an ambulance. She ignored it.

She found an annotated map in a drawer next to his soiled bed. She put it in the bag with the money.

The walk down the stairs could have lasted years. With each step, his shattered form came closer and clearer, even in the dark. It was only when she reached the bottom that she realised he was still breathing, feeble and uneven. His flickering eyes found her.

As she passed him, he managed a word.

'*Maggie.*'

CHAPTER ONE

About a year later

Maggie sensed danger the moment the man walked through the door. Standing behind the dimly lit bar, polishing a pint glass, she glanced up and felt the slightest warning prickle across the back of her neck. It wasn't that he looked especially threatening; he was middle-aged in a dark blue suit without a tie and hair slicked back in an apparent attempt to hide how little there was of it. Maggie saw plenty of guys like him come through here every night. No, the danger lay in the way he held himself. He stood in the doorway, hands on hips, wide-set eyes lazily scanning the bar, a thick-lipped smile suggesting people should know who he was and be scared.

Maggie wasn't about to please him on either of those fronts. But she did watch as he swaggered in, running a finger along one of the empty tables and inspecting it for dust. He glanced at the four other customers tucked away in booths lit only by low blue lights, talking quietly over beers, the sound of their conversations dampened by the crawl of mournful country music. The bar wasn't a happening place. Which was precisely the reason Maggie liked it.

The man took his time strolling to the bar. He placed both hands on it and turned his smile to her.

She kept polishing the glass.

'Scotch.' He pointed one ringed finger to the top shelf behind the bar. 'The single malt. Two cubes of ice, thanks.'

'Eighteen dollars,' Maggie said.

The man didn't move or react. His smile stayed where it was.

Maggie finished polishing the glass and put it away. She picked up another one.

'Getting thirsty,' the man said.

'Eighteen dollars.'

'New?'

'Ish.'

'Andrew hasn't been doing his managerial duties then. I don't pay.'

The man waited, but she just kept polishing. His smile didn't waver but Maggie saw the hot rage in his eyes. She finished polishing, put the glass away and picked up another one.

'Maggie.'

Andrew stood behind her, watching the man in the suit. He almost always looked pale and worried, and his grey hair and light blue eyes made him appear washed out. Tonight, however, was different. There was genuine fear in his expression.

'It's alright,' he said. 'Just get the drink.'

Maggie didn't bother to look back at the man in the suit. Smug smile or grim satisfaction; it meant the same thing. *You've been put in your place, bitch.* Maggie poured the drink and slid it to him.

'Are you hungry, Len?' Andrew asked, the quake in his voice almost hidden by determined loudness. 'We've got some good cuts on tonight. Could do you a—'

'Might just have a couple of drinks while I wait,' Len said.

Maggie had returned to her polishing, but she was almost certain Len's eyes were still on her.

'Wait for what?' Andrew asked.

Maggie looked at Len. His eyes were cold and hard on Andrew. 'For us to chat, mate.'

Len made for an empty booth. Andrew's mouth hung slightly open as Len settled himself. Without acknowledging Maggie again, Andrew hurried out the back. Maggie watched after him until the glass was gleaming and she returned it to its usual spot.

'Any idea what that was about?' Evie sidled up next to her, spinning a tray between her hands. Evie was around Maggie's age with a mass of dark hair barely tamed by a scrunchie.

Maggie shrugged.

'When Andy saw that man he nearly ran for the door,' Evie went on. 'What do you reckon? Spurned lover? Grim reaper?'

'Something to do with taxes probably.' Maggie poured herself a glass of water from the tap. Movement in Len's booth snapped her eyes back to him. He was heading for the hall behind the bar where Andrew stood with a bad attempt at an easy smile on his face. Len nodded to Maggie as he and Andrew disappeared out the back.

'Mind watching the bar for a sec, Evie?' Maggie asked. 'I need to go to the bathroom.'

The staff toilet was tucked away in a dingy room where nobody had ever bothered to clean the cobwebs. Maggie shut and locked the door behind her then turned her attention to the small, barred window above the toilet that Evie regularly joked made her feel like she was in prison. Maggie flipped the toilet lid closed then climbed up onto it. The window was high and she doubted anybody would see her from outside, but she was still careful as she leaned close and listened.

'... told you, I need another couple of weeks,' Andrew was saying, fast and low. 'Jane's interstate for work and I can barely afford the babysitter—'

'Another couple of weeks wasn't the deal,' Len replied. 'You were supposed to have the lot to me last Monday.'

'You changed the price. That wasn't fair.'

'That's interest, mate. You already had an extension. It's my money you're spending to keep this shithole afloat.'

Silence for a moment. Maggie leaned a little closer.

'You gave me too much.' Andrew sounded on the verge of tears. 'I only wanted a couple of grand.'

'For fuck's sake, what's wrong with you? You're complaining about getting a better deal than you planned for? You needed the money to pay for advertising, and to hire those pretty girls out the front. A couple of grand would have cleaned the dust off the kitchen and not much else. And I don't remember you complaining when I offered more.'

'Please, Len,' Andrew said. 'We're friends, right?'

'Sure, mate. As good as family back in the day. But that makes it a bit worse. You can't just go around fucking over family.'

'I haven't made the money I thought I would. I haven't—'

'You've got customers in,' Len said. 'There's some money, so that's what I'll take. Tonight's earnings, and every night's until we're square. And *because* we're friends, I'll come in myself to make sure the transaction goes smoothly. I'll come in and be served drinks and at the end of the night, you'll hand me the cash and thank me for being so considerate. How does that sound?'

'It'll kill me.' Andrew sounded strangled, faint. 'I won't be able to pay the staff. I can't ... please, Len. Please, just two more weeks and—'

A gasp, then a brief, loud crunch that made Maggie jump and then a quickly stifled cry.

'Shut it,' Len said.

She heard whimpering, then a thud as Andrew hit the ground.

'Come see me at the end of the night.' Len sounded bored. 'Get one of the girls to set that for you. You don't want it healing dodgy.'

Maggie slid from the toilet, unlocked the door and moved swiftly back into the bar. She glanced at one of the mirrors behind the drinks shelf. She looked composed. And, as she'd taken care to ensure, unmemorable. No makeup, shoulder-length dark hair – the only thing about her that might stand out were the clothes that covered her whole body in the heat of Port Douglas, but even those clothes, jeans, boots and a black, loose-fitting collared shirt, were plain and forgettable.

Evie was no longer in the bar and a customer was waiting, tapping his finger impatiently. Maggie adopted an easy smile and walked over to him just as Len swaggered past her.

The rest of the night dragged on. Andrew appeared after about half an hour; his nose a swollen, angry red. Usually, he checked the state of the bar and pointed out things that needed tidying. Tonight, he barely even looked at Maggie. He seemed to just drift in and out, staying very clear of the corner where Len waited like a shadow.

Predictably, Andrew told her to leave early, before she'd even mopped the floors. Maggie didn't argue. She walked out with her hands in her pockets and even nodded to Len, who just watched her as she left.

Out on the street, she took a deep breath of the warm, salt-tinged air, then scanned the cars parked out the front. One caught her eye immediately: an oversized black, shiny thing with the silhouette of a driver in the front seat. A gangster, then. Maggie didn't look at the car for any longer than any passer-by would. She put her head down and walked.

She could hear the rumbling croaks of cane toads sheltering from the cars. Above her, the shadows of countless bats burst from a tree, filled the night and were gone. She didn't even jump anymore when that happened. The bar sat on a side street. It was close enough to the centre of the town to be accessible, but away from the noise of Port Douglas by night. Not that the noise was ever unbearable in this little tourist town, but tourists liked to get loud and drunk. They just seemed to prefer doing it away from Andrew's bar.

But she hadn't chosen Port Douglas for the noise or quiet. She'd chosen it because she had never lived anywhere warm before, and the change of scenery felt somehow symbolic. A new place for a new life. She had driven into town a couple of months back, worn out and sick of the road. Her plan had been to have a few drinks, crash in a motel and leave, but she needed the rest more than she'd realised. Or rather, she needed time to heal.

A few drinks in a quiet bar had led her to meet Andrew, who was looking for staff and, a little tipsy, Maggie had taken the opportunity she wasn't aware she was looking for. Within a week, she had a job and a little apartment in a resort town that somehow managed to toe the fine line between tacky and beautiful. The smells of the ocean and fruit were thick on the air, and the people wandering down the palm-tree-lined main stretch always seemed relaxed. The glass-fronted shops and stalls sagged with bathers and beads, and all-around easy smiles flashed in greeting at the cafés and pubs that had the look of having once been brightly coloured but now were slightly sun-bleached. Everything here was just that little bit spaced out, as though even the buildings were giving each other room to breathe.

Maggie had arrived in the middle of summer, when the air was heavy and humid and the rain would bucket down in relentless torrents. She would sit under cover watching and marvelling at how somewhere so hot could be so far from dry. But as the weeks crept past the rain had slowed, the heat became that little bit less oppressive and she found a whole new rhythm to a life that was, if not normal, then at least pleasantly unremarkable. She had been surprised by how quickly she found herself fitting in. Life here was lazy and unassuming, and nobody looked twice at another young woman working behind a bar.

Maggie's apartment was essentially a bedsit: one room and an adjacent bathroom with mouldy smell in the air. Her flat was tucked away behind a shop on the main street, accessible only by a narrow alley. It was the opposite of fancy, but Maggie liked the simplicity of it. Everything she owned could fit into one duffle bag if she needed to leave in a hurry.

She never hung around long in the apartment, and tonight was no different. Once inside she went to the tiny bar fridge and took out a couple of beers. She didn't bother to turn on the lights before she was back out the door and on the main street again. Some of the bars still had sound coming from inside, but it was muted and the town was largely empty. A weeknight.

Usually, she enjoyed her nightly stroll down the main street, but there was a twinge in her chest that she didn't like. That feeling tended to precede trouble of some sort, and Maggie's initial interest in staying here had been to avoid trouble. That was half the reason she'd chosen to work for a man who could be knocked over by a light breeze.

Sometimes the beach near the town still had a few drunk idiots staggering about, or else a couple enjoying a romantic, moonlit walk, but tonight, as Maggie preferred, it was empty. The white sand stretching away under the shadows of trees and the clear, starry sky met the dark, lapping, languid sea. It was as though a blanket had been draped over the place to keep it preserved until dawn, and with no nearby people, it was easy enough to assume the blanket was covering them as well, leaving Maggie the only person awake and aware.

She sat about halfway down the beach and cracked a beer. She took her first sip and waited for that familiar sense of tension unwinding, of another day having passed without being recognised or hunted.

It didn't come.

Whatever was happening with Andrew and the gangster had nothing to do with her. It shouldn't affect her life in any way. It was, simply put, none of her business. Andrew was obviously terrible with money and had appalling taste in friends. Those were his problems to deal with.

And yet.

Even thinking this way was dangerous. She had managed to stay ahead of any pursuit for a long time, and it had taken every second of that time to gain enough confidence to settle even in this limited way. Tenuous as it was, this peace was the definition of hard won and Maggie had no interest in doing anything that might upset it.

And yet.

Without Andrew, there would be no peace. He had offered her the fragile infrastructure she needed, even found her the apartment. She was under no illusions; it was no act of great charity, but it mattered to her. What she knew was this: Andrew was a good person, and beyond that, without his bar, she would lose what little she had.

Her first beer was finished. She ground the bottle into the sand until only the top half stuck out. She looked at it for several seconds, considering. The twinge in her chest had built into a low thrum, something electric and angry and simmering, something that she knew, left unchecked, would only keep building. She cracked the second beer.

What did she have?

She lurched awake in the early hours of the morning, then lay there, heart pounding, her eyes on the roof.

She got out of bed and walked to the door. Opening it a crack, she saw that the first touches of light had entered the sky, the clouds turning a vivid blue in the dark grey. She sat down on the front step and leaned against the doorframe. The air was still cool.

There was no point in trying to get back to sleep. There never was, after one of the dreams.

They varied but the effect was always the same. Whether it was the blood and the laughter and the guns, the tiny figure falling from the rock or the clawing hands slipping away into the dark, it didn't matter; they burned through her like acid and poisoned the whole day ahead.

This time it had been her parents. That had happened before. Fractured images of her father and his bottle, the blur of dark hair and maybe-smiles that was all she had left of her mother. In this dream she had been standing in a burning house – maybe her childhood home but it was hard to tell – as her father poured petrol on the flames and she begged him to stop but the fire didn't affect him and then through a window unobscured by smoke and flame, her mother watched and Maggie tried to reach her but then the fire built and Maggie was sinking into it but still her father stood clear and determined, pouring that petrol.

In life he had never operated with such determination. His bursts of violence had vanished as soon as they arrived; forgotten the moment he took another swig from that newly opened bottle. Sometimes he asked her where the bruises had come from.

Her mother, for all she knew, might as well have been lurking outside windows, watching and doing nothing to help. Maggie had been maybe five when her mother had slipped out of the door and never come back, escaping her husband's fists but leaving her daughter to them.

It had been about a year since the decision to try to find her, the decision that sent her father down the stairs and Maggie on the run. So far she had found only trouble. The last solid clue to her mother's whereabouts had led to a torn-up leg, more fuel for the nightmares and the vague hint that her mother had gone 'north'. So Maggie had done the same, except 'north' could mean just about anywhere and so she had ended up here, pouring drinks and keeping quiet and hoping that the dreams would stop.

For a while, they had. Then Len had walked into Andrew's bar.

There was a hint of sunrise over the buildings now, a slight touch of red in the pale blue. It was pretty. It looked, to Maggie, like spreading blood.

She went straight to her car that morning, skipping the run that had become a daily ritual once her leg had healed enough for exercise. Her car was parked on a residential street about a ten-minute walk from both her apartment and the bar in either direction.

The car was a station wagon, probably around twenty years old. It was a drab tan colour and fairly battered along either side. Its licence plate was the third Maggie had used – a fake, unregistered.

She didn't keep much in the car. An old, worn book of maps and a few other odds and ends: rocks and a couple of knives tucked under the front seat, rope, a crowbar and a chisel in the back along with some other spare licence plates. Maggie liked to be prepared. She locked up the car and leaned against it, thinking through the slowly formulating idea. It wasn't a great one. It couldn't be without her knowing more about Len. But she had tools at her disposal, and that was a start.

She had breakfast at a small café on the main street, watching families in garish Hawaiian shirts and bathers pass by, the occasional car moving in either direction towards the beach or the nearby city of Cairns.

Generally her days weren't spent doing much of any use. She'd bought a pile of books – nothing intellectual, pulpy crime novels – and would read them down by the marina, until the first splashes of sunset on the still water and the windows of the boats told her it was time to head to work. On the days when she didn't work, she might catch a bus to the Daintree rainforest, or even Cairns. A couple of weeks back, she'd got a boat to a small island about an hour off the coast. She'd walked around all of it, relaxed under trees in the centre and had only just caught the last boat back. Not because she'd lost track of time but because part of her genuinely considered staying. Stupid idea. But a nice one.

Much of the rest of her time was spent at the gym. At first it had been purely to gain her strength back, but she soon went beyond that; a new tautness to her already lean body that she liked. Preparation not for anything specific, but preparation all the same.

By the time she arrived at the bar that night, she was no clearer on her plan. Like a scattered jigsaw puzzle, she had a few pieces that fitted together reasonably well, but the key was gaining information. She didn't ask Andrew about his bandaged nose and pretended not to notice his eyes darting to the door every time he ventured out of his office. She got to work, kept her head down, laughed at Evie's snide comments about customers and didn't blink when Len entered, wearing the same suit and smile as the night before. She made his drink before he could try to talk to her and only looked at him when she was sure his back was to her.

She gave it about an hour before, clenching her teeth and moving gingerly, she told Evie she was feeling sick.

'Are you shitting me?' she exclaimed. 'You can't bail in the middle of service.'

'It's a quiet night,' Maggie said. 'You'll be fine.'

'Andy won't be happy,' Evie warned, which seemed to Maggie like projection, especially as Andrew barely reacted when Maggie told him she had to go home. He was leaning against the wall out the back, drawn and distracted. More to keep up appearances than anything, Maggie asked if something was wrong. He didn't react.

Maggie let herself out through the back door. In minutes she was around the front of the bar. The black car sat in the same place as it had the night before, the bulky figure of the driver again in the front seat, waiting. Len had to be paying well. That told her something. She glanced at her watch. Nine.

She walked fast to her car. She made it there in seven minutes, then got straight in and started the engine. She had dressed in black – dark jeans and a hoodie – just in case.

She drove slowly back towards the bar. She parked well down the road, where she was sure the driver wouldn't notice her. She could only see the vaguest dark outline of the car, but it was a clear night and she would know when it left. She leaned back in her seat and waited.

It was just after eleven when Len strode out of the bar and got into the back seat. The car pulled away from the curb. Maggie started the engine and followed at a distance. Len's car remained a dark shape ahead, and that was how it would have to stay for now. Despite the temptation, she didn't turn off her headlights. Doing so would draw more attention than just an old car trundling along the road.

They drove for about half an hour, away from the tourist-courting centre of Port Douglas, heading towards Cairns. They took one turn then another, down narrower streets fringed with towering fences behind which sat squat, shadowy warehouses. Maggie didn't know this area. Probably for a good reason.

Because of the distance between them, it took Maggie a moment to realise that Len's car had stopped. She killed the lights and pulled over. Her heart picked up. She was rusty. If they had noticed that they were being followed, she had just confirmed any suspicions.

Maybe there was movement around the car, but it was hard to tell. After a few minutes, it became obvious that nobody was approaching her. Maggie gave it another ten, then got out, a knife in her belt and a rock in her pocket. She kept low and watched. There was no movement, but a dim light came from near Len's car.

Keeping to the shadows of trees on the footpath, she moved forward, eyes sweeping the road for any sign of somebody watching. There was nothing. Her heart was getting louder and faster, but she ignored it. She couldn't control a physical reaction, so there was no point in letting it affect her any more than it absolutely had to.

About a hundred metres from Len's car, she stopped. It was parked near an open gate in a fence, through which a sloping driveway led down to a large warehouse. Inside the car she could see the driver, alone again. Len must have gone inside. The only light came from the warehouse.

She watched and considered for a moment, looking between the car, the driveway and the warehouse.

She hurried back to her station wagon. She slung the loop of rope over her shoulder, grabbed the crowbar, then moved back towards the warehouse. She wasn't sure how much time she had. She wasn't even sure if she should be doing this now. The only thing she knew was that this might not be Len's destination every night, and she could do something with what she had here.

A couple of vans were parked about five metres away from Len's car on the opposite side of the road. She ducked behind one and tried to steady her breathing. She looked towards the warehouse again. Light shone from the high windows and under the door.

She took the rock from her pocket, aimed and threw. It hit the back of Len's car with a clatter that made her wince.

The door opened and the driver, a gun in his hand, stepped out into the night. He was a thickset, towering man. A bodyguard too, then. He looked around, eyes narrowed, then walked towards the back of the car. He came around to the side Maggie was on. He spotted the rock and knelt.

Swiftly and silently, Maggie ran across the road then hefted the crowbar and brought it down hard on the back of his head. He staggered, raised a hand, started to yell, then she hit him again and again until he was down. Maggie ignored the blood as she looked towards the warehouse. No sign of movement. The driver remained still on the ground. He seemed to be breathing.

She walked down towards the door of the warehouse. There were no guards outside; evidently the driver was supposed to suffice. Maggie paused near the door. A low buzz of voices, but nothing discernible. She moved closer then put her ear to the metal.

'... anyway, mate, once the shipment comes in, we'll be as good as gold. We've got people wanting product all over the place.'

'You hear from Melbourne?'

'Melbourne is *gagging* for it, Len. Ever since the Ford shit, they've been looking for an edge and they know this could be it.'

Maggie darted back up the slope to the car. The driver remained still on the road; she dragged him onto the footpath, trying not to grunt with exertion. She searched his pocket and found a set of keys. She glanced towards the warehouse again. Nobody was leaving yet.

She got into the car and started the engine. She looked out the window. No movement. She reversed the car, then swung it around and rolled forwards onto the driveway. She applied the handbrake and killed the engine. She stepped out. The wind lifted slightly. The warehouse remained still.

She unscrewed the fuel cap and took the rope from her shoulder. She cut a length of it, then, resisting the urge to check the warehouse again, fed it into the tank. She kept pushing until she held only a couple of centimetres. She pulled it out again. It dripped with petrol.

Letting the rope hang from the tank, she returned to the front of the car and pushed down the handbrake. The car didn't shift. She took a lighter from her pocket and moved back to the rear. She pushed.

It took a moment before it started to move. As soon as it did, she flicked the lighter on and touched it to the rope.

Flame danced and Maggie ran. She ran as the car rolled forward, as the fire raced up the rope, as she heard the collision, the yells, then the familiar rush of ignition and the surge of heat as the car went up in flames and the explosion filled the night.

CHAPTER TWO

For the first few days after, Maggie bought the newspapers and scoured them from top to bottom. There was nothing about a destroyed warehouse or a dead gangster. She wasn't sure if that was a good thing. The first night after had seen Andrew watching the door nervously. Maggie, her head down over her work, had kept her eye on the entrance as well, but there was no sign of Len. Whether this was because he was dead, incapacitated or trying to work out who had attacked him, Maggie didn't much care. Although her preference leaned towards him being dead.

As the week went on and the bar stayed quiet and calm, Maggie felt the undercurrent of tension slowly start to unwind. On the fifth night, sitting on the beach as the cool wind lifted her hair, sipping her beer, she finally felt like she could relax again.

The sixth was Evie's night off, which always meant she would turn up at the bar with a gang of locals – surfers and casual workers, all around Maggie's age, bleached blond and speaking in relaxed drawls. That was, when they weren't laughing at every apparently outrageous joke they threw at each other. Andrew's bar was hardly their usual scene but Evie got free drinks and could usually swing discounts for the others. They gathered around a couple of tables, buying jugs and telling stories and all the while Maggie went about her work and tried not to pay them much attention.

One of Evie's surfer friends, Mike, physically almost identical to the rest but a little quieter, had taken to wandering over to the bar in between rounds to order drinks despite the fact that he'd barely touched the ones he'd left at the table. He was good-looking in that stereotypical beachy way, choosing to wear close-fitting shirts that showed off his muscles. His shaggy, salt-thick blond hair sat back from his tanned face and he pretended not to notice Maggie until she neared him. Then he smiled. It was, Maggie conceded to herself, a nice smile.

'Thought I might get a rum and dry,' he said.

'To mix with the beer? You're brave.'

'Closer to stupid, but I'll take it.'

At least it wasn't Scotch. Maggie poured him the drink. Mike sipped it but didn't return to the table. Maggie could have played coy and pretended to work. Instead, she waited.

'What time do you finish?' Mike asked finally.

Maggie shrugged.

'There's a party, a little later on,' he said. 'Down at Jamie's beach house.'

'Jamie has a beach house?'

'Jamie's parents do, and they're in Ibiza.'

'Port Douglas not tropical enough?'

'Guess not.' Mike drank. 'So.'

'So.'

'You want to come?'

'Did I miss an invitation?'

'You're invited.'

'Speaking for Jamie?'

'To be honest, for me.'

He was forward. Relatively. Maggie liked that. He didn't ask again but just watched her with that slight smile – confident but not cocky. If she told him she wasn't interested, he would take it with ease and wander back to his friends and that would be it.

'Alright,' Maggie said. 'I'll come.'

The smile broke into a grin. Mike finished his rum and returned to the table. Maggie watched after him. There was a tingle of something in her stomach, something daring and unfamiliar.

Apart from Evie's crew, the bar was quiet and before long Andrew, a slight slur to his voice, called for a free round for everyone and told Maggie to knock off. His good mood had lasted, then. Maggie sat next to Evie and drank her beer. Mike was glancing at her from across the table. She didn't look at him. She gave brief, polite answers to the questions from Evie's friends and then somebody said they should head to the party and together they moved out into the night. Maggie hung slightly back from the others. Usually, she would go home around now. But then what? She'd lie in that narrow single bed staring at the peeling roof until she fell into a sleep she'd likely be thrown from by nightmares.

The beach house looked like some rich person's idea of easy seaside living realised by an overpaid interior decorator. There were light-blue curtains and lots of wicker with big windows looking out over the dark mass of the ocean and the sand in front of it. Already the air was thick with music and talking. It didn't take Maggie long to decide she'd be happier out the front. There were people out here as well, loud and boisterous, but there was fresh air and the sea as well. She leaned against the balcony and watched it as she drank.

'Bit much?' Mike asked as he joined her.

She sipped her beer. He asked if she wanted to go for a walk.

She didn't reply. Just straightened up and moved for the stairs that led down onto the sand.

Together they wandered up the beach, away from the pulsing music. Other houses sat up from the sand, mostly dark and quiet. The beach usually felt peaceful to Maggie, but not tonight. She didn't begrudge Evie's friends their party. She just wished she could enjoy it as much as them.

'You're a bit of a mystery, you know,' Mike said.

'That so?'

'Evie reckons you just like to cultivate the taciturn stranger thing,' Mike said. 'But that doesn't seem right.'

Maggie was impressed that he knew the word 'taciturn'.

'You can't be much older than us,' Mike said. 'Probably the same age, right? Early twenties? But Evie says you live alone and you don't talk to anyone. You work and sometimes you hang out in town and that's it.'

There was a question underscoring everything Mike said, of course. He was throwing out the bait because he was too curious not to, but he didn't expect a bite and he was okay with it.

Maggie slowed. She looked out at the water.

Mike didn't say anything but he stopped when she did. He was deliberately not looking at her. But he wanted to. And, Maggie realised, she wanted him to.

He moved a little closer. She turned her head. Caught his eyes. He was nervous.

It would be so easy, really. The right reply. Maybe they would go back to the party, they'd laugh, they'd drink more, then stumble back to someone's house. Or maybe they would skip the party altogether. If she asked him right now to come back to hers, he wouldn't hesitate. For all that she was mysterious and 'taciturn', Mike had no reason to think she was, in the end, all that different from the rest back at the party. Someone with a story, sure, but someone too young and too real for that story to be anything outside of the ordinary. And she could let him believe that. The likelihood of him learning the truth was slim. For tonight, maybe more than tonight, she could be one of those girls back at the party. She could laugh and drink and take a guy home and do all the normal things.

But she knew she wouldn't. Because even in the dark he couldn't miss the scars. She was careful to wear clothes that covered them, but there was no way to do that if this night went the way she was imagining. And while he was probably too decent to say anything about them, he would remember. Then all it would take was somebody asking the right questions and for Mike to think he was doing the right thing and even this tentative quiet would collapse from under her, or else become some lingering snare that would catch her down the road, a marker of where she'd been for anyone who cared to look.

'Come on,' she said. 'Let's head back.'

She knew he was disappointed, even if part of him hoped that the turnaround didn't mean what he knew it did. She talked idly with him as the lights of the house grew nearer and the music got louder. Back at the party, now packed with raucous dancers and stinking of sweat, she got another beer and had polite conversations with people whose names she quickly forgot. And Mike, who could have stuck close with her and tried to change her mind, told her he'd be right back and didn't return.

The night got late. Most people now were too drunk to notice or remember Maggie. That was fine. She leaned against the balcony with her beer. Through the sliding glass door, she saw Mike huddled on one of the wicker couches with Evie. Mike was leaning close, saying something. Evie laughed and tucked some hair behind her ear. Her eyes were half closed. Enjoying the attention. Knowing where it would end.

Maggie finished her beer, placed the empty bottle on the balcony then, hands in pockets, left.

She didn't walk along the beach. Instead she made her way up the dark road, under shadowy palms and the cries of bats.

Friends and parties, relationships, steady jobs that grew into careers and all the rest, all the accepted milestones of a respectable life. She generally operated under the assumption that those things were out of her reach, but maybe they weren't. Of course, there were realistic considerations, passports and tax file numbers and the rest, but nothing was insurmountable with the right money and the right connections. If she really wanted to, she knew, she could adopt the guise of somebody innocuous and everyday. It would take time and effort, not least to shed the impression of 'mysterious' that even Evie's friends had picked up on, but it could be done.

At what point, she thought as she swatted away an overhanging branch, was enough enough? Would there ever come a time when she had adequately made penance? When the past would become something faint and distant, something that might as well have happened to someone else? Her own mistakes, many and ugly as they were, at a certain point had to be left behind. Already, realistically, had been. There was no direct way to make up for the things she had done, the people she had failed. The boy, not so different to Mike, who she'd led down the wrong road in blind pursuit of her mother. The road she had returned from alone.

Wind moved through the trees. The air was touched with cold now, a hint of impending winter. Not that winter meant much up here, which was one of the reasons she liked Port Douglas.

If she was going to stay, then she couldn't keep going the way she had. Her solitude was having the opposite effect to what she wanted, making her stand out. Maybe the only practical option was to, at least for a while, pretend. To play the part without being it. And if, over time, the lines between the pretence and the reality became blurred, well, she could live with that.

Another gust of wind. Maggie stopped. She turned. She scanned the empty road behind her, the still buildings, the gentle sway of the trees. For a moment there, she was sure she had felt eyes on her.

She was a shadow with no last name and a first generic enough to seem fake if anyone decided to dig a little deeper. She had cut off the past at the root and thrown away all the things she could have been in exchange for a life on nobody's radar or record. The problem was how fragile that life could be and how thoroughly she had risked unbalancing it by following Len to that warehouse.

Paranoia was the consequence of the way she lived. One of them. The street remained still. She started walking again.

Having her coffee the next morning, Maggie again felt somebody watching her.

She read her book, had a second coffee, paid and left. As she walked up the busy street, she casually glanced over her shoulder. There were lots of people out; the weather was typically perfect and there was a carnival on down at the beach. It would be hard to spot anybody conspicuous even if she tried.

By the time she arrived at work, she was almost certain it had all been in her head. Still, she found herself checking the door more often for signs of Len or one of his cronies. She even looked a little closer at every person who came into the bar, but as far as she could tell they were the usual combination of regulars and tourists, none of whom paid any abnormal attention to her.

She turned down Andrew's offer of a drink that night. Standing in the cooling night air out the front of the bar, she waited for several seconds, looking to either side. The street was empty. She listened. Distant snatches of conversation and music. Leaves in the wind. A car passing, several blocks away.

She started to walk. She kept her hands in her pockets. She wished she had brought the knife with her. In the first days of this job, she had, every night. She'd become complacent.

There it was again: that feeling, so distinct and so hard to define, of eyes on her. A shiver, a sense of crawling across the back of her neck. She didn't slow or turn. She glanced at a car ahead. The reflection in the windscreen was dark and distorted but enough to show nobody behind her. She stopped and turned. Her eyes swept across the road. There was no rustle in a hedge or flash of movement as somebody ducked behind a car. The road was as still as it had been when she had left the bar. She picked up her pace. The sense grew again. Ahead was a narrow alley. Briefly, she considered ducking down it, doubling back and taking the long way home. She could lose whoever was there – if, indeed, somebody *was* there. But she was unarmed and for anyone who meant her harm, a narrow, dark alley was practically a gift. She passed the mouth of it. Ahead, a rock lay to the side of the pavement. Without slowing, she picked it up. It didn't make her feel much better.

Most nights she took a shortcut to her apartment along a back road. Tonight, she went via the main stretch of the town. She glanced behind her as she passed the dark shops. There were a few people still out, talking, laughing, stumbling. Good. Witnesses were a strong deterrent.

She locked the door the moment she was inside and stuck her chair under the handle. She put her knife beside the bed. The apartment had one window. She placed her only glass on the sill, deliberately precarious. If somebody tried to come through, even silently, she would know. Once she was sure she had done everything she could, she got into bed. She lay there, wide awake, staring at the roof and feeling the simmer of hot, uncomfortable anger. She didn't want to live this way. She didn't like being forced into a position where she had to.

She wondered if the person following her could guess just how far she would go to do something about the fact.

The next morning, she was sure of it. Somebody was tailing her. The feeling remained strong as she took a corner seat in her usual café and watched the street. What frustrated her was that whoever this person was, they were very good. She had glimpsed nobody who stood out, no eyes quickly moving away from her, no overly casual figure rapidly shifting their attention to a phone or nearby store.

She didn't lend much credence to the idea that it was happening in her head. Some people laughed at the notion that you could feel eyes on you, but Maggie took the feeling at face value, especially when it lingered like this. There was some strange imbalance to the air when somebody was tracking you; it was a sense that the world wasn't just moving around you in the way it usually did. Somebody had noticed you.

By early afternoon, she had decided what she was going to do. Whoever was following her obviously had a decent idea of her day-to-day movements in Port Douglas. Their ability to elude her suggested that they also had a reasonable knowledge of the town itself. Therefore, her best option was to act as unconcerned as possible, then do something that would draw the person out, throw off their understanding of her routine and force them into a location where they weren't as comfortable.

Getting ready for work that afternoon, she took her old backpack from where it was secured under her bed. More from habit than anything, she checked inside. Once it had been full of cash. Now there was about half left of what she had started out with. She packed her knife as well, then slung the backpack over her shoulder.

She kept her eyes forward and took her time as she walked to her car. The day was warm but mild. Even so, she felt like the heat was closing in on her, leaving her stuffy and uncomfortable. She checked in the boot. Everything where she had left it.

She drove to work and parked down the road. It would have seemed a strange choice, given she could easily have walked, and that was what she was hoping for. If she was still being watched, this slight change in routine would be noticed. And that, hopefully, would prompt the person to do exactly what Maggie wanted.

It was an unusually busy night in the bar. Even Evie didn't have as much time for gossip or annoying questions. Andrew's glances towards the door were fewer. Again, there was no sign of Len. Or, Maggie felt, anyone else suspicious. She worked hard, polishing and serving faster than she usually would. Unbidden, the image of a dark figure creeping over to her car, a flashing device in hand, eyes on the door of the bar, kept playing out in her head.

It was nearly midnight by the time the whole bar was clean and Evie asked if they could have a couple of staff drinks. Maggie declined despite Andrew, who she suspected might have been swigging from a flask out the back, merrily urging her to stay. Instead, she hefted her backpack over her shoulder, smiled, waved and walked out the front door.

The street looked empty again. Her car was exactly where she had left it. She crossed the road and rested a hand on the roof. She looked behind her, towards the distant lights of the main street. She walked to the back of the car. She popped the boot and lifted it. Nothing moved. She retrieved a pen from her pocket. It slipped from her fingers and hit the road with a slight clatter. She swore, got to her knees and leaned down sideways, as if it had fallen under the car.

In the dark, it was hard to see, but there were no flashing lights or unfamiliar shapes. She picked up the pen and stood. She closed the boot. Then she went to the driver's side door, opened it and got in. She waited only a moment before starting the engine.

No bomb. No stalling. She pulled the car out of the park then hit the brakes. No cutting either, it seemed.

She drove.

It only took a few turns for her to get on the Captain Cook Highway. It was roughly an hour's drive to Cairns, give or take, and the highway went straight there. At this time of night, there weren't many other people out. That made her tail easier to spot, but also made her more vulnerable.

By day, it was a nice drive; the left side gave way to the ocean, while on the right sat vast fields of towering sugar cane and, further along, a stretch of rainforest-covered mountains. During her first week, Maggie had stopped there and taken a cable car up into the trees, where the tiny village of Kuranda, all wooden boardwalks and shops that seemed to grow between the trees, was tucked away like a secret hideout that tourists kept exposing. She'd liked Kuranda and found the trip to and from peaceful and pleasant. At night, however, all she could see was darkness hemming her in: the trees and the hills' looming shadows, the water a writhing void.

And behind her, distant but close enough to see, a pair of headlights.

It clicked home with a flicker of hateful vindication. He was real and he was here.

She didn't speed up or slow down. She suspected that if she stopped, he would kill his lights and wait – knowing, then, that she was onto him. He was taking a risk having them on at all. He was hoping, perhaps, that she would assume he was just another late-night driver while avoiding drawing the attention of a passing police car. It was the same tactic she'd employed with Len the other night.

The obvious answer to the *who* was one of the gangster's men, but she doubted it now. Mainly because Len had no reason to link her to the attack, but also because he would have been arrogant and brazen. If he was going to come for her, he wouldn't be afraid to act fast and draw attention.

Which begged the question of who the fuck this was.

There were several potential answers Maggie could think of, and none of them boded well. A thug would be easy enough to deal with, but the other options created a whole pile of new problems. Namely, that she had been found. That it was naive to have thought she could fly under the radar. Maybe the truth was that the past always found a way to get its hooks in and drag you back.

Well, it could try.

Maggie slowed as houses and buildings started to appear around her, and she entered Cairns. There were more cars on the road now, but the pair of headlights in her rear-view mirror remained. Or had they got closer?

Cairns didn't feel much bigger than Port Douglas. There were very few skyscrapers; most of the buildings were low and throughout it had the feel of a fashionable suburb in a major city or else a resort town grown too big, with the waving palm trees and ocean sounds under the bustle.

She parked as centrally as she dared, near a line of closed restaurants and bars. She knew she was near the sea and the expansive public spaces around it. The noises of the still-open nightclubs were faint and there weren't many people on the street. She checked the rear-view mirror. The one advantage of the highway was gone here. She had no idea where her follower was. She could only guess he was still on her tail. She stepped out of the car, bag over her shoulder in case she had to run, covering the knife with her jacket. She breathed in the warm air and looked behind her. Then, locking the door, she walked towards the sea. She put both hands in her pockets and kept her head down. Nobody spoke to her as she passed. Maybe one or two giggling teenagers gathered around a rubbish bin stopped to watch, but they said nothing.

Not far from the ocean was a vast stretch of courtyard fringed with art installations and palm trees. In the midst of it all was a giant public pool, the water barely touching your feet in some places, deep enough to swim in others, electric neon blue under the streetlights. Sticking out at various intervals were towering stainless-steel poles, at the top of which were triangular fish. Whether they were weird fountains or just for decoration Maggie had no idea. She walked along the edge of the pool to the furthest point, close now to where the ocean began after a paved walkway. The streetlights kept everything illuminated; the steel fish gleamed against the sky. She stopped and turned.

At the other side of the pool stood a man. He was in the shadows, but beyond that made no attempt to hide himself. Maggie's hand went to the knife. Her heart had picked up. She didn't move.

The figure approached, stepping into the light. He was dressed simply in a blue business shirt, sleeves rolled up, and dark trousers. From a distance, she could see that his sparse hair was closely cropped. He was slow but he didn't falter as he came closer.

The wind picked up, rustling the trees. Neither spoke. In the distance, Maggie heard a yell followed by raucous laughter.

Whoever she had been expecting to emerge from the shadows, it was not him. And she couldn't deny the pang of something keen and aching, something so unfamiliar she'd almost forgotten what it meant, something that slammed into her the moment their eyes met and he smiled.

CHAPTER THREE

The last time Maggie had seen Harrison Cooper, she'd still been at uni. She was in theory headed to class but was hungover enough to know that she'd likely go lie down in a park somewhere until the headache subsided. Still, she'd stopped in at a café near campus to at least make one serious attempt to wake herself up.

She knew, waiting in line, that the booze was only one part of the sour taste in her mouth and the throbbing behind her eyes. The night before, watching Ness and that prick, had been a harsh reminder of just how out of her depth she was here. Hence the drinks.

She hadn't recognised Cooper immediately. She'd glanced at him, felt a sense of some vague familiarity, then a jolt as she realised who he was. He stood to the side, waiting for his order, frowning down at his phone. His face was more lined than before and he'd clearly given in to his encroaching baldness by cutting his hair close, but there was no mistaking him. Her coffee forgotten, she'd stood there, rigid and uncertain. It would have been easy enough to just shuffle forward, order and leave. He hadn't seen her since she was a kid. He wouldn't even glance up as she left. The line moved and Cooper stayed where he was. Maggie tried not to look at him but she couldn't help it. She was waiting for his name to be called out, for the moment he'd take his coffee and leave. She was waiting but she didn't want that moment to come and so once she'd ordered her own, she stood beside him and said, quietly, 'Hi.'

He looked up at her. His frown deepened and she went to make some excuse, a mistaken identity or something else but then his eyebrows went up and in a voice that sounded just slightly choked he'd said her name.

The rest was awkward. He collected his coffee but asked if she wanted to sit. She hadn't said yes, exactly, but he'd taken her half-shrug to mean as much. Maggie held her own coffee tight but didn't drink as they faced each other across the table. She didn't want to make eye contact, but she made herself do it anyway. She might not have been able to pinpoint what she was feeling, but Cooper didn't need to know that. She wanted him to see confidence and solidity. She wanted him to know that none of what had happened had broken her. Nor had his failure to ever intervene.

So she asked casual questions. Was he still a cop? Was he still on the drug squad? He'd answered briefly, then tried to steer the conversation to her. How was she? What was she studying? Did she have friends? The subtext always – *but you turned out okay, right?*

Part of her wanted to be direct. To tell him about the foster homes, about the fights and the bruises and the scars. About the missing years after his regular appearances at her father's house during her childhood. But she didn't. She gave brief, innocuous answers and as she did something dawned on her.

The earnestness in Harrison's expression, the guilt that he was trying to assuage, could be used in her favour. A comment about the prick, about her fears for Ness, and Harrison would jump into action. It would be an easy way for Harrison to feel like he had done something. And she could make it so that Ness never even realised she'd been the one to tip off the cops.

But, as silence fell between them and she watched Harrison struggle to work out what to say, she knew that she didn't want his help. Not now. He didn't deserve to be let off the hook, even in his own mind. If something was going to be done for Ness, Maggie would do it herself.

She'd told Harrison she had to get to class. He'd given her his card, told her to stay in touch. The moment she was out the door she threw it in the first bin she saw, along with her untouched coffee.

Now they sat across from each other in the corner booth of a small bar that was Hawaiian-themed and tacky, all bamboo and Tiki statues and draped leis. Elvis played on the speakers – 'Always On My Mind'. Harrison nursed a light beer but Maggie had gone for water. She didn't want to dull her senses even slightly for this.

'You've been following me,' she said.

The twitch of an embarrassed smile made him instantly younger. 'Sorry. I had to be sure it was you. And to work out if it was safe to make contact.'

Maggie decided to gamble, just slightly. 'Why wouldn't it be?'

'Partly because I haven't seen you in years,' Harrison said. 'But mainly because several nights ago you blew up a drug dealer's warehouse. It didn't occur to you that there were cameras?'

'I didn't see any.'

'You didn't look across the road, then.'

'The footage reached Melbourne?'

'Clearly you didn't know who you were blowing up.'

'I knew he was a scumbag.'

'That much is true,' Harrison said. 'Still is, probably, given that we didn't find his body. More's the pity. For a long time most of the gear on the market came through a massive Melbourne syndicate, but recently things went south for them. Namely, somebody got the better of their main operator and burned him alive. Cue revenge killings, cue the wrong people getting shot and that's the end of the Melbourne monopoly. Suddenly Len Townsend's cartel contacts make him the man of the hour and he goes from low-rent thug to major player.'

'So you've been after Townsend?' Maggie said.

'Not me,' Harrison replied. 'Just trying to deal with the impact back home. But then his warehouse got attacked. Local cops pulled the footage from the neighbouring joint and there's this Jane Doe turning a car into a bomb. Nobody had any idea who you were. But I recognised you straight away.'

Her mind wasn't moving fast enough. *If Harrison had passed her identity on to the Queensland police ...*

'Nobody knows apart from me,' Harrison said. 'I put two and two together then flew up. Based on the location, I figured you'd be living in Port Douglas. I sussed out a few different options: namely, the kind of new bar that might be paying cash in hand. In the rarest ever case of a cop being in luck, there you were.'

Maggie considered a couple of different responses, then settled on the only one that mattered. 'Why?'

'First, to make sure that you were okay.'

'And second?'

Harrison didn't speak straight away. His brow was furrowed slightly, as if considering what to say.

'Second, I need to tell you something.'

'I know he's dead,' she said.

Harrison leaned back. He interlaced his fingers on the table and looked at them. 'Do you have any idea who killed him?'

She gambled again. 'I thought he fell.'

'In the eyes of the coroner,' Harrison said. 'But I'm reasonably confident they're wrong.' His hands parted, suddenly. Maggie flinched, but he just put them on his knees. If Harrison noticed her reaction, he gave nothing away. 'Years back there was this case. At first it was written off as a bunch of unconnected incidents. Some dead junkies and low-rent prostitutes, probably killed in fights or whatever. But after a while, some kid barely out of training noticed similarities between all these murders. Facial mutilations, knife wounds, stuff that wasn't too far out of the ordinary for a fucked-up speed freak. But there were specificities and eventually your dad got sent to look into it. Did you know any of this?'

Maggie shook her head. Her father had never spoken to her about his job. Not that there was anything especially unique in that. He tended to use his fists for whatever messages he wanted to convey.

'Just about every cop I've ever known has one case that just … I dunno, eats at them. Maybe it's because you see patterns other people don't; maybe it's overpowering gut instinct; maybe it's just this singular reaction to what you're faced with. But Eric became obsessed with this. Especially after one of his informants got hit. Even after you were born, he barely spent any time at home. He was out on the streets, interviewing potential witnesses, canvassing suspects, all of it. It took him a while but eventually he thought he'd found his man. Terrence Adams was a drug dealer with a record and a reputation for enjoying his own supply a little too much. He knew some of the victims, he moved in the areas they were found and he'd been in prison ten years back for a stabbing that went a bit beyond the basic. Your dad went in to speak to him.' Harrison grimaced. 'It got ugly. Eric killed Adams.'

Maggie thought she knew where this was going, but she kept her mouth shut. Let Cooper tell his story so she could work out what she was going to do.

'Then, a year or so later, another body turned up.' His voice was flat, resigned. 'Most of us figured it just looked similar. Your dad didn't think so, though. As far as he was concerned, he'd got the wrong guy.'

Silence, heavy and fraught.

'There were no more bodies,' Harrison said, 'and most of the higher-ups were willing to go with coincidence. Not Eric. His obsession made him hard to work with. His reputation slipped, the drinking got worse and then your mum walked.' Harrison rubbed his eyes. Maggie wondered what he remembered. How much he remembered. The grime, the bruises. 'I tried, Maggie,' he said. 'I promise I did. I wanted to be his friend and help, but fuck, it was hard. Eventually I gave up.'

Maggie knew that much. As a kid she had always looked forward to Harrison's visits. No, more than that. She had hoped for them the way a drowning person hopes for air.

'Anyway,' Harrison said, 'about a week before Eric died, he got in touch. We had a drink together. He had evidence, he said. He was sure he knew who the real killer was. By this point, I'd heard that a lot. Always a different suspect, never anything that would make a judge look twice. A couple of times before, I'd looked into it for him, but I never found anything. But this time, he said, it was solid. He showed me this portable hard drive. I told him to give it to me but he refused. He was rambling a bit by this point; it turned out he had information about your mother on there as well. He ranted about how he was going to find her this time and … you know. That was the final proof I needed that he had lost it.'

Maggie didn't move. 'What kind of information?'

'Can't say for sure. He said he had photos, names, a few potential locations. Given that he'd been looking for her for years and never found her, I wrote it off as another wild goose chase.'

Except there were things Harrison didn't know. That some of Eric's previous information had been a long way from wrong. That Maggie had left Melbourne to follow her mother's trail and found nightmares hidden away in the darkest corners of the country, nightmares her mother had been part of. A community left alone to curdle and become savage, a community her mother had lived in – until she ran. Since then, Maggie had let the pursuit of her mother fade away to a pipe dream that maybe was best left unfulfilled. Maggie had wanted to face up to her and ask why, to finally know and understand how she could have been left alone with him. Knowing what her mother had been part of – and that she had nowhere else to look – had dampened that need somewhat. But now … Her heart was beating faster. She willed herself to keep still, to keep her face calm.

'I told him to take a shower and get help,' Harrison said. 'He got angry. I gave him the number of a good shrink. He took that about as well as you'd expect. A week later, someone pushed him down the stairs.' Harrison's gaze went to the roof. 'He had a tonne of booze in his system. Everyone was happy to write it off as an accident. The problem was, that night in the pub he had told me who he thought the killer was. And that was half the reason I told him to fuck off. He was going up against the kind of person who could catch wind of someone gunning for them and decisively act.'

Maggie clenched and unclenched a fist under the table. When she trusted her voice not to waver, she spoke. 'You think this person killed him?'

'I think I owe it to Eric to find out.'

It was strange how quietly and unknowingly Harrison had blindsided her. The assumed foundation on which she had built her current way of life had suddenly collapsed. If Harrison was telling the truth, if Maggie hadn't woefully misinterpreted something, then she was not under suspicion. The reason she had run, the thing that had kept her moving and on edge for so long now, may never have been real. Possibilities she had never even considered were opening in front of her. Picking up where she had left off. *A normal life.*

But beyond that was the biggest and most complicating factor in whatever she did next: the hard drive. The thing that Harrison wanted also might hold the answer to her question, the question that had led her to leave Melbourne in the first place. Over the past year, it had never once occurred to her that her father, with his disdain for technology and reliance on old-school notebooks, might have more information than the maps and scribblings she had taken from him that night. That there might be something current, something meaningful, something that would allow her to finally face the woman who had abandoned her.

It took her a moment to realise Cooper was still talking. 'The only reason anybody looked into your father's death was because you went missing two months beforehand, around the time he was investigating a potential killer.'

The two months. Her smartest move, even if it had been more insurance than anything. She had moved into the kind of dingy sublet where nobody cared about your last name as long as you paid your bills. She had kept her head down and used only cash at the most tucked-away stores. Then she waited. After two months of living like a ghost, she visited her father. Not planning to kill him. But if it went that way, at least she wasn't vanishing right after, and in the process branding herself a suspect.

Harrison didn't seem to have noticed her drift off. 'There was this idea that you'd been kidnapped to try to put Eric off digging any deeper, but nobody was taking his suspicions particularly seriously, so, while you technically remained a missing person, the general belief was that you'd run away.'

'General,' Maggie said. 'Not yours.'

Harrison shook his head. 'I didn't know for sure. But whatever else Eric was by the end, he was a good detective, and I'd let myself forget it. If this person had killed both of you ...' His expression twitched in a near wince. 'The point is I didn't listen to him when I could have. And when I saw you on that video, I had to be sure.'

Maggie would have been touched if she didn't know something else was coming.

'The thing is,' Harrison went on, 'the man Eric named is still free. The man he claimed to have evidence on. At the very least, I want to see what that was. All of Eric's belongings have been under lock and key since he died.

He left everything to you, and as it isn't an active murder investigation, I can't take a look. But I reckon that hard drive is still there. Somewhere.'

There was a tightness to her limbs, a fearful tension that she knew better than to ignore. A warning. She had kept clear of Melbourne for a long time and for good reason.

'You want me to come back,' she said. 'To prove I'm alive so you can find whatever evidence he might have had.'

'That's what I'm asking,' Harrison said, without looking at her. 'You're within your rights to say no. But before you do, I would argue it's in your best interests as much as anyone's.'

'How?'

'To put it bluntly, the money,' Harrison said. 'And the house, which you could sell. Eric was no millionaire, but he had a bit put away.'

More than a bit. For every dollar her father had in the bank, he kept another in the hidden safe in their house. His drunken-paranoia fund. What was left of that stash was in the backpack at her feet. The rest – whatever she could get for the house – could give her security. A future.

But no matter what Cooper said, she found it very hard to believe that nobody on the police force had ever considered that she might have killed her father. And beyond that, selling the house and accessing the money would not be as simple as a signature and handed-over keys. For one, she would be announcing herself to the world again. The flashing arrows she had managed to avoid until now would surround her.

But the hard drive would be hers before Harrison's. Without a warrant, he could do nothing to dispute that, especially if she vanished right after claiming it. And, she found herself reasoning, it *was* in her best interests to secure it. Harrison's pursuit of this 'killer' might well lead him to the realisation that, like Eric, he had the wrong person. And that in turn might lead him to think differently about who the right person was.

Looking at Cooper, at his expectant, hopeful expression, she felt the tiniest prick of pre-emptive guilt. But it was swiftly offset by the truth she had reminded herself of again and again over the years. That he had known what Eric was and done nothing.

'What do you think?' he asked, a slight waver to his voice. 'Will you do it?'

CHAPTER FOUR

Maggie drove alone through darkness. Even the vague outlines of familiar markers melted away into the night, so insignificant they might as well not have been there. All she saw ahead was the illuminated road fringed with the dark.

Cooper had to return his rental car to the airport and Maggie had gone back to the apartment to pick up her things. From there, the plan was to meet at a location Maggie had given Cooper, a quiet lookout on the road. It hadn't taken much time to convince Cooper to do things her way. He was clearly just happy she'd agreed to return to Melbourne with him, happy enough to forego flying back and take the long drive down with her. Maggie had pointed out that Cooper could fly alone, but he clearly didn't trust her to keep her word, just like Maggie wasn't quite ready to put herself on the radar as thoroughly as taking a plane would do. Cooper must want to catch that killer pretty fucking badly. Or, and this alternative had danced around her thoughts like an ugly taunt, he was lying to her. It was pathetic how much she didn't want to believe that, especially considering she fully intended to claim the hard drive for herself. But there was some comfort in the fact that it was also unlikely; if he *did* suspect her, it would have been far easier to bring backup and arrest her straight away.

That was another reason to take the drive together; it would give Maggie time to fully evaluate Cooper's intentions.

Arriving at the lookout, she parked between trees then turned her attention to the ocean and the dark sky. At this time, the view didn't look much like the slice of tropical paradise she knew. It looked cold and unpredictable. She sank a little lower in her seat. She knew she was tired, but it was a distant, clinical knowledge rather than any demand on her body's part that she get some sleep. Even if she'd been drifting off, she would have kept herself awake somehow.

Harrison Cooper. Maggie remembered all too well the instant rush of joy and relief she would feel whenever she heard his distinctive knock on the door – two quickly consecutive knocks, a pause, then three more. Later, in the first of her foster homes, she had emulated that knock herself.

He was usually in a jumper and jeans, a sixpack of beer under his arm. His hair hadn't been thin back then. It was always messy and his eyes crinkled in a small but real smile when he saw Maggie. Her dad would be a different person around Harrison, laughing and telling stories. Maggie would hang around, almost unnoticed, eyes on Harrison as he relayed little anecdotes from work or home, telling them about the latest trouble his son Aaron had got into.

Maggie had once asked if Aaron could come for dinner too. Harrison had changed the subject. That night her father backhanded her as they were standing in the hallway after Harrison left, telling her never to ask such a fucking stupid question again. *'What, you think we're some kind of fucking restaurant here?'*

She remembered the little exchanges she and Harrison would share when her father stumbled off to the bathroom. Always silly and brief, but silliness wasn't something Maggie got a lot of back then.

'Did you get any bad guys today?' Maggie would sometimes ask.

'If by "getting bad guys" you mean "finished off a huge amount of paperwork", then yeah, I got heaps. You should have seen me.'

'They're gonna make a movie about you.'

'They already have. Haven't you seen *Dirty Harry?*' Harrison would laugh and make his fingers into a gun. '"Do you feel lucky, punk?" Only problem was that Clint Eastwood wasn't quite tough enough to be me, you know?'

She wondered what Harrison thought when he looked at her now. It had been a long, long time since she had even considered how she came across to another person. But seeing Harrison, it was hard not to feel, on some deep and not quite buried level, like that kid waiting with pained hope for every sporadic visit.

Light spread slowly, turning the ocean from grey to glittering blue with veins of flame red dancing through it. Maggie didn't move. She watched until the sun was up, the sky was clear, and she saw movement in the rear-view mirror. Automatically she reached for her knife, but it was just Cooper, small suitcase in his left hand, his right in his pocket.

Maggie said nothing as he put his bag in the back seat then opened the passenger door and sat beside her. For a moment, they just watched the ocean. Cooper glanced at the knife, sitting in the cup holder.

'I have to ask,' he said. 'Because I need to know what I'm dealing with here. Blowing up Townsend's warehouse ... that was an extreme move. Very extreme.'

Maggie said nothing.

'Who ... I mean, who were you working for?'

Maggie almost laughed. 'No-one.'

'No-one,' Cooper replied, unconvinced. 'Then why?'

'He broke my boss's nose.'

Silence.

'He broke your boss's nose,' Cooper repeated.

Maggie nodded.

Cooper laughed. After a moment, Maggie grinned and started the engine.

The landscape slowly changed around them; rainforest replaced by wide fields and the occasional paddock. They stopped for fuel when they needed to and ate in silence outside busy petrol stations, hemmed in by semitrailers and trucks. Then it was back in the car. For hour after hour, neither spoke.

She knew that, when Cooper felt he had a sense of what he was dealing with, the questions about the last year would come. Where she had been, how she had been looking after herself. She hadn't given much thought to the answer, apart from knowing that it would likely be some vague and logical lie about backpacking and cash-in-hand jobs.

When he finally broached the topic, it was phrased as a comment. 'You must be getting a bit sick of the road.'

'What makes you think I've been on the road?'

'You had to get from Melbourne to Queensland somehow.'

Maggie shrugged, eyes forward and hands on the wheel. She could feel Cooper looking at her. He was waiting for more, but she didn't plan on giving it to him.

'Where else have you been?'

He asked it easily, in a way that could be written off as small talk. But a quiet voice in her head was asking, *How much does he know?* Surely not a lot. But then, he was a cop and some of the situations Maggie had found herself in since leaving Melbourne would be on the radar of Australian law enforcement officers, wherever they were.

She went to brush the question off, but something stopped her. An impulse with the flavour of a memory. Because it *was* a memory.

There had been times when Harrison had visited when her father, after finishing off the regular sixpack offering and rifling through the empty cupboards, would announce a bottle shop run. Harrison would usually make some noises about how it was getting late, but her father would insist and Harrison would stay as Eric lurched out the door.

Maggie would always feel a rush of excitement in those times, because, with Eric gone, Harrison's attention and smile would be all hers as he sat across the table and asked her about school, her friends, what she wanted to be when she grew up. All the questions nobody else ever had. And how he *listened*.

In response to her probably stupid answers he would say nice things, about how smart she was or how her teachers at school must either love or hate her for the way she thought. Maggie was too pleased to tell him that her teachers didn't notice her. That she kept quiet to stop anybody at school from noticing her.

In those moments, moments Maggie would replay in her head again and again, she could let herself believe that there was somebody in the world who looked at her with pride and maybe even love.

And as something tangled and thorny and too big for her to understand rose in her chest, she would find herself wanting to answer the one question he never asked. Because maybe if she told him, he would do something. He would take her away from there, maybe to his own house, to a family that would embrace her as one of their own. And everything would change. If she just found it in herself to tell him the truth.

But something always stopped her. In later years she had assumed it was the fear that she wouldn't be believed. But in time she came to understand it was really the fear that she *would* be believed but that it would mean nothing. That Harrison would simply shrug and tell her it was none of his business, or worse, that she deserved it. That he would stop talking to her when Eric went on his bottle shop runs. That he would no longer like her.

Now, sitting in the car, Maggie felt an echo of that old desire. There was no reason to think Cooper would believe she was a liar if she told him about the town she had found while looking for her mother. About the hunters in the night, about the people who died and the ones who didn't. About Frank and Allie. Simon. About the things she had done to survive. Maybe, some tiny part of her even hoped, he would be proud.

Except, a bigger part countered, he wouldn't. Harrison's world was a different one. He lived according to law and order and went home at the end of the day. For Maggie, it was as though the death of her father had opened a doorway to a kind of shadow world, a twisted reflection of the reality she knew in which nothing made sense and danger was around every corner. The myth of the lawless west, Maggie now knew, was as real as it was alive. People were just very good at looking in the opposite direction.

And Maggie had done bad things. Selfish things, things that still ate at her, things that innocent people died because of. Harrison Cooper didn't need to know about those things.

He was still watching her, expectant.

Maggie kept her eyes on the road. 'Here and there,' she said. 'I've been here and there.'

Thoughts and warnings circled uneven and half-formed through her mind. She tried to focus on the road but as late afternoon crept towards evening her body started to protest. She was running on servo food and no sleep.

'Maggie.' Cooper's voice was low, gentle. The sky was pale, the sunset creeping away. 'Maggie.'

She didn't look at him.

'You're about to pass out. Pull over.'

She shook her head.

'Maggie.' Soft but insistent. She glanced at him. He looked tired too. 'Should we find a motel?'

'No.'

'Then let me drive. You've been behind the wheel all day.'

She wanted to say no, but she couldn't think of a reason. She pulled over. Her eyelids were drooping. Off to the side was a vast expanse of tall grass. Cooper's door opened, then he was gone. She watched the grass. She heard her own door open. She got out of the car. The air was cooler. She looked back the way they had come, up the stretch of highway. She didn't know how far from Port Douglas they now were.

'Maggie.' Cooper touched her shoulder.

She looked at him.

He smiled. 'Get some sleep, yeah?'

She nodded and rounded the car. She got in, put her seatbelt on and put the seat back. Beside her, Cooper had restarted the engine. Pale blue was darkening through the windscreen. She could see the occasional star.

The car wasn't moving. She looked at Cooper. Brow furrowed, he seemed to be staring at the steering wheel. Maggie waited.

'I didn't know,' he said. 'What he was doing. I promise you I didn't know.'

Maggie watched him.

'But I …' He closed his eyes and exhaled. 'But I wondered.'

'You knew about the drinking.'

Cooper nodded.

'So why did you bring him booze?'

He looked at Maggie, and even through her half-conscious haze it hit her how old he looked now. It went beyond the worry lines or the lack of hair. It was the tiredness.

'There was one time I didn't,' he said. 'Eric asked if I wanted a drink. I told him we should just have a coffee and chat. He was like a cornered animal. Men like him, they know. They know they're wrong. But they don't know how to stop so they act blind and hope that we all fall into line around the lie. And we usually do. The moment somebody suggests the smallest thing that might indicate change, or judgement, they lose it. I knew then that your Dad would rather have no friends at all than one who was honest with him. I thought he needed a friend, so I compromised. I fucked up.'

'Even though you saw me,' Maggie said. 'Every time you turned up with your sixpack.'

Cooper looked away. 'Yeah. Even then. Because it was easier to pretend no damage was being done. Or that the damage wasn't …' He grimaced, and when he spoke again his voice was disgusted. 'Or that the damage wasn't as bad as it could have been.'

'So … what?' Maggie could hear the steel in her voice. 'Because it wasn't sexual, it was okay?'

Cooper shook his head. 'No. It wasn't okay at all.'

They sat in silence for another moment. Maggie turned away. The car pulled back onto the road.

* * *

Maggie swapped with Cooper early the next morning. Her sleep had been fitful but had more or less lasted through the night and she felt, if not much better, then at least like she could think. With Cooper asleep in the passenger seat, she stopped at a roadhouse and sat cross-legged on the car's bonnet, eating a doughnut and drinking a metallic coffee as she watched clouds move across a mostly overcast sky. They were definitely out of Queensland, down where autumn meant something more than a lack of torrential rain.

Cooper woke up around midday. Maggie gave him a bottle of water, which he accepted with a grunted thanks. She glanced at him as he drank. There had been one question that, in all that had happened, she had forgotten to ask.

'This killer,' Maggie said. 'Who do you think it is?'

Cooper finished off the bottle and screwed the lid back on. He didn't look at Maggie. 'I don't *think* it's anyone, as such. I don't have the evidence.'

'My father gave you a name.'

'He gave me a name, not a reason to think he was right.'

'But reason enough for you to come north.'

'My job is finding the truth. That's all. Right now, as far as I'm aware, this man is completely innocent.'

Maggie kept her eyes on the road. 'Who is he?'

'I'm not going to tell you that.'

'Why?'

'Because I'm not associating a potentially innocent person's name with a killer.'

'Who am I going to tell?'

'That's not the point, Maggie. It's ...' Cooper sighed. 'Listen, imagine if it was you. If a drunk was going around telling people you were a murderer, but you knew you were innocent. Would you want *anybody* hearing it?'

'That's very conscientious.'

'Cautious. I've seen enough cases where cops think they're onto a sure thing, speak about a suspect like they're a lock, then some exonerating evidence comes in and next thing the lawyers swoop down on them for defamation. And fair enough, really. I don't think you're going to tell anyone. But that doesn't change the fact that I've got a rule about these things. If your dad had real evidence, then I'll share it with you. Until then, there's nothing to share.'

Maggie didn't push the issue. But she couldn't shake the feeling that Cooper's reasoning was well-thought-out bullshit.

CHAPTER FIVE

They drove. Sometimes they stopped; sometimes they alternated. Neither said very much. During her turns in the passenger seat, Maggie would look out the window, noting the turn-offs to Sydney, then Canberra. Already she missed Queensland. Here, brown hills gave way to scrubby forests then extensive paddocks. Sometimes the trees hemmed them in, obscuring little settlements that could barely be called towns, other times the landscape rolled out to either side of them, populated only by grazing cows and the occasional farmhouse. Maggie noted the long grass and gentle slopes, ochre combinations of yellows and oranges as the minutes and kilometres slipped quickly away.

Maggie tried to ignore the green signs which, each time they passed, marked how much closer they were getting to Melbourne. Nothing was stopping her from changing her mind, from telling Cooper to get out of the car before she headed off in a different direction. But despite the decreasing kilometres on those green signs, she never did.

As afternoon neared evening, Cooper turned from the wheel. 'I don't know if I can drive through another night.'

Maggie felt the same. The car was stuffy and she really wanted a shower. She also wanted to get to Melbourne and get this over with as soon as possible.

'There's a town up ahead,' Cooper said. 'Holbrook. Let's stop. Get some food, stay overnight in a motel, then leave in the morning. We can easily be in Melbourne by tomorrow afternoon.'

A tightening in Maggie's chest at the thought. Maybe slowing the process down wasn't the worst idea in the world. 'Okay.'

The exit wasn't far ahead. A narrow road arced away from the highway, through trees and into a tiny township.

'I used to bring my son here,' Cooper said. 'Back in the day, when he was younger. He loved it.'

'Why would he love it?' Maggie asked. All she could see up ahead were a rundown corner pub, a dilapidated supermarket and— 'Oh.'

To their right, glaringly out of place among the small-town Australia trappings, was the bulk of a long, black submarine, half-buried in the neat grass of a public park. It took Maggie a couple of moments to be sure of what she was seeing. From the bulbous nose to the tapered far end, it had to be almost a hundred metres long.

'HMAS *Otway*,' Cooper said. 'Ultimately, it's just a weird feature in a park, but it gives the town a bit of a tourist attraction. We used to run up and down it pretending to be sailors.'

'I'm not doing that with you.'

Cooper looked sideways at her. 'Thwarted. Can I at least convince you to grab a burger with me and eat it on the sub?'

'Purely because I never expected to hear that sentence in my life.'

Cooper laughed as they took the side street towards their motel.

They checked in, with Cooper paying for two clean but plain rooms, then headed to the little fish-and-chip shop. Cooper ordered burgers while Maggie stood outside, watching the road. A couple of teenagers kicking a footy passed her, but otherwise the town was still.

Up close, the size of the sub was striking. The dissonance with its surroundings seemed especially pronounced here. Cooper pointed to a ladder on the side. Maggie climbed up and sat cross-legged, facing the setting sun as she unwrapped her burger. Cooper joined her. For a few moments, neither spoke.

'You seem on edge,' Cooper said finally.

'A lot has happened,' Maggie said. 'I've just learned to be careful.'

'But that's the thing.' Cooper's voice had risen slightly. 'You shouldn't *have* to be careful. You should be living your life in Melbourne, partying with friends, meeting guys or … I dunno. How old are you now, twenty-three? I still remember you as this little kid. And now I see you blowing up warehouses and … I mean, surely on some level you want to return to something easier than this? Once everything's sorted out you could go back to uni, get a job, have a life, you know? Stop being ...' He faltered. He clearly didn't know how to describe what Maggie was now. She couldn't blame him. She didn't either.

The sun was dipping below the horizon now. Maggie and Cooper finished their burgers in silence.

'I've got this theory,' Cooper said. 'The amount of years in either direction tends to dictate where your focus goes. In your twenties, everything's about building a future, laying foundations or whatever. In your fifties and up, it's all about contending with the past. Tying up loose ends, atoning for your screw-ups, making sure you've arrived at a place where you can live with yourself and die knowing you've done alright.'

'Jesus,' Maggie said. 'You're not *that* old.'

'No,' Cooper said. 'But I'm getting to that stage. And hindsight is starting to show me that I've got more than my fair share of regrets. What I'm saying is that I'd hate to see you end up in that same boat.'

'I don't have any regrets.'

'Not yet. But when you start killing or meting out punishment with impunity ...' Cooper shook his head. 'I knew guys who went down that road. Cops who aren't cops anymore, thank God. What I'm saying is I don't want you to end up in a place where I have no choice *but* to arrest you.'

The sun was gone. The night had turned cold around them. Maggie looked at Cooper. His eyes were on the stars.

'Feel like a beer?' she asked.

Cooper looked surprised. 'Really?'

'I reckon we've earned it.'

'Sure, but ...' Cooper shrugged. 'I'm just surprised you even drink.'

Maggie went to speak. She stopped. The wind picked up. She stood.

The pub was directly across the road from them. It was an old-fashioned, mustard-coloured building sitting on a street corner. Quiet music played inside and there were only a few other customers, mainly old men watching the footy on a wall-mounted TV. Maggie ordered two pints and joined Cooper in a booth off to the side. They both sipped.

'How's Aaron?' Maggie asked.

Cooper paused, mid-drink. 'You remember his name?'

Of course she did. All the nights she had imagined the world where Cooper took her home, where Aaron was introduced as her new brother. All the little snippets of information about him that Cooper had let slip that she had clung to, just in case. She knew he liked riding his bike and drawing, that he played guitar but was bad at it, that his favourite book as a kid had been *Alice in Wonderland*.

She nodded.

Cooper drank. 'He's fine. Good, really. He's finished off his degree, making his mother and me look like a couple of uneducated idiots.'

'What was your wife's name?' Maggie asked, even though she remembered.

'We're divorced.'

'Sorry.'

Cooper shrugged. 'Long time coming, really. My job isn't kind to relationships.'

'Why do it then?'

'That's the million-dollar question.' He smiled ruefully. 'Probably you watch one too many movies as a kid, get it in your head that the pursuit of truth and justice is what you were put on this earth for, then you start pursuing truth and justice and you realise that they're both fucking complicated. Justice, for example, doesn't make most people happy. Most people want revenge, not justice.'

'Is there a difference?'

'I used to think so. Now, I dunno.' He drank again. 'You can drive yourself crazy trying to work out those distinctions.'

The door to the pub opened. Maggie looked over. Three men had entered. They were large and bearded, and wore leather vests – their 'cuts' – adorned with dark red scorpions.

'Bikies,' Maggie said.

Cooper didn't reply. Maggie glanced at him. He was watching the bikies, unblinking and intent. One of them looked back at him. A small nod. Maggie returned her attention to Cooper. His brow had knitted, just slightly.

'Same again?' Maggie asked.

'I'll get them,' Cooper said.

He slid out of the booth and made for the bar. Maggie watched him go. One of the bikies had turned away from his mates and was watching her as he sipped his pint. He winked. Maggie turned her glass in her hands then knocked back the last of the beer.

How likely was it that Townsend had sent them after her? She felt like she would have noticed several bikes on their tail, but then the trip down had been largely a blur of unending road and little sleep. She hadn't been at her most vigilant. She tilted the glass with a finger, balancing it on the edge of the base. She could throw it, hit one of them, then be out the door before they realised what had happened. She looked over at the bar again. Cooper was paying. The bikies were back to their conversation. They hadn't acknowledged each other any further.

Cooper returned with two more pints. 'So this is what I'm thinking,' he said. 'We'll get into Melbourne tomorrow afternoon. I'd invite you to stay with me, but right now it's a one-bedroom bachelor pad and the couch isn't much fun.'

'I'll get a motel.'

'I'll arrange to meet the lawyer straight away,' he said. 'Find out what the process is, how quickly we can have everything sorted. If it goes smoothly, I should be able to get the money transferred and the papers signed overnight. Then we can get access to the house and the storage unit and we're done.'

'Storage unit?' She was only barely listening. In her head, she was working through the layout of the pub and its immediate surrounds: entrances, exits.

'Yeah, the contents of the house have been moved to one. Standard procedure, apparently.'

Maggie stopped listening, catching only snatches from Cooper about how much money she could expect. She eyed him as he spoke. She thought about the nod. Could have been nothing. Probably was. Cooper might not have been in uniform, but it would hardly be a surprise if men like that could recognise the way a cop looked and held himself. But she had not mistaken the slight bunching of his shoulders, nor the tension that had held him the moment the bikies walked in.

Maggie didn't speak much as they headed back to the motel. She said a brief goodnight then headed to her room. She didn't unpack or undress. She sat on the bed, looking at the curtains that hid the window.

Melbourne tomorrow. The trip had been long, but not enough. And in that time the certainty that she had hoped she would gain regarding Cooper's intentions had not come. If anything, it had been shaken. Shaken through moments that could have meant nothing. His refusal to name the suspect. His reaction to the bikies. The way he had looked back even as they left the pub, glancing at the empty road behind them the whole way to the motel. There could easily have been a good explanation for his worry – Maggie could think of several – but what bothered her was the fact that he hadn't shared it with her. That made her wonder if the nod had been not a casual acknowledgement but instead one of recognition. And if so, what that meant.

Holbrook did not seem like the kind of town that was home to bikies. It probably wasn't; after all, bikies travelled. But why stop here, in this strange town off the main highway? Unless there was something they were looking for. Something they knew would be here.

If she got in the car with Cooper tomorrow morning, then that would be it. Her choice, which she now knew to be less certain than she had thought, would be entirely made. And if things went wrong, if she had let her tangled childhood feelings blind her judgement, then she really was fucked.

She picked up her bag and got to her feet. Hesitated by the door. Then opened it and moved quietly back up the hall and out into the parking lot and the cool night air. Clouds had crept across the dark sky. There was a bite to the wind, harder now that they were further south. Winter meant more down here than it did in Port Douglas, and winter was almost here.

She would feel bad about leaving Cooper. But he could get a bus home or something. If he had meant everything he had said, then he would have every right to hate her. But that risk, to her, seemed safer than the alternative. She moved for her car, eyes forward, not giving herself the chance to reconsider.

Then.

An explosion of pain behind her eyes, spiralling through her head from the place where something had hit her. Her vision blurred. She felt hot blood running down the back of her neck. She tried to turn. She staggered, then her face was in the dust.

A voice in her ear.

'You made it pretty fucking easy for me there.'

Hands rolled her over. She was on her back, looking at the sky, but something blocked her view. A face, narrow and pockmarked, nicotine-stained teeth bared in a grin. Something pulled tight around her wrists, something biting that did not give when she tried to pull free. The face vanished and she felt her ankles bound too. She tried to struggle but her body was reacting far too slowly. The face was back. Something musty smelling was shoved into her mouth. She tried to bite his fingers, but he pulled them clear, leaving the gag.

'*This* is some fucking luck,' he said, eyes moving over her. 'Your picture's been doing the rounds. Big reward for whoever finds you and makes the call. I couldn't fucking believe it when I saw you wandering over to the pub. You know how much you're worth?' He shook his head. 'The fucking *chances*.' He stood, taking out his phone. 'Gotta work out where to keep you, but that should be fine. Mr Townsend's gonna send someone quick when I tell him.'

The consistency of the eyes on her in Port Douglas. Of course it hadn't just been Cooper.

'And if you try to fuck with me …' He kicked her hard in the stomach. Maggie snapped inwards. Pain reverberated through her gut. She didn't make a sound.

'Nice and quiet,' the man said. 'A quiet little bitch.'

A creak. The man looked up.

Maggie rolled over. Cooper stood in the doorway of the motel.

He held up his badge. 'I figure Len Townsend sent word out through the usual channels?'

'That's none of your fucking business,' the man spat.

'Sure.' Cooper pocketed the badge. 'But she is. You can tell me to fuck myself. Except I'm pretty sure you're not carrying a gun and I am. I'm well within my rights to intervene.'

'Show me.' There was a waver in the man's voice. 'Show me your gun.'

'Or maybe I don't have one,' Cooper said. 'But, given that she's part of an important case, I wouldn't be doing my job if I didn't try to step in. You and Townsend directly interfering in a case is one thing, but hurting a cop? How has that ever worked out for anyone?'

The man said nothing.

'You can be stupid if you want,' Cooper said. 'But that's a big, brave gamble, my friend. How much is Townsend offering? Fifty grand? Less? Worth jail time? Or being cornered in an alley and kicked to death by a gang of detectives?' Cooper took a step forward.

'Stay back!' the man snarled.

Maggie turned her head. He was holding a knife.

Cooper took another step forward. 'You want to try this? Really?' Another step. He was close now. 'Or do you want to cut her loose and walk away?'

The man didn't reply.

Cooper stopped. 'Your choice, mate.'

For a moment, everything was silent.

Then a tug at her wrists as the man cut the zip ties, followed by the ones at her feet.

With some difficulty, Maggie stood. She pulled the filthy rag from her mouth. Her head throbbed. She put her hand to where she'd been hit and it came away sticky with blood. She looked at the man. He was staring at her, open-mouthed, as if he had no clue of what he was supposed to say or do now.

Then Cooper stepped past her and punched the man in the face.

He went flying with a squawk. He hit the ground and

Cooper was on him, punching again and again, his fist coming back bloody until the man was still.

Unsteady, Cooper stood, shaking his hand. He turned to Maggie. 'You okay?'

She said nothing. Her eyes moved to the fallen knife.

'No.' Cooper's voice was hard. 'He's more use to us alive. If word gets out that you're under police protection, fuckwit thugs like him are gonna think twice.' Cooper glanced at the dumpster. 'So let's just inconvenience him overnight.'

'Fine by me,' Maggie said. Her head really hurt.

The man was unmoving but breathing. They found the zip ties in the pockets of his torn, faded jeans. He stank like old booze and weed. Maggie bound his wrists while Cooper did the ankles. Then he tied the rag tight around the man's mouth. He groaned slightly but didn't rouse.

Cooper lifted the lid of the dumpster. Maggie met his eye, he nodded, and together they lifted the man's limp form and dropped him in. Maggie slammed the lid. They stepped back together.

'The people you worked with in the bar,' Cooper said. 'Would they have given Townsend your photo?'

Did Evie or Andrew *have* her photo? She had tried to avoid cameras but maybe she'd missed some promotional shot of the venue, maybe …

Heat raced through her as realisation hit.

'He wouldn't have hurt them,' Cooper said, seeing her expression. 'Not badly, anyway. With all the attention, he can't afford an investigation into a civilian death. He would have scared them, maybe, but that's it.'

The pain felt distant and dull. Maggie exhaled. She wasn't sure she entirely believed Cooper, but for now she'd take it.

Townsend was hunting her. In the midst of everything else, this fact felt almost insignificant. Despite the throb in her head Maggie's awareness of her surrounds seemed sharper, keener. She cast an eye over the parking lot, as if searching for another attacker lunging out of the dark. But the night stayed quiet. For now. If word of Townsend's bounty had reached this far south, then there would almost certainly be opportunistic thugs in Melbourne who would take their chance if they saw her.

'We should get clear before someone finds him,' Cooper said. 'As much as I was looking forward to a bed for the night. How's the head?'

'I've had worse.'

'No concussion?'

'Don't think so. Just a nasty headache.'

Cooper nodded. 'Good. Let's move.'

Maggie hesitated. Then she followed him to the car.

The pain in her head had subsided, but she was still resisting falling asleep. Not that resisting was too hard. She lay back on the seat, eyes out the window on the dark trees rushing past. She glanced at Cooper. He was focused on the road. His brow was furrowed. She thought of the violence with which Cooper had set upon her attacker, the protective rage in his expression.

Sometimes, as a kid, lying in bed listening to the buzz of the television and her father's occasional hoarse yells at whatever had so grievously offended him, she would imagine that she was in a different house listening to a different TV. It was warmer there, and beneath the TV she would hear the current of quiet conversation and laughter. She would close her eyes as the door opened and Cooper stood there, watching to make sure she was safe. In the mornings he would take her to school, hugging her as she left, telling her that he loved her and was proud of her, telling her without having to say the words that he would be there no matter what happened.

She would open her eyes hoping that she had willed herself into this different life, that if she wanted it enough it would happen. She would let herself believe that she had, until the next yell from downstairs.

Maggie knew that the gap between dreams and reality could never be closed. But now Cooper was here, and as hard as she might try to keep her guard up, she couldn't chase away that aching sense that maybe, finally, some long-accepted injustice was going to be put at least a little bit right.

CHAPTER SIX

Maggie had tried at uni. After barely scraping through high school, it had seemed a chance for a fresh start. Something almost like freedom shot through with the potential of a new start. The chance to be anyone. The chance for a normal life. And after all those years of foster homes and shitty schools, hadn't that been the thing she had wanted most?

She'd got into a basic arts degree, signed up for classes and done all the readings. She lived in a tiny apartment without windows and worked in a faded old suburban restaurant, living frugally. When she had enough money, she would go out with Ness, the friend she'd made during O-week, to bars with student discounts, bars that were loud and dingy and served beer that was clearly watered down. But none of that mattered because this was what people did. Maggie had never been great with flirting or making friends, but Ness, with her cascading blonde hair and booming laugh, had all of that covered. Maggie stuck close to her and occasionally got talking to someone who'd been drawn by Ness but wasn't getting her attention.

On other nights, the nights Maggie preferred, she and Ness would hang out alone. They would sit in Ness's room on campus, drinking cheap wine and talking. Occasionally they'd share a joint, but Maggie soon found she hated weed. What alcohol dulled, weed heightened. One night, after a particularly rough episode of unstoppable recurring thoughts and the shakes Maggie tried so desperately to hide, Ness promised they'd stay away from weed in future. She told Maggie she didn't need to know what was going on, but she would listen if Maggie wanted to talk.

Which, Maggie found to her own surprise, she did. She told Ness about her father, the foster homes and the rest. About the persistent worry that she could never be normal. And Ness hadn't tried to talk her out of thinking that way or told her she was wrong but instead just gave her a hug and said sorry and asked if she wanted more wine.

For a while, that was enough. Better than enough. Then came the prick.

His real name was Elliot. He dressed well and, by the looks of it, visited an expensive hairdresser every couple of weeks. The way he carried himself, not to mention his lazy smirk, screamed rich kid. But Maggie seemed to be the only one to notice. Because Elliot had the kind of charm that offset questions of class. He had the ability to seem at ease wherever he was. He was good-looking with a deep voice that made him come across older than he was. And Ness, with her atrocious taste in men, had fallen for him quickly.

Maggie had seen it coming the first time they'd met at the campus bar. But she had figured – hoped – it would be a one-night stand and nothing more.

The next time she saw him, he was sitting in their usual booth with his gaggle of mates, arm slung around Ness, holding court and talking to Maggie as if *she* was the one who had to win him over.

'So what are you studying?' he'd asked with an indulgent smile, as if Maggie was lucky to be receiving any of his attention.

'Arts.'

'Anything specific in there?' He laughed, so loud that anything specific Maggie might have said would have been drowned out. So she just shrugged.

'Maggie's sussing out her options,' Ness said.

'I had this English teacher,' Elliot said, 'who told me that any story that is about everything is really about nothing. That's basically the deal with arts degrees, right? People do them to keep their options open, then end up working at Maccas. Except for you of course.' He said the last part to Ness as his cronies guffawed. 'You've got that particular focus. That drive. It's what I like about you.'

Ness had blushed as Maggie sipped her beer and wondered whether she could make smashing it over his head look like an accident.

'But no, seriously, I envy you,' he'd said to Maggie, taking on a conspiratorial tone. 'Doing science just kind of locks you into one career path, you know? I mean, don't get me wrong, that's what I want, but I *wish* I could just, you know, go with the flow. See where life takes me. I think it's really cool to not care about the future until it arrives.'

The prick moved fast. Within the fortnight of what could loosely be called their relationship, he had convinced Ness that this was love, that they didn't need more time to think it through or test it out. When you knew, he would say, you knew.

Ness had laughed about his request at first. She said it as an aside to Maggie as they grabbed a coffee after the one class they had together – if you were trying to offload MDMA, where would you go? She tried to treat it almost as a joke. But Maggie heard the unsteadiness in her voice. And while she knew better than to lecture Ness, she wasn't about to let it drop. A couple of quiet prods and Ness came clean.

'It's not much,' she said. 'You know, he deals a bit to pay for uni.'

His parents clearly paid for uni, but Maggie didn't point that out.

'And why shouldn't he?' Ness had said, sounding like she was trying to justify it to herself. 'I mean, students will always want to get high, right? And if El can make sure the stuff they get is pure, then that seems fair enough.'

'What's not fair enough is him pulling you into it,' Maggie had said.

'That's not …' Ness shook her head wildly. 'No. It's not that. He just had a meet that fell through and needs to move some stuff to make rent. He needs someone he can trust and … it's nothing. Really.'

But then he had asked again.

* * *

The dissolution of Maggie and Ness' friendship was, at least at first, only surprising in how long it took. Maggie had got used to people quietly cutting ties when they realised that her 'intensity' wasn't some act calibrated to make her seem interesting.

For a while she had let herself believe Ness was different. There weren't many people who could make Maggie laugh, or just feel slightly at ease, but something about Ness had achieved that from early in their friendship, some singular alchemy that made Maggie cling to Ness with a need verging on desperation.

But when Ness stopped replying to messages, only occasionally sending back brief, terse replies, Maggie suspected that this was a different kind of distancing. That Ness wasn't pulling away because Maggie had scared or embarrassed her, but because things in her own life had taken a turn for the worst. It was obvious whenever she saw her at uni; Ness had lost weight and her usually lustrous hair was stringy. But nothing made Maggie more certain than the tightness in her face and the way her eyes looked either glazed or too sharp and darting. Maggie knew those looks.

She didn't think Elliot had turned violent. Not physically, anyway. What Maggie suspected was that the little favours had turned into bigger favours, bigger and more frequent. Offloading a bit of product to help with rent had become a succession of parties at which Ness was being pushed to sell whatever Elliot had, pushed because that was what doting girlfriends did when they loved somebody. Pushed because maybe the lack of violence had started to look less like a given and more like an axe that would only need a slight provocation to fall.

Maggie didn't know for sure. And she didn't try to find out. She wasn't entirely sure why this was. Maybe it was her sense that getting involved would disrupt the fragile semblance of a normal life she was trying to construct. Or else it was that Ness's distance, whatever the reason, stung more than she cared to admit. Just another person Maggie had let herself love who had dropped away.

Then the call came.

It was three in the morning and Maggie jerked awake with the first vibration of her phone. Her heart raced and sleep vanished in seconds.

'Maggie,' Ness sounded breathless, choked. Wind and footsteps in the background – wherever she was she was moving fast.

Maggie said nothing. Her heart was yet to slow down.

'Mags, I fucked up.' Ness was crying. 'I fucked up really bad. I was … oh God, I was at this gig and I was trying to …' her voice caught. 'There was a cop. Undercover and … and I ran but I think he knows who I am, I think he was tipped off and … oh fuck, fuck, Maggie, what do I do?'

Maggie slipped out of bed. 'Get back to college. I'm on my way. Any gear you have in your room, toss it.'

A jumper and jeans tugged on in seconds and Maggie was out the door. She flagged a cab rather than record her movements with Uber, counting out the few notes she had in her wallet. Ness lived on campus and Maggie could walk there in half an hour, but they might not have that long.

As it turned out, they didn't. Maggie saw the white and blue of the police cars parked outside the halls of residence well before the driver pulled over. She gave it a split second of thought then, as the driver went to indicate, told him to keep going another block. She kept her voice light, made it seem like an arbitrary request.

Hands in pockets, she had walked back towards the halls. Meandering, just a girl making her way home on a cold city night. She slowed a little as she passed the building. She identified the light on in Ness's second-storey room. The shapes moving inside. The one cop waiting down in the car. Waiting for anyone who might have hurried to help.

Maggie didn't linger. She walked back home. Sat on her bed and watched out the window until the sun started to come up. Her phone never rang. Then she had a coffee, a shower and headed into class as if nothing had happened.

Maggie had hoped that Ness would give up Elliot, but she never did. It seemed the police had hoped the same – they'd known for a while that somebody was running a pretty efficient operation on campus, and while they had their suspicions, they didn't have enough to prove Elliot was anything other than a casual fling for Ness. He'd covered his tracks too well.

Ness stayed with her parents through the legal proceedings. She dropped out of uni before she could be expelled, not wanting to face the staring and the muttering and, inevitably, the laughter. Maggie had been questioned about the 3 am phone call but claimed Ness had been drunk and incoherent, something the police apparently accepted without question. She'd half-expected to hear from Harrison Cooper in the middle of this, given her tangential connection to what could have been a major drug bust, but she never did.

She visited Ness whenever she could but found the experience more frustrating than anything. Ness would sit on the bed, staring into space, and only shook her head when Maggie urged her to turn in Elliot. This made Maggie start to wonder what Elliot had on her. Photos, maybe. Or else something more, a dangling threat, implicit or not.

Whatever the case, it was Elliot who had pulled Ness into this, Elliot who was to blame for the fact that she could be facing prison time.

What made it all the worse was the fact that whenever Maggie saw Elliot at uni, he seemed entirely unfazed. One night, she even glimpsed him at the pub, getting cosy with some new girl, laughing and whispering something in her ear that made her blush. He didn't notice Maggie. Not even when she started turning up in the same places as him, as she began to work out what exactly his routine was. He never so much as glimpsed her sitting with her nose in a book across from him on the grassy uni lawn or in the shadowy corners of pubs. Always with the rounders bat hidden under her jacket.

CHAPTER SEVEN

Melbourne came into sight just before midday. Cooper was driving; he thought it was better Maggie didn't after the blow to her head. Maggie felt fine but kept quiet. She didn't trust herself to hold the wheel steady when the towers came into view beyond the stretch of highway that had seemed never-ending.

The sky behind them was overcast, a dreary grey against which the buildings looked stark and unwelcoming. The weather made the fields and hills, interspersed with the occasional half-built housing development, appear washed out, like all colour had seeped away and the only thing with any solidity was those fast-approaching towers.

Melbourne was the kind of city whose aesthetic value varied depending on where you were standing. Or, perhaps more pertinently, who you were. Ness, for example, had regularly waxed lyrical about the beauty of the city. To her it was a bohemian paradise full of boutique cafés hidden away down artfully cluttered alleys, of tree-shaded walks along a river that shone in the sunlight, over which the towers of the city stood proud and gleaming. Sometimes, when they'd had a couple of drinks, Ness would drag Maggie to the bridge overlooking the Yarra to bask in the brilliant lights of the bars along Southbank that were so perfectly reflected in the water. She would tell Maggie that in that spot the electric possibilities of the city, the vivid *life* that characterised it, became all you could see. It was obvious that Ness was trying to win Maggie over to feeling that same love for the place. Maggie did appreciate the effort but that didn't change the fact that all she tended to see were grimy swathes of worn concrete, a river that was muddy and full of rubbish and alleys that were more likely to be full of overflowing dumpsters and stink than hipster cafés and elaborate graffiti murals.

From here, watching the cluster of towers grow nearer, devoid of colour or conveniently reflected sunlight, her perspective seemed the right one.

It was hard to ignore the sense that she was heading straight into danger. There was no real reason to believe that this couldn't be straightforward, that she wouldn't be able to find an easy way to disappear the moment she had the hard drive, but a fitful uncertainty lingered. Uncertainty over Cooper's motives, over her own ability to betray him, over whether a return to Melbourne had been in any way a good idea to begin with.

The fields vanished. The suburbs became all she could see, then the shops and train stations started appearing and soon Melbourne sprouted around them. Maggie felt the occasional spike of recognition seeing bars and restaurants she knew, parks she'd walked through, but it all seemed so unreal, like the set of a play she'd once appeared in but had since forgotten all the lines for.

Cooper pulled over near the bottom of the long, vibrant stretch of Sydney Road. Maggie tried to keep from looking around the worn kebab stores and ramshackle bars like a tourist. Faded furniture shops and convenience stores with signs that had not been changed in what seemed to be thirty years were jammed together with upmarket pubs and record stores that erred on the side of rundown but in a way that was all too self-conscious, like they were trying to project an air of underground authenticity. The combination of people on the streets was eclectic – hipsters in paisley shirts with immaculate quiffs and rolled cigarettes passed older men stumping along with their scowls and their stained aprons, back to wherever it was they were working. The mutual glances of disdain were all too obvious.

'Home sweet home.' Cooper glanced at his watch, then leaned back in his seat. 'Still a while until we have to see the lawyer. I'm gonna head home quickly for a shower then we can meet at the pub.'

'Pub?'

Cooper nodded. 'Ms Darch likes a drink. I figure after a couple of glasses, she might be a bit more willing to help without too many questions. And I don't want the meeting going on any record.'

'For the police?'

'For anyone. If we can get this all handled informally, then we're good.'

'How likely is that?'

Cooper glanced at the rear-view mirror. 'Reasonably. She was your father's lawyer for a long time, so there's likely at least a bit of nostalgic affection there. Eric could be charming when he wanted to be.'

'Guess I never saw him want to be.'

Maggie drove to an old motel that she knew from memory, up the other end of Sydney Road. It sat near a busy intersection, adjacent to a 7-Eleven across from a tram stop. It was a blocky, two-storey building shaped like a squared-off C, with carparks in the centre. It was plain and uninspiring, but she didn't need much else. She paid for one night, then took her stuff to her room, on the second floor.

She sat on the bed and checked the clock. She felt wired, like she needed to burn off some excess energy. And she knew well enough that the only way that was going to happen was to get this meeting over and done with. So she sat and watched the clock, fidgeting until it was finally time to head across town. She considered taking the backpack with her, but instead left it under the bed. Although she didn't like leaving her money behind, it was generally better not to carry thousands of dollars in cash.

The address Cooper had given her was a couple of blocks off the famously trendy stretch of Smith Street, which Maggie had avoided like the plague during her brief uni stint. Overpriced bars where the staff were clearly trained to be coolly unpleasant and 'retro' clothes stores that sold second-hand stuff for three times its original price had never, despite how Ness insisted, had any appeal for Maggie. She parked a decent distance from the pub, down a side street, before walking the rest of the way. The trees lining these streets were almost bare, the remaining leaves red and gold. The wind came in occasional icy bursts. It wasn't winter yet, but autumn in Melbourne was very different from autumn in Port Douglas. Over the houses and phone lines ahead of her Maggie could see the towers of the city. She slowed, watching them for a moment and feeling the first flecks of rain. She could hear the trundle of trams nearby. *Melbourne.* Her home, until it wasn't. Until it couldn't be anymore. Maybe tonight that would change. She kept walking.

The pub Cooper had chosen seemed, at first, like a bit of a joke. It was a narrow corner venue with a strong stale beer smell in the air, low lights and decorations largely made out of empty bottles with skulls atop the taps. The bartender, a shifty-looking punk with a towering blue mohawk and a ragged denim jacket, gave Maggie a bemused stare as she walked in. Cooper was already waiting at a side table with a bottle of red wine and three glasses.

'It's close to her office and we're not going to be disturbed,' he said, by way of explanation.

'Disturbed by who?' Maggie eyed the bartender.

The door swung open and, nose wrinkled, a woman entered. She looked to be in her sixties, dressed in a pencil skirt and suit jacket, skin leathery, no makeup, hair silver and short. Her eyes landed on Maggie.

Cooper stood. 'Ms Darch.'

'Harrison.' Her voice was low and gravelly. She walked over, taking the glass Cooper offered and sitting without hesitation. 'Interesting venue.'

Cooper sipped his wine. 'Cops get used to out-of-the-way places. The décor becomes a secondary concern.'

'My concern is a bit more than secondary, but we'll let it slide.' Her gaze fixed on Maggie and for a moment they just looked at each other. She extended a long-fingernailed hand. 'Stephanie Darch.'

Like a punch to the gut, recognition struck. Maggie didn't take her hand. The memories were flooding in; she was eleven years old, the musty smell of the too-large courtroom, the judge watching with cool disinterest, her father shaven and sombre across the room, and beside him, this woman. Never once looking at Maggie, speaking about her as if she wasn't there. *She has a history of lying and emotional problems. My client is innocent.* This woman had almost stopped the state from taking her to something close to safety, something that had seemed possible after her teacher finally noticed the bruises. Maggie had hated that voice, without any remembered name to give it, almost as much as her father himself.

'I remember you,' Maggie said.

Darch's hand didn't lower. Maggie felt Cooper's eyes on her, felt the silent plea.

She took Darch's hand. The woman's skin was dry and brittle.

'Look at you now.' Darch touched her wine glass to her lips. 'All grown up.'

Maggie put her hand around her own glass and held it tight.

'Thanks for meeting us,' Cooper said. 'As I mentioned on the phone, we're in a slightly precarious situation. It's of the utmost importance that we access Eric's estate quickly and quietly.'

'For the inheritance?'

'More than that,' Cooper said. 'It's a police matter, but we believe somewhere in Eric's possession is a crucial piece of evidence for an ongoing investigation.'

'So get a warrant.' Darch drank.

Cooper topped up her wine. 'Our prime suspect is a dangerous and well-connected individual, and while I respect and expect the best from my colleagues—'

'The police force and secrecy go together like water and a sieve,' Darch said.

'Call me paranoid, but a warrant causes a lot more noise than an heir receiving her inheritance.'

Darch finished her glass. 'Depends on the heir.'

Cooper leaned forward. 'I understand that this is out of the ordinary.'

'Do you?' Darch said with an expression of slack amusement that made Maggie want to punch her.

'This goes beyond protocol,' Cooper said. 'This is about Eric.'

Darch's eyes narrowed slightly, but she didn't retort.

'My working theory is that the suspect set up Terrence Adams,' Cooper said. 'That he used his influence to point the police in the wrong direction. The same wrong direction that Eric ran in.' There was a bite of anger to Cooper's voice now.

Any amusement was gone from Darch's face. She watched him with something not far off fascination.

'Eric was not a forgiving person,' Cooper said. 'It's part of what made him such a great cop. At the start he was downright zealous. Didn't rest until he'd got his man. And he usually did.' Cooper raised his glass but didn't drink. 'But that inability to forgive extended to himself.'

Darch cleared her throat. 'Eric—'

'Is dead,' Cooper said. 'You don't need to defend him. What he became is not the man he started out as. If I'm right, then the person I'm looking for is the person responsible for that.'

Nobody spoke.

'What I'm asking for,' Cooper said, 'is discretion. Maggie is the legal heir to Eric's estate. There is no reason she shouldn't be allowed to access it.'

Darch's gaze flicked to Maggie.

'I know you're not naive,' Cooper said. 'You know the force isn't perfect. Which is why I'm asking you to help me. Get whatever documents you need together, let Maggie sign them. I believe Eric's possessions ended up in a storage unit somewhere?'

Darch nodded.

'Then we just need the key. Without letting anyone else know about it. If I'm wrong, all you've done is your job. If I'm right, it's justice. For Eric.'

Another stretch of silence. Cooper was watching Darch. Maggie kept her eyes on her drink.

Darch looked at Maggie. 'You've been quiet.'

Maggie shrugged.

'He was a charismatic man, your father.' A playful note had crept into Darch's voice. 'I always thought he was like something out of a classic western. The take-no-prisoners sheriff. Shoot first, ask questions later. He was old-fashioned, in some respects, but chivalrous.'

A surge of billowing hot rage. 'Yeah.' Maggie could hear the tremor in her voice. She didn't care. 'He was really fucking chivalrous when he held my hand over the stove for dropping a saucepan. When I was *seven*.'

Darch's gaze was steady. 'Sometimes people misremember. They exaggerate.'

Maggie was up and out of her seat. Cooper's hand was hard around her wrist.

'The past is past,' he said firmly. 'What matters now is doing the right thing.'

Darch's eyes gave nothing away. Through the throbbing rise of hate, it struck Maggie that this woman was a lot cleverer than she let on and clever, in this situation, meant dangerous.

Maggie sat. Cooper let go.

Darch looked between them and took another long swig of wine. She wiped her mouth and nodded. 'Alright. The keys to the storage unit and the house are at my office. We can meet there tomorrow and—'

'Tonight,' Maggie said. She didn't want to see Stephanie Darch again. 'We'll go tonight.'

For a long moment, Darch looked at her. Finally, she nodded. 'Tonight it is.'

'Did you drive?' Cooper asked.

'Walked,' Darch said. 'But you two drive. I need to make a phone call.'

'We'll walk with you,' Maggie said.

Another moment of consideration, then another nod.

Outside the air was cool and the night sky thick with dark clouds. A light rain was falling. Cars rolled by, and the occasional beeping of a horn was punctuated by a yell from somewhere back on Smith Street. Cooper stayed close to Darch, talking to her about paperwork and details. Maggie lingered behind them, eyes on Darch. Involuntarily, her right hand opened and closed.

Darch hadn't gone for her phone.

Something had been building the whole time they'd been in the bar, something more than the pulsing hatred that grew with every second in Darch's company. It was a sense that she'd been carrying since Cairns, a hard-to-define sense of something being missing in all this. It was the same sense that had flared up with Cooper's refusal to name his suspect, and the moment in Holbrook with the bikies. Paranoia, maybe, but Maggie doubted it. Whatever the case, she had to play this next part very carefully.

Especially considering that if Darch was true to her word, she'd be getting the keys tonight. And then what? Maggie had parked her car at a slight distance to avoid the risk of Cooper knowing where to follow her to, but to get back to it she'd still have to evade him. And even then the key was only the first step. She would then need to reach the storage unit and search it without him finding her there.

Darch led them right around a corner, onto a narrow, shadowy street. There was no-one else in sight and the lights in the row of old shops were all out. Even the distant horns were now only faint snatches. Darch stopped at a glass door through which Maggie could see only crumpled blinds. There were faded gold letters on the window. Darch's first name was missing the T. She didn't look at Cooper. Focused on the layout of the office.

The waiting room smelled musty. Drab beige chairs lined the off-white walls. Dog-eared magazines sat on chipped coffee tables. Maggie wondered if anyone ever sat behind that empty reception desk.

'Wait here a moment,' Darch said.

She pushed through a door behind the desk and shut it.

'Relatively painless,' Cooper said.

There was something about his voice. Something almost surprised. Maggie's eyes moved to the closed door to Darch's office. Then back to Cooper, who was looking at the window.

Maggie followed Darch. Cooper said something but Maggie ignored him. She shoved the door open.

Darch was hunched over her desk, phone halfway to her ear. She gaped at Maggie, then went to speak but was cut off by Maggie's fist. Darch's head hit the table. Maggie grabbed the phone, throwing it across the room. Gasping, Darch tried to push herself up on the desk. Maggie's eyes landed on a letter opener. She picked it up and, fist clenched around the hilt, pushed the tip hard into Darch's middle finger, splayed on the desk.

'Maggie.' Cooper was in the doorway, hands raised, eyes wide.

'Who were you trying to call?' Maggie said.

There were tears in Darch's eyes. 'N-no-one, just a—'

Maggie pushed the letter opener harder. Darch squealed. Cooper didn't move.

'The police,' the lawyer cried.

Pounding in Maggie's ears. 'Cooper is the police.'

Darch shook her head. 'He's not on your case.'

Her case.

'Maggie, please, listen to me,' Cooper said.

The bikies. The evasions.

Keeping the letter opener pressed into Darch's finger, Maggie turned to Harrison Cooper. 'Who the fuck are you working for?'

Cooper didn't reply. His jaw was tight as he tried to think, tried to work out the explanation that was eluding him.

'The keys,' Maggie said to Darch. 'Now.'

'I can't.'

'Why not?'

Through her tears the lawyer looked up at Maggie and there at last, burning through the alcohol and the smug condescension was pure acid spite. 'Because you killed him.'

The heel of Maggie's left palm slammed hard into her clenched right fist. A crack of severed bone, a burst of blood and Darch was screaming, falling, clutching her hand.

Maggie sensed movement and pointed the letter opener directly at Cooper.

'The keys, now, or it will be more than a finger,' Maggie said, without looking away from Cooper.

Spluttering and sobbing, Darch fumbled for the drawer to her desk.

'Maggie, this isn't what you think,' Cooper said.

'Fuck you.'

A clatter on the table as two keys on a ring were dropped. Darch hit the floor again, quivering. Maggie snatched up the keys and as she did, in that moment of distraction, heard the click of a cocked gun.

CHAPTER EIGHT

Cooper's aim wasn't wavering. 'Give me the keys.'

Maggie didn't reply.

'Please,' Cooper said. 'Give me the keys and I can let you leave. No-one will know you were here, but you have to give me the keys before—'

From outside, the low rumble of an engine. Then another and another. Behind Cooper, bright light fractured by the blinds filled the waiting room.

Cooper's expression was pained. 'Please.'

Maggie didn't move.

They both turned as the front door opened with a creak. Maggie dropped her arm, turning the letter opener up inside her wrist, concealed. She moved back as Cooper stepped aside.

A man stood in the doorway to Darch's office. He was tall; his slicked-back hair almost brushed the doorframe. His amused blue eyes stood out in a clean-shaven, sunbeaten face as he looked them all over. His leather cut, with a patch inscribed *Vice President*, strained slightly against his muscled torso.

'Evening.' His voice was a deep, low drawl. 'Threw a party and didn't invite us, Harrison?'

'It's under control, Byrne,' Cooper said.

The bikie – Byrne – glanced from Cooper's gun to Maggie's letter opener to where Darch was crumpled shaking in the corner. 'Clearly,' he said. 'Lucky for you, Rook wanted us to keep an eye on things. Can we step out into the waiting room? This office is a bit fucking claustrophobic.' He moved backwards. Cooper shot Maggie a look that urged her to comply before he followed Byrne. Maggie hesitated, then did the same.

Two more bikies waited out there, a skinny young one with straw-coloured hair and wide eyes, and an older, bearded man with a shotgun.

'Who the fuck is *she*?' the young man said.

'Hoping to get answers to that myself, Nipper.' Byrne looked steadily at Maggie.

Maggie said nothing.

Byrne nodded to Cooper. 'Well?'

'She's Eric's daughter.'

Byrne looked back to Maggie, eyebrows raised. 'No shit.'

'How did you know my father?' Maggie asked.

'Figured you'd keep a few key details from her?' Byrne said to Cooper. Then to Maggie: 'Your dad was a mate of ours. Just like Harrison. Just like—'

'That's enough.' Cooper's voice was hard.

Byrne's lip curled up in a smirk. He crossed the room and sat in one of the chairs, resting his right ankle on his left knee as he leaned back. 'Seems there's a lot you've been keeping to yourself, Harrison. Were you gonna tell us about the girl? Or were you just gonna let her slip off into the night the moment you had the keys?'

'She's got nothing to do with this,' Cooper said.

'Was that the tune you played her?'

Cooper looked away.

Byrne's cold gaze moved to Maggie. 'Problem is, this does have something to do with her. More than something, now. Rook's gonna need to hear what she might know.'

'I haven't told her anything,' Cooper said.

Byrne's eyes didn't leave Maggie. 'We'll be the judge of that.'

Maggie tried to gauge her distance to the door without looking. She'd have to get past the two other bikies to get out. And even then, she'd be on foot and they'd have bikes. She didn't imagine they'd conveniently left the keys in the ignitions for her.

'This is what's gonna happen,' Byrne said to Maggie. 'You'll hand over those keys. Then you're gonna come with us back to the clubhouse. If you say no, we'll kill you.' There was no change in tone on the last part.

'Oh yeah, no worries,' Maggie said. 'And after you've taken me to your clubhouse and presumably tortured me, you'll let me go of course.'

'Depends on how forthcoming you are.' Byrne stood. 'Now. Keys.'

Maggie kept her eyes from darting around the room. That thrum of energy was building again. Her senses felt heightened; the light a little too bright, outlines a little too sharp.

The bearded older bikie moved for Maggie. She held out the keys. He went to take them.

Distantly, she heard a siren.

The bikie glanced at the door just as just as Maggie grabbed his hand and brought the letter opener up hard through his wrist.

The bikie screamed. Maggie pulled him around just as Nipper fired off several shots, shots that silenced the bearded man immediately as he slumped against Maggie. She yanked out the letter opener and dived for the door, past a shocked Nipper and a frozen Cooper. The sirens were louder. Then more shots and glass shattered as she stumbled into the night.

The rain had picked up. At one end of the road, the flashing lights of a police car screeched into view. Sirens were coming from the other end as well. Behind her she could hear Byrne's bellowing. She ran across the street, weaving as another volley of bullets turned the night into an explosive cacophony. She clocked the mouth of a narrow alley between shops and ran through it just as the buildings behind her were bathed in red and blue and more yells filled the air.

Maggie ran down the slippery alley. Ahead was the bulk of a dumpster and then—

A glare of light and a growl of engine as a bike pulled into the alley.

Maggie flung herself behind the dumpster. She tried to slow her breathing. Her heart pounded. More roars from the street behind her, almost drowned out by the shrieking sirens. The wall of the alley across from her turned bright with the headlight. The bike slowed to a crawl as it approached. Maggie closed her eyes. Focused. She waited for the sound of the engine to drown out everything else, then opened her eyes as the bike pulled into view and lunged.

She slammed into the rider, who shouted as he was carried sideways and the weight of the bike crushed his leg. Everything came in fragments: the helmet, the Scorpion insignia on his jacket, the letter opener in Maggie's hand, the blood as she drove it into his neck again and again.

The bikie was struggling feebly but there wasn't time to finish the job. She pushed herself up and away from the still-vibrating bike. The yelling and sirens from behind hadn't slowed. She moved fast and quiet the way the bikie had come, slipping the bloodied letter opener into her pocket as she did.

Maggie exited the alley into another street; also still, the various takeaway stores and cafés closed for the night. A couple of lights above shops had turned on, awakened by the noise. She hurried up the street, alert for any sign of movement, any shifting shadow. She continued until she reached the turn-off for another main street then kept going, now into a residential area, all jammed together townhouses and cramped front gardens. She couldn't hear the sirens anymore. She kept moving. She held her hand out, hoping the rain would be enough to do something about the blood.

Her heart hadn't slowed. She could feel the shaking she was barely holding at bay. But she couldn't let it overwhelm her, send her curling into a ball ready for the police or the bikies or anyone to come and take her away. For now, she had to move, to get away from these side streets to somewhere more public, somewhere where even the boldest bikie wouldn't attack and even the savviest cop wouldn't think to look.

Darch must have called the police. Ignored and injured in the office, she'd taken her chance. Maggie might have been impressed, even grateful, but that didn't make her regret severing Darch's finger.

As she turned right again onto a wider, better lit street, Maggie pulled off her jacket despite the chilly air and slung it over her arm, as if she'd got too warm and was carrying it. She didn't seem to have much more blood on her, but for now she would just have to hope she looked innocuous enough. With her other, clean hand she ran her fingers through her wet hair, pulling as much as she could over her face without obscuring her vision.

There were more people around here, clumps of laughing drinkers and the occasional old man veering with a bottle of something cheap. None of them seemed to have the slightest idea of what had happened just several blocks away. Good. That meant none of them would think to associate her with it. She kept walking until she hit Smith Street. She was near the top of it now, and it was alive with lights and tables that scattered the pavement as people downed beer, talked shit and staggered to the next bar. Nobody paid her the slightest bit of attention as she moved fast through them all.

Down the street, distinctly louder than the cars, the roar of a bike. Several.

Maggie didn't turn or speed up. Somewhere in the night there were sirens, but that didn't mean they were coming for her. Still, she needed to be away from here. The bikes were getting louder.

From behind her came the tell-tale ding of a tram. There was a stop up ahead and she moved for it. The tram was new, she saw, all vivid green paint and a well-lit interior. It slowed and she stepped on. It was crowded with people, mostly standing, talking loudly over each other. She wished that she had a phone she could look at. Instead, she tried to smile vaguely, a slightly drunk girl headed home from a night out. She found a seat up the back. She didn't look out the window. It was harder to make out the sounds of bikes in here, but they had to be close and she had to look inconspicuous.

What had she learned? Not much, apart from the fact that Cooper was almost certainly working for the bikies. He had said it wasn't what she thought, but what the hell did that mean? His motives seemed inconsequential in the face of the fact that, again, he had let her down. With a swell of boiling rage, she realised that he had known his lies would bring her into danger. Now here she was, stuck in the city she'd spent so long running from, hunted by bikies and cops and Townsend all at once with no clue of where to turn or how to get out of this. The only advantage she had, and it wasn't much of one, was she had the keys that everyone wanted so much.

Sitting across from her was a young boy, wide-eyed in the face of everything around him. His mother's protective arm was over his shoulders even as she looked at her phone. The boy was looking at Maggie.

Then, from outside the window, the distinctive roar of a bike.

Maggie sank a little lower in her seat, didn't look, despite her racing heart, despite the feeling that every inch of her was vibrating with the energy of a building explosion. The bike was louder, then gone, past the tram.

The boy was still looking at Maggie. Specifically, at the jacket covering her hand. At the bloom of blood on it. Maggie rearranged the jacket to hide it. She raised her clear hand, put a finger to her lips and winked at the boy.

The tram turned, moving off Smith Street and towards the city. Voices nearby. Maggie looked up and immediately wanted to scream. Three burly men in outsized jackets were showing off their badges as they moved through the crowd of groaning passengers. 'Just checking tickets. Have them ready for inspection,' the lead one was saying.

Maggie stood up and worked her way through the muttering throng towards the tram door, keeping her head down. *Surely the bikes had gone. Surely there wasn't another one coming.*

'Hang on there, miss,' the man said, approaching her. 'Just gotta check your ticket.' Up close, his face was broad and flabby, barely managing to contain his smug glee at catching someone. His cronies, smelling blood, were moving over to join him as other passengers shifted out of the way.

'Where's your ticket?' the inspector asked her.

'Don't have one.'

'That's an offence.' He said the last word as if it gave him almost sexual pleasure. 'You are aware it's illegal to travel without a valid ticket?'

The tram was slowing.

Maggie shrugged.

'Well, there's a pretty decent fine for this, which should teach you a lesson.' The inspector reached for his notebook as the tram stopped and the door slid open. Maggie went for it. The inspector, instinctively, reached for her. She threw the jacket in his face. The inspector stumbled back, colliding with one of his cronies as the third lunged for her, but Maggie stepped backwards off the tram as its door slid shut and it started to move again.

She spun on the spot, looking for bikes, but there was none. Adrenaline still pulsed through her. Maggie's eyes landed on a nearby bar, lights dim and music slow. Hands in pockets, she moved fast towards it. It was one of those places that was clearly supposed to seem old-fashioned and rustic, all wooden furniture and fairy lights and expensive craft beers. The tables, predictably, were packed with drinkers. Looking as casual as she could, Maggie walked through them all, as if searching for a friend. She caught sight of a young couple in a booth, whispering to each other. Beside the guy was the bundled-up shape of what looked like a hoodie. Maggie slowed as she neared them. Another guy was passing, carrying two pints. Maggie stuck out a foot. With a squawk, he went flying, all eyes on him as Maggie snatched the hoodie and kept walking.

At the rear of the bar was a hall, down which, to Maggie's relief, a *Staff Only* sign adorned the door next to the toilet. She slipped through it into a narrower, musty hall lined with shelves straining under boxes, along which she moved until she found a screen door. She slipped through into an alley. She stopped, giving herself a moment to catch her breath.

She wanted to find somewhere to hole up for the night, to hunker down and close her eyes and try to work through everything that had changed so rapidly and violently. Or if not changed, then just revealed itself for what it really was. There was a flood of bitter emotion that was close to overwhelming her, but she had to fight that with everything she had, just like she had to fight off the sneering voice telling her that she should have guessed Cooper couldn't be trusted, that there was more going on than she had let herself believe. She had been wilfully blind, wanting so much for him to prove himself the heroic good guy she had so desperately wanted him to be as a kid.

Through all of this a couple of things gnawed at her. Byrne and the bikies, for one – Maggie was now almost certain that whoever her father had evidence on must have been from among their ranks. But then how did Cooper come into it? Was it as simple as longstanding corruption, or something else? And beyond that, what had been her father's relationship to the gang?

The water on the ground, the grime on the walls, the voices from inside – everything was heightened, *more*, brought to vivid life by whatever this current running through her was. She needed to get away from here and fast, but there was some small, strange urge telling her to get back out there and take them all on – the police, inspectors, bikies, anyone stupid enough to try to fuck with her now.

She shook it off and hurried into the rainy dark.

* * *

Sticking to the shadows and the alleys, she took the long way back to her car, never straying too far from Smith Street, always listening for the rumble of a bike or shriek of a siren. She kept the hood up and her hands buried deep in her pockets. Caution was what would keep her alive.

If Cooper or Darch had survived the shootout, then the police would know about her. This meant that for now her job was to stay ahead of everyone. If she could get back to her car and her money, she could be on the road and out of Melbourne before the morning. It stung to think that she couldn't go after the hard drive, but there was nothing to be done about that. The storage unit would be watched, and besides, she had no clue where it even was.

It took a couple more turns down dark, empty streets to work her way back to where she had left her car. There was still no-one in sight. She paused as she neared it. Nobody, as far as she was aware, knew where she had parked. But still. She approached slowly and checked through the windows then under the car. Nothing out of the ordinary. She opened the boot and found her spare licence plates. After a quick look around, she got to work swapping them over. Still no sign of anyone nearby. Breathing slightly easier, she slid into the driver's seat and turned the ignition.

Nothing.

She tried again, then again. She stopped. Looked at the small panel under the ignition. She went to open it just as the back door opened and she heard the click behind her.

CHAPTER NINE

Maggie looked in the rear-view mirror. Green eyes in a haggard face.

'G'day, girl,' the harsh voice said. 'Do me a favour and keep calm, would you?'

'Do I seem not calm?'

'You figured out the fuse quickly enough.' The eyes in the mirror flicked downwards. 'Now, how about I give it back and we take a drive? There are a whole bunch of cops out looking for you.'

'I'd rather end up in their hands than Len Townsend's.'

His laugh was harsh. 'Jesus, is *that* the impression I'm giving off? I'm not taking you to Townsend. Or the cops, for that matter. I want you to drive so we can get clear of the bastards and talk somewhere safe. Let's go with whatever shithole motel you've been holed up in.'

For a moment, Maggie didn't move. She held out her hand and he dropped into it the small piece of plastic with its two protruding metal prongs. Maggie opened the panel and, replacing the missing fuse, started the engine and pulled out on to the road. 'Have you been following me?'

'Just putting two and two together. Old Cooper went home without you before and I was fairly sure you weren't going to hide out anywhere that would require online booking. It had to be a cheap motel that would take a fake ID and cash in hand.'

'Who are you?'

In the rear-view mirror, Maggie caught a glimpse of a crooked grin. 'Jack Carlin, love. I knew your dad way back when.'

'He arrest you?'

'The bastard wished. We did the arresting together, back in the halcyon days of yore.'

'What do you want from me?'

'We'll get to that. Stay off the main roads, will you? Don't wanna risk some trigger-happy cop seeing us together.'

Maggie pulled onto a side street. She figured she was heading in the direction of the motel, but it was hard to focus.

'You've managed to piss just about everyone off,' Carlin went on. 'Got the attention of my old police comrades, of the most dangerous bikie gang this side of, well, anywhere, *and* on the wrong side of Len Townsend right after he started wearing his big-boy pants. In my best years, I'd have been happy with one of the three, but the lot is just asking for a metric fuckton of trouble. You'll need to be very, very lucky to get clear of Melbourne.'

Maggie didn't even try to keep the irritation out of her voice. 'Would you mind telling me what the fuck you want?'

'Sensing your father's temper there, love. That's not a good look on anyone.'

'I don't have the key. If that's what you're after.' Maggie glanced in the rear-view. Held Carlin's gaze for a beat. 'Are we done?'

'Not quite. Where's your motel?'

Maggie turned down another side street; they were almost there and she figured she was better served parking away from it. Especially if she had to work out a way to get rid of this prick. She pulled over.

'Alright,' Carlin said. 'The one across the road, yeah? We walk there nice and calm. Just going for a stroll. Don't try to run or pull any other bullshit, alright? I promise it won't be worth your while.'

She got out of the car. Seeing him fully now, Jack Carlin looked something like a rangy, matted old wolf. He was tall but slightly stooped. His tangled mane of grey hair sat back from his thin face. He wore an old leather jacket and ripped jeans. He looked one step from homeless, but there was a keen intelligence in those green eyes that Maggie didn't like at all. Nothing about him indicated ex-cop.

Carlin gestured. 'Shall we?'

It was less than a five-minute walk to the motel, but it felt a lot longer. Every step Maggie was aware of Carlin's calculating gaze, of the weapon he had concealed and just how easily he had managed to get the better of her. He might not have been one of Townsend's goons, but Maggie almost would have preferred that.

The moment they were through the door of the motel room, Carlin lit a cigarette and offered one to Maggie.

'It's a non-smoking room.'

'Well, God forbid you should ever bend the rules.' He sat in an armchair facing her.

'What do you want?'

'Those keys in your pocket would be a great start.'

'Fuck you.'

Carlin whistled and leaned back in his seat. 'You kiss your mother with that mouth?'

The amused glint in his eye told Maggie that the pointed jibe was very deliberate. It also told her that Jack Carlin knew more than she was comfortable with.

'Who are you?' she said.

'I thought we'd been through the introductions.'

'A name doesn't count for much. Who are you working for?'

'You reckon because Cooper's in the pocket of the bikies everyone has some hidden agenda?'

'Given that you're yet to tell me your agenda, hidden seems like the right word.'

'My agenda is my own,' Carlin said. 'Suffice it to say I'm not working for Townsend, or the bikies, or the cops. Which right about now makes me your best friend in this city.'

'Alright, *friend*,' Maggie leaned forward. 'How about you shed some light on this whole mess. What's on that hard drive?'

'Evidence.'

'On who?'

'You survive a shootout with bikies and you're still wondering that?'

'So my father knew something about the Scorpions.'

'More than something, but more than he should have about one Scorpion in particular.'

'Somebody important?'

Carlin took a long drag. He seemed to be weighing her up. 'How much do you know about the criminal underworld?'

'More than most.'

'But not enough,' Carlin said. 'The truth that people fail to grasp is that it's an ecosystem the police are very much part of. In a perfect world, they'd be stamping out gangs left right and centre, but that's neither realistic nor profitable.' Another drag of his smoke. 'Yeah, you have your hero cops here and there, but ninety percent of the time they don't last very long. Not without compromise. Not without the understanding that gangs are like hydras – cut one down, see five more sprout up in their place. Five that might not be as predictable as the one they replaced. So as counterintuitive as it might seem, there's often good reasons certain major players don't get taken down.'

Maggie wasn't sure corruption counted as a 'good reason', but she didn't bother pointing it out.

'But,' Carlin went on, 'let's say that along comes one of those crusading hero cops who reckons that whole approach is bullshit. Say that rockstar Detective Olivia Dean doesn't give a fuck about the policy of vague tolerance adopted by her colleagues towards a hydra head that's a bit more reasonable than the others. And say there was proof, proof that *could not* be ignored, that a rogue member of that group had done something really fucking bad. Something that nobody could hand-wave away. That member wouldn't have to be important. They'd just need the patch.'

'So a bikie, what, moonlights as a serial killer and—'

'Moonlight*ed*,' Carlin said. 'He's been dead a while.'

'So why—'

'Think,' Carlin said.

'Yeah, okay.' She was tired and pissed off and wished she'd stayed in Port Douglas. 'Bikie gangs are careful never to give the cops anything actionable. All your detective needs is proof of one being a killer and she can tear the whole operation apart. But given what happened tonight, I don't understand how the cops don't have grounds to take them down.'

Carlin smirked. 'You think Rook Gately and his boys got this far without ever having a run-in with the boys in blue? I'm reckoning they dropped their weapons and politely pressured that lawyer into backing up whatever absolving story they came up with. Might cop an illegal firearms charge or two, but that just doesn't pack the same punch, legally speaking, as serial murder. Just watch. Now' – Carlin brought his hands together in a single loud clap – 'let's talk mutual benefits.'

'I don't have the key,' she said.

He stubbed his cigarette out on the arm of the chair. 'Problem is, girl, you're lying.'

'You don't know that.'

Almost lazily, Carlin drew a pistol with a screwed-on silencer from inside his jacket and pointed it at Maggie. 'Turn out your pockets.'

Maggie didn't move.

Carlin grinned. 'Yeah. Lying.'

'You're not going to shoot me in a motel.'

'Try me.'

Maggie held Carlin's gaze. Any amusement was gone from it. And watching him, Maggie knew that for all that he was an unknown quantity, one thing was certain: he was a killer. Whether he would hesitate to shoot her or not, banking on the latter was a gamble Maggie wasn't willing to take.

She reached into her pocket, withdrew the keys and tossed them towards him. Carlin caught them without looking, then lowered the gun.

He stood. 'Now, here's what's happening. I'm gonna go have a dig around at this storage unit. See what I can find.'

'You know it'll be watched.'

'Not an idiot, girl. Meanwhile, you'll stay right here and try not to kill anyone. Before you tell me to get fucked, consider two things. One, I have eyes everywhere and will know if you try anything. Two, I can help you out of this. All you have to do is nothing. Reckon you can manage that?'

Maggie said nothing.

'I'll take that as a grudging yes,' Carlin said. 'See you soon, Maggie.'

The door slammed behind him. Maggie stayed put, her eyes on the cigarette butt, still smoking, bent and twisted on the arm of the chair.

Every instinct in her body was telling her to give Jack Carlin the middle finger and walk out the door. She hated this too-small room. She hated the sound of the shrieking baby a few doors down. She hated that she was trapped here by the fact that she had no idea whether Carlin was capable of everything he had threatened.

She got to her feet and paced the room.

What would Carlin do if she left? That depended on his reasons for wanting the evidence. If his aim was to get his old job back, then chances were there was only so much he was willing to risk. If he wasn't after reinstatement, then that made him far more unpredictable. Which meant the only option was to get as far away from him as possible. She didn't want to leave Melbourne without the hard drive, but it seemed like that ship had sailed and at a certain point survival had to come first. Whatever Carlin said, the motel was a public place and any attempt to harm her risked witnesses. His scare tactics might have worked on petty crooks and burned-out junkies, but this was far from Maggie's first rodeo.

She snatched up her backpack and slung it over her shoulder. She crossed to the door, took hold of the handle and leaned against it, listening. Distant trams and beeping cars.

She could move fast and she could move quiet. Get away from the motel and down the side streets. If Carlin *was* bullshitting, then she could be back on the highway in under an hour. By morning, she could be anywhere.

She opened the door and stepped out on to the balcony.

The rain was still falling, but lighter now. There was no-one else in sight; all she could hear was the still crying baby. Low light shone from beneath a couple of the doors across from her, but otherwise the motel sat in darkness. She looked to her left; the staircase down to the ground was just a few metres away. She looked to the right. Nobody was waiting. She turned left and started to move, just as a figure came up the stairs.

For a second, for one strange, mad second, she thought it was a ghost. It was tall and thin, with no discernible features, and so dark that it blended into the night and only snatches and slivers of light from the rooms cast it into relief. The face was an inky extension from the body and yet Maggie felt the eyes on her. Involuntarily, she stepped back as the figure slowed, surprised.

Reality snapped into place. A man, all in black, face covered by a stocking. And in his hand ...

He raised the machete as he started towards Maggie.

She turned and ran. She heard heavy, pounding footsteps and knew without having to look that he was close, that he was fast enough to cover the distance. She felt air across the back of her neck as he swiped the machete and a renewed rush of panic made her try to run faster, even though she knew she couldn't, even though she knew he would be on her in seconds. She careened around the corner and bolted along the balcony, her eyes finding the staircase on the opposite side. It was less than two hundred metres away and yet it might as well have been on the other side of the world.

The swish of the machete came again and she felt something snag and pull her back. A snarl of tearing fabric as her backpack gave way and hundred-dollar notes were caught by the wind and thrown up around her.

It didn't matter. She ran.

She rounded another corner and the staircase was just metres away. She lunged for it just as something hit her back and for a moment there was only the feeling of dull collision and then the pain slammed into her as something hot and wet drenched her jacket and, with a yell she couldn't help, she fell forward and tasted concrete. The baby was still crying, the noise louder now. The stairs were ahead. She tried to pull herself forward. She sensed movement behind her, the raised machete. She pushed herself up despite the feeling of her skin being torn apart; a foot took her hard in the stomach and she was thrown forward. She hit the edge of the staircase, went over and then concrete edges pummelled her from every direction, blows glancing off her head, arms flung up to protect herself as she went over and over again until she hit the bottom.

She saw night sky. She saw clouds. Then the glint of metal. She rolled as the blade glanced off the pavement. The figure dragged it back up, coming towards her again. The letter opener was in front of her, fallen from her pocket. She grabbed it. She knew, distantly, that she was bleeding and battered, that she was in pain and needed help. It didn't matter. What mattered was the machete and the shadow wielding it.

It came down again. She got clear, just, the tattered backpack swinging from her shoulder. She snatched at it, threw it at him. He faltered as the machete went up.

She rammed the letter opener through his foot. He yelled out in pain, and warm, spurting blood coated her hand.

She rolled away as he staggered and fell to his knees, just centimetres from her. The machete hit the ground with a clatter. The man was breathing heavily, groping for the weapon.

Maggie snatched it clear as she stood. She swung the machete up, then embedded it in his skull.

He didn't make a sound. He swayed, half-raised a hand, then toppled and was still, the blade wedged in place.

Maggie looked up at the motel. There was no commotion, no doors opening or people investigating. The attack, for all the time it had lasted, hadn't made much noise. The baby was still crying.

With some difficulty, Maggie picked up the heavy machete. For a moment, she considered making straight for her car. The pain told her she needed to at least bandage her back, and she needed to be away from here to do it.

And yet.

She gathered up the remains of her backpack, what notes she could. Then she was back up the stairs, tripping and faltering. The notes from her bag were spread around the landing; plenty had blown away, but she had to salvage what she could. It was all she had.

Wincing, she crouched and started gathering them up in handfuls. She kept a hold of the machete as she did. Moving along the walkway, stuffing notes into her pocket, her vision blurred. Her head spun. It occurred to her, distantly, that she might have lost a large amount of blood. She glanced back, saw the trail of moonlit black she'd left and as she did another man came up the stairs.

She didn't need to think twice. His face was covered and in his hand was a gun. He raised it as Maggie threw the machete.

It spun through the air. The man went to move; it bounced off his skull with an audible crack. He made a guttural noise and staggered. One hand went to where the blade had hit as the other lifted the silenced pistol again.

Maggie dived to the side as he fired. The gunshot was muffled but the bullet hitting concrete behind her wasn't.

Veering widely, the man fired again.

Maggie ran towards him. Her eyes on the fallen machete.

Another gunshot. A yell from one of the rooms. The man was less than two metres away.

She ducked his next shot and grabbed the machete just as his hand caught her throat. She had no time to attack as he pulled her upwards, his grip strong, so strong, impossible to fight. The baby still crying. Everything was spinning; she was moving fast; she couldn't breathe. She kicked out, hit metal and realised that he had hoisted her *over the balcony*, holding her by the neck.

She tried to draw breath but it was impossible. Black spots filled her vision; the biggest among them could have been his face, featureless and terrible but for the wide eyes in the holes that now leaked blood.

Brief clarity. *He had her in his right hand. His left, wavering, lifting the gun.*

At that moment Maggie remembered the machete.

She swung wild and hard. She didn't know if she would hit anything until she did, until the man let out a strangled, gurgling cry, she saw the blade half-buried in his neck, and his hand let go of her.

She grabbed for whatever she could, whatever was in reach. She felt the top of the stocking that covered his head and the hair beneath it as she fell. She held tight and her fall stopped part way. Her legs flailed in empty air. Her fingers were slipping. She tightened her grip as best she could and as she did she heard a horrible, wet tearing sound that made her look up.

The man's neck was bent over the bannister, head wrenched down by Maggie's hold, the machete lost in the chaos. His open wound pointed upwards, gaping, red and widening by the second.

'Oh, *fuck*,' Maggie managed as the wound tore, the head came off, and she fell in a shower of blood.

There was a brief rush of blurred light and colour and then came the impact that raced through her body, turned the pulsing pain into something overpowering, something that blasted all thought from her mind as she tried to move but couldn't. She knew she had to stand but wasn't sure for that moment what standing was.

Vision returned. The empty sky above. Something clutched tight in her hands. And around the fringes of her vision the lights and the slowly closing circle of gasps and whispers and screams.

She stood. Her left leg buckled and she was down again. She didn't even feel the impact this time. She closed her eyes and clenched her teeth and tried again. She was up, the world tilting on either side. She lifted what she held and looked into empty eyes and blood. Her grip had mostly pulled away the stocking. She could see his face. Not one she recognised. She threw the head away. She saw shapes approaching, shapes that warped and grew in her fractured vision. Then she was moving without knowing how, away from the motel, away from the lights and the shouts, away.

Maybe there were sirens. Maybe people were staring at her. She moved into shadows and bushes. She moved in the wrong direction until she didn't think anyone was looking and then it was the dark streets and the looming houses and finally, she registered with a rush of relief, her car. She dug her keys out of her pocket with a shaking hand. She shouldn't have been driving. She was anyway. Streetlights and headlights, the stretch of empty road, a beeping horn, then the dark late-night houses of a different street in a different suburb. Lights grew in her vision, colours changing, shifting into new and terrifying forms. The road ahead tilted, the windscreen rippled and everything beyond it was grey and formless. She couldn't feel her hands around the wheel.

She needed to be gone, back north. But she was moving out of the car and through the long grass of a forgotten lawn until she found the loose brick to the left of the door and the key behind it. Hand on the doorknob, then the dark of the hall, the smell of mould and mildew, the foot of the stairs in shadow. She didn't close the door behind her. She fell. She looked at her hands. Dark. Maybe the night, maybe the blood.

Up the stairs then, half-crawling, half-walking until she reached the landing and passed it, passed the doors she knew until she reached her own. Her room was empty. There was no sign of the little girl left. Cobwebs and dust. She collapsed on the floor. Sleep reached up and took hold of her, so gently that the pain started to slip away and all that was left was the darkness and then the little girl she'd left behind.

Huddled in the wardrobe, eyes on the door. She could hear the heavy footsteps up the stairs. They stopped two doors up, at his room. Then they kept coming. She closed her eyes. The creak of the wardrobe door. She wondered what she had done, what he would do and then the sobs, so quiet she almost missed them, so strange a sound that she opened her eyes and looked at him and he looked at her and then he collapsed and held her as he wept into her shoulder and again and again whispered that he was sorry while she stared at the wall and thought about the day she would kill him.

CHAPTER TEN

Maggie had bought the rounders bat because of its size. Easy to obscure, relatively light but still solid. Still wood. She liked the weight of it in her hand. She liked that she could have it tucked in the back of her jeans, hidden by a jacket, then out and swung hard and fast in seconds.

But the night she made her move, she didn't hide it. She didn't need to. She had placed herself in an alley, dressed in black and with a balaclava over her head, the shape of her body disguised by an oversized hoodie. By then she had worked out that after a round of smokes with his mates out the front of the pub, the prick tended to walk home down quiet back streets by himself. Sometimes he'd have a girl with him, but that wasn't as often as he probably liked.

She would have preferred to have placed herself inside the pub, or at least to walk past it a few times to be across anything that might be outside the ordinary, but she didn't want anyone to later be able to place her. She was fairly good at not being noticed if she wanted to, but a girl drinking alone always stood out at least a little to anyone who cared to look. Luckily, Elliot never had.

Standing in the dark shadows of the alley, Maggie rocked back and forwards on her heels. She hefted the bat. She felt the comforting weight of the Swiss Army knife in her pocket. Just in case. She was about to check the time again when she heard footsteps. Heavy and uneven. She sank back. Waited.

And there he was. Cigarette in mouth, laughing at something on his phone as he walked. He passed the alley and was gone. Maggie lingered just a moment, then stepped out. The night was cool. Elliot's head remained down. There was no-one else around.

Light on her feet, Maggie moved. Elliot didn't even know she was there. She brought the bat hard across the back of his head. With a yelp, he staggered forward, his phone falling from his fumbling hands as he hit the pavement and then Maggie was on him, the bat coming down again and again – on his back, his legs, his arms. He wailed something incoherent, cried, tried to roll over. Maggie let him and then cracked him across the face. He spat blood and teeth. His kneecaps were now exposed. In quick succession, Maggie hit both of them. Elliot screamed. Maggie glanced behind her. Still no-one. She looked down at him. Bloody and pathetic, trying to sob and beg and threaten all at once. She wanted to hit him again so she did. His cry was high-pitched. Maggie took out the knife.

The hate had flared billowing and all-consuming, stoked by every sound the fucker made. This man who ruined lives and got away with it because he was charming and connected enough to pull the wool over all the right eyes. This man who had destroyed the only friend Maggie had ever had. Lured her in with his pretty face. He'd have a hard time doing that without those looks.

She hit him one more time to keep him down, then knelt. She took Elliot's wallet from his pocket. The knife was already open in her hand although she didn't remember doing that. She lifted it. Her hand was steady. The blade glinted in the glow of a streetlight. She lowered it.

Then, from nearby, 'What the fuck are you doing?'

Pounding feet came towards her and Maggie was gone.

She ran until she reached a better-lit street then tucked the bat away and pulled off the balaclava. She slowed but kept going, steady and casual and easy. Nobody worth taking any notice of. Once she reached the city, once the people started bustling around her and the lights turned bright, she dropped Elliot's wallet in the nearest bin, followed by the bat.

The day before Ness's court appointment, Maggie had gone round to her place. She found Ness lying on her bed, staring at the roof, eyes blank. Until she saw Maggie.

'What the fuck were you thinking?'

Ness didn't sound angry. Not overtly anyway. Closer to worn-out.

Maggie played dumb, but Ness wasn't having any of it.

'He didn't tell the cops he thought the mugger was a girl,' she said. 'But he told me. You pulled a fucking *knife* on him?'

'You're still talking to him,' Maggie said.

'I wasn't,' Ness said. 'Until I heard about the attack. And I had a feeling it might not just be some random junkie. So, again, what the fuck were you thinking?'

'I was thinking this is all his fault. I was thinking you should have turned him in but since you won't, someone had to do something.'

'Someone had to – can you *hear yourself*?'

And there the anger was, wild and exasperated and finally erupting from under all the late nights and endless fretting about the future. Maggie didn't move. She didn't know what to say or do.

'Maggie, it was *my choice*,' Ness said. 'Do you understand? Elliot didn't force me to deal for him; he asked me and I said yes. Do you have so little respect for me that you think I'd put up with it if he tried to push me around?'

Maggie didn't have an answer for that.

Ness slumped back on the bed. 'Jesus Christ. Jesus fucking Christ. All this time I've defended you. Told people that you weren't this broken, fucked-up mess. Maggie, he thought he was going to die. He thought you were going to kill him. Can you understand that?'

She could, but she didn't voice the fact.

'At what point,' Ness asked, 'are you just your father all over again?'

The words didn't hit hard. Not at first. But over the following days Ness's voice, as clear as if she was hearing it again, repeated in her thoughts. And as it did, something seemed to happen to the world around her. The old sandstone buildings of the university, the perfect green of the grass and the laughs of the students, became flimsy and artificial. Maggie moved through it all and with every step saw it for what it was, a performance of some half-arsed concept of normality that nobody could pinpoint the origins of because it had just been roundly accepted and these people let themselves believe that what they were doing somehow mattered, that their lives and pointless dramas and fractured fears meant something. That they didn't all just contribute to the pretence, the smoke and mirrors, that convinced the easily led that the world was fundamentally good, that cruelty and danger were far away rather than occurring behind every second closed door.

She stopped paying attention in class. Then she stopped turning up. When Ness eventually called again, Maggie ignored it. She didn't even know how the court case had gone. She never saw Elliot again. She just wandered through the collapsing artifice, and as she did, slowly, her thoughts turned to her parents.

Maybe they had done her a favour. Her father's violence and her mother's abandonment had disabused her of the false notions that the rest of the world lived by, the notion that fairness and decency would win out if you just followed the rules. But it was hard to feel grateful when Maggie wished with painful desperation that she *could* delude herself, that she could worry about marks and flings and mortgages. Not when she had been through what she had.

In those long, empty days without Ness, answers seemed impossible to find, as impossible as the idea that she could just go back to uni, pick things up and live a normal life. It had never once occurred to her not to hurt Elliot; just like, so long ago, it had never occurred to her not to trip into a fire the vicious foster brother who could also turn on the polite charm when he needed to. On both occasions she had felt justified. But after what Ness had said, she wasn't so sure anymore.

She had assumed on some level that violence was her birthright. That her father's capacity for harm and her mother's carelessness were what had shaped her. That notion had persisted even during the time that she, at least at a surface level, had attempted to pursue a normal life. But if she didn't *want* her past to define her, then what options were left to her? Could she ever overcome such ingrained instinct?

She left her job and her apartment. The university stopped emailing her. She scraped together what little money she had and moved into the dingiest share house she could find. And there an obsession grew. Because if what she was had been caused by her parents, then maybe the only way forward was to understand what had caused *them*.

Her father wouldn't have answers. None he'd share, anyway. The last she'd heard he had descended fully into booze and incoherence. He'd sooner backhand her again than tell her anything.

But, she slowly understood, that didn't mean he didn't know anything. After all, his biggest fixation during the last years Maggie had lived with him had been finding her mother. For revenge, spite or love, Maggie didn't know. But his need to find her had never shown any sign of abating.

And on some level, he *had* once been a good cop. Which meant that if anyone knew where to start looking, it would be him.

The thought of seeing him again was unpleasant, tinged partly with fear but also with something else. Some vague sense of the potential to put things right.

CHAPTER ELEVEN

The first thing she knew, before her eyes even opened, was the pain. It was everywhere, from the throb in her leg to the persistent tearing in her back to the pounding in her skull. She didn't move. Minutes, maybe, crept past. Flashes of the night before returned to her. She couldn't deal with them even if she wanted to, and she was a long way from wanting to.

She was in her father's house. She was only partly sure of how she had got there and less sure of why. But here she was. Home. The thought would have made her laugh if laughing didn't hurt so much. She shifted, slightly, and the pain swelled. She heard a whimper but wasn't sure if it had come from her.

'Easy, girl. You've taken more than your fair share.'

The voice was familiar and with it came a dull sense of warning.

'Carlin,' she croaked.

'Stay still. I bandaged you up, but I'm no doctor and you're in a state that needs a fair bit more than a couple of Band-Aids.'

She opened her eyes. Carlin was slumped against the wall, cigarette in mouth, eyes on her. She glanced down. Her shirt was gone but heavy bandages wrapped around her stomach and the wound on her lower back. Her bra and bloodstained jeans were still in place.

'I didn't send the bastards,' Carlin said. 'Before you start losing your shit. The obvious money would seem to be on Len Townsend. The machete tells me it was supposed to be messy. A warning to anyone who might try to pull the same shit you did. Between the lawyer's office and the motel, cop radio's been going crazy all night.'

Maggie closed her eyes. She wanted to sleep.

'Sorry, love.' Carlin poked her with his boot. 'We've got no time for that. Far as I know, nobody's officially linked you to the motel fuckery yet, but that's only a matter of time and the first place anyone will look is here, if only to cover their bases.'

'Fuck off, Carlin.'

'Listen.' His voice softened.

Maggie opened her eyes.

'I'm sorry,' he said. 'Believe it or don't, but there it is. I'm used to getting my way by putting the fear of God into brain-dead fuckwits scared of any police attention, official or otherwise. Instinct overtook sense. You'd have been long clear of that motel if it wasn't for me.'

'Good cop, now?'

Carlin snorted. 'Fuck, no. My plan hasn't much changed, girl. And if there's anything worthwhile in this house you can tell me about – for example, a tucked-away hard drive packed with incriminating evidence – that'd be tops.' He paused. Maggie said nothing. He shrugged and continued. 'Still relying on the storage unit, then. Let's hurry up and get you somewhere safe so I can find it. It's just lucky that whatever conscience most will tell you I don't have happens to line up with my self-interest. I don't want you dying or arrested, and that means I need to help you get clear and get well. Either you trust me to take you somewhere relatively safe, or I'll leave you for the cops or Townsend or both. That ain't blackmail. It's just what it is.'

Maggie rolled onto her back, staring at the ceiling. 'Who are you working for?'

'I'm not,' Carlin said. 'The hard drive incriminates somebody I want incriminated. Now, are you coming or not?'

She closed her eyes again and exhaled. She wasn't getting far alone, and if Carlin was about to betray her, then he had her in the perfect corner for whoever was paying the most.

She nodded.

More carefully than she would have expected, Carlin helped her up, slinging his arm around her back and gently guiding her to her feet. She cried out as she put weight on her left leg; it felt like it had been torn apart. She leaned against Carlin and step by tentative step he guided her out of her old room and into the hall, collecting a plastic bag as he did.

'Your cash,' he said. 'You left a trail of it from your car. It rained last night, so most of it was washed away. Whatever I could find is in here. Speaking of which, I've moved the car to a different street, but if there's anything you need in there, speak now or forever hold your peace.'

Maggie shook her head.

Together they moved down the stairs, Maggie biting back the yelps that threatened with every movement. It was slow, frustrating going but together they reached the landing.

'Hang here for a sec,' Carlin said, guiding Maggie to lean against the wall. 'I'm gonna take a quick look and make sure the coast is clear.' He let go of her and headed out the door. Maggie watched after him for a moment, then her eyes moved back to the stairs. In the light of day, the house was dusty and sparse. There had never been much in the way of furniture or decorations, but now it just looked a few steps from dilapidated. Not like the place where she had grown up. She had imagined coming back would fill her with horror and dread, that she'd sense her father over her shoulder or see him stalking the abandoned halls. But here, now, all she saw was an empty house.

'We're clear,' Carlin said from the door. 'Let's go.'

Maggie didn't look back.

Carlin drove an old black van, the back windows painted over. The reason became clear as he helped Maggie in; a mattress and a few ragged blankets had been piled inside. It smelt of stale cigarette smoke. Maggie lay back on the hard mattress, looking at the peeling upholstery on the roof as the van hummed to life around her.

'I'll try to drive gentle,' Carlin said from the front, 'but I wanna get clear of the city fast, so if there are any bad bumps, don't let 'em kill you, fair?'

Maggie didn't bother to reply. There was, she knew, a very real risk that this was as bad an idea as returning to Melbourne in the first place had been. But she was hardly overflowing with alternatives. Her options boiled down to jail, death or Carlin.

He drove without a word. In the dark back of the van, Maggie had no idea where they were and she wasn't interested in prompting conversation by asking. As the first hour passed, she let herself fall into a light doze, occasionally jolted awake by a sudden stop or the jerk of a speed bump. Despite the renewed protests from her back and the fact that she could feel warm, fresh blood through Carlin's makeshift bandages, she said nothing.

She hadn't even realised she'd fallen asleep until the car stopped and her eyes flickered open. Her whole body felt stiff now, like it was going to protest even the smallest attempt to move. She sat up anyway as Carlin opened the side door. She smelled fresh air and gum trees. He helped her out onto soft grass.

In front of her was a weatherboard house in the middle of a small, overgrown field. Swaying gums became more frequent the further past the house she looked, until they were thick behind a barbed-wire fence. The forest sprawled across a backdrop of deep green hills beneath a light grey sky. She looked to the side. The view wasn't much different.

She took a deep breath. The air was cool and fresh. They were a long way from the city.

'Home away from home,' Carlin said, guiding her towards the front steps that led up to the porch.

'Where are we?'

'Just out of Warburton. A good hour clear of Melbourne.'

'Were we followed?'

Carlin gave her a withering look. 'Yeah, I noticed a couple of shady-looking pricks on the road behind us. They're probably gonna roll up any minute now.'

As they neared the house she stopped; somebody was waiting on the front steps. A middle-aged woman in ripped jeans and a thick, green jumper. She had short, mousy hair; a cigarette in her mouth; a weathered, suspicious-looking face; and a large, fluffy, brown dog panting happily next to her.

'Julie,' Carlin said, by way of explanation. 'You made great time.'

Julie took a long drag of her cigarette, dropped it on the bottom step and trod on it. 'You didn't.' Her voice was hoarse. 'Can't wait around all fucking day to cater for you. Argos and I have places to be.'

Maggie looked at the dog. She couldn't see its eyes through the shaggy fur. It didn't seem much bothered by the wait.

Julie opened the door and walked through as Argos ran up to Carlin, who greeted him with a scratch behind the ears before helping Maggie up the stairs and into the house. It was plain inside, but homelier than Maggie expected. The scrubbed wood of the walls and rustic, slightly uneven homemade-looking chairs and tables put her in mind of an old hunter's cabin, as did the mingled smell of wood smoke and eucalyptus.

'Jack fancies himself a carpenter,' Julie said. 'Too bad he's shit at it.'

Carlin took her into a side room, with only a narrow, single bed low to the ground and a table over which Julie went through a leather bag, taking out more bandages and several small bottles. Argos sat at the foot of the bed, watching as Carlin lowered Maggie down onto it.

'Beer, Julie?' Carlin asked.

'Gin if you've got it. Just the one for now, but I'll thank you for a few more glasses once the girl's stuck back together.'

'On it.' Carlin departed, leaving Maggie alone with Julie. She wasn't sure what to say so she said nothing.

Julie turned to her. 'First things first, I'm gonna have to see the damage. What you've done to yourself and what I can do to fix it. If I can do anything.'

'Are you a doctor?'

'Vet,' Julie said. 'Now, take off that bandage; I'm getting an infection just looking at it.'

Maggie obeyed, wincing as the dried blood tugged at her wound. She tried not to look at the rags as she threw them aside. They were mostly red and black.

Julie leaned over to examine her back. She gave no audible reaction. 'Cleaning and stitching. Figured as much. I'll see to that first and then we can work out what's broken.' She returned to her table and set about preparing a syringe that made Maggie flinch. 'Gonna stick you with this first,' she said. 'Won't stop the pain, but'll make it a bit easier to deal with. Machete?'

Maggie was too tired to ask how the hell Julie knew that. She nodded.

'Hold still now.'

Something about Julie put Maggie close to at ease. Maybe it was the fact that she showed no interest whatsoever in putting Maggie at ease.

Carlin returned with a beer in his hand and a gin for Julie, which she ignored as she started stitching up Maggie's back. Carlin remained in the doorway, watching and drinking without a word. For her part, Maggie kept her face impassive even as it felt like she was being flayed.

When Julie was done, she crouched in front of Maggie and took a hold of her leg. She looked up. 'This could hurt.'

Maggie nodded.

Firmly, Julie felt one then the other. Maggie clenched her teeth as she checked the left.

'Could be a crack in the bone here,' Julie said. 'Hard to tell without an X-ray or anything, but it doesn't need setting. That said, I wouldn't be running anywhere for a while.'

'You might struggle to stop her,' Carlin said, finishing his beer. 'The girl took a machete in the back rather than stay put in Melbourne.'

'If she doesn't want to be in a world of pain, she'll stay put here.' Julie straightened up, surveying Maggie with crossed arms. Argos plodded over and placed his chin on Maggie's knee.

'How's the head?' Julie asked.

'Hurts, but not as bad as the rest of me.'

'Avoided a concussion then,' Julie said. 'You slept through the night and you're not dead, so I'd say that's alright. But yeah, you've lost plenty of blood and you've taken a royal fuck of a beating. So don't do anything stupid. Or do, but I'm not a fan of seeing my handiwork put to waste.'

'Doctor's orders,' Carlin said.

'Shut the fuck up, Jack,' Julie said.

'Thank you,' Maggie said.

Julie took her gin from Jack and knocked it back. 'Now I'm owed a few more of these, and you,' she nodded at Maggie, 'need some rest. No escape attempts.'

Maggie weakly saluted, then lay back. The bed creaked as Argos jumped up and lay next to her, head resting on her shoulder. Julie paused in the door for a moment. 'Argos likes you. That's usually a good sign.'

She left. Maggie looked down at the shaggy dog. She got halfway through scratching him behind the ears before sleep claimed her with a vengeance.

Days passed. Or maybe they didn't. It was hard to tell. Maggie drifted in and out of sleep. Sometimes it was day; sometimes it wasn't. At first, she only left the room to use the bathroom and eat. Food was always out of a can, something Carlin heated up or left for her when he wasn't around, which was most of the time.

She couldn't have run if she had wanted to. Whatever had seen her through the night at the motel was thoroughly depleted. It didn't matter how long she slept, she remained tired and sore. So she lay in bed or read one of the three books Carlin left for her. All she had to wear were old clothes of his and some cheap basics he'd picked up from a supermarket somewhere. The clothes were far too big, but at least not covered in blood. Carlin made only the briefest of appearances, and when he did he had nothing to report about the hard drive, her father, the bikies or the police.

When she felt almost well enough, she took a faltering walk outside. The house was even more buried in the bush than she'd first realised; trees closed in all around it from every direction, the only gap being the narrow dirt road they'd presumably driven in on. Maggie would sit on the front stairs, watching the dark opening in the trees, waiting for Carlin, the police or Townsend's men to come trundling through. Good luck to her if it was the latter; Carlin had left nothing around the house that could be used as a weapon, unless she planned on taking on her assailants with a spoon.

Using a stick for support, she started doing wider and wider rounds of the house, bringing herself right up to the edge of the trees. She would look through them as if for a stalker or watcher, but she knew there was no-one. That feeling that had persisted on the streets of Port Douglas had not reappeared. What she felt here was the opposite: an almost eerie lack of humanity. She didn't mind it. There was something peaceful about it, although that sense easily slipped away when she thought about the circumstances that had led her here.

Working out her next move would be a challenge. Her car had been left back near her father's and she had no idea whether the police had found it. All she had here was the handfuls of notes she had salvaged from the motel. It would be enough to get her away from Melbourne, but not much more than that. Without a car, she didn't have mobility, and without a weapon, her chances of survival crept too close to zero for her liking. As much as the fact made her feel unwell, she had to at least partly rely on Jack Carlin.

It had been about a week, she thought, when Carlin came home early. This time Maggie was up and waiting at the small kitchen table, sipping one of his beers. Carlin nodded to her and got his own.

'Well, you've made a right fucking mess of things.' He joined her at the table and cracked his beer. 'You've also handed Olivia Dean her warrant on a silver platter. I didn't find anything in the storage unit, but then I didn't have much of a chance to look before Dean and her crew arrived wielding signatures.'

Maggie sipped her drink. If the hard drive wasn't in the storage unit or the empty house then there was only one place she could think of that it might have ended up, but that place made far less sense than the others.

'Cooper's alive, by the way,' Carlin said. 'So is the lawyer, although her signing days are probably over.' His expression turned briefly amused. 'But, predictably, she's sticking to the story the Scorpions gave her.'

'Surely the police know that story's fucking stupid,' Maggie said. 'Darch called them.'

'And said you had attacked her. Not the Scorpions, who are probably claiming to be good Samaritans who stepped in and tried to stop the lawyer's de-fingering. The police know that's bullshit, but what can they do? Two bikies are dead and the lawyer's missing a finger. All remaining fingers are pointing at you. Rook's playing the outraged patriarch card, demanding the police bring you to justice. Without Darch's testimony incriminating the Scorpions, the police can't do much except lob those illegal firearm charges around. Which still, I guess, adds fuel to the fire of Olivia's crusade.' For a moment, Carlin looked deeply bitter.

'You don't want her to bring down the Scorpions?'

'I want the Scorpions burned off the face of the planet,' Carlin said. 'I just wish I could be the one to do it.'

'Why?'

'Long story that I'm not itching to tell.'

Maggie drank, thinking. 'My father was involved with them. Cooper is as well. Were you?'

A heavy silence hung over the room.

'That,' Carlin said, 'is the kind of question that any cop would rightfully get pissed off by.'

'Except you're not a cop.'

'They can take the badge but that doesn't take why you wore it.'

'But they *did* take the badge. Because you were crooked?'

Carlin's smile curled a little too far to be genuine. 'Ask Harrison Cooper why they took my badge.'

'But I can ask you.'

'You can ask. Doesn't mean you're gonna get an answer.' He leaned forward. 'Ancient history doesn't change your circumstances, girl.'

'No,' Maggie admitted. 'But it might explain my circumstances.'

Neither spoke. Carlin drank. Maggie gave him a moment but it was clear he didn't plan on saying any more.

'What's happened to Cooper?' she asked.

'He's in trouble, of course,' Carlin said. 'But not because of the bikies. Because of bringing you back to Melbourne. I'm hearing he's trying to claim he was going to arrest you, but that holds about as much water as a net. Dunno how he plans to worm his way out of this.'

This isn't what you think. When Cooper had said that, Maggie had been too angry and blinkered to consider what it meant. Now, she wondered if it was in fact a missing puzzle piece.

'So what now?' Maggie said.

'Now, I'm gonna really hope you have some other idea about where that hard drive might be.'

To her surprise, she almost wanted to share her vague theory. It wasn't that she liked Carlin, exactly, but for all the posturing and threats, he had protected her. Maybe Carlin would at least let her take the information that pertained to her mother before he did whatever he wanted with the rest. Maybe. But she still didn't truly know what kind of person Carlin was or what he would do once he had the hard drive.

Maggie shook her head.

Carlin drank. 'Square one again, then.'

Julie returned on what Maggie estimated to be her tenth day at the house. She was sitting on the porch, reading, when she heard the approaching car. She felt a low buzz of unease when she didn't recognise Carlin's van, but relaxed upon seeing Julie's face through the windscreen of the Jeep, the panting shape of Argos next to her.

The dog bounded around them, chasing flies as they walked the fences and Julie asked gruff, routine questions about how Maggie was feeling. The answers seemed to please her; the tiredness and lingering pain were still very present, but Maggie was walking without the stick now and able to sleep through the night despite her back.

'You'll have a scar,' Julie said. 'But then, it won't be the first. I saw your leg. Dog bite?'

'Something like that.' Maggie watched a rosella jump from branch to branch, calling out as it did.

'Some dogs shouldn't be underestimated,' Julie said. 'People reckon they've got 'em tamed then all it takes is the wrong move and those animal instincts come flooding back.'

'This dog was trained to do exactly what it did.'

'That's worse,' Julie said. 'Some piece of shit beats an animal until it attacks because it can't do anything else.' She nodded to Argos, now sniffing around the fence line. 'That's what happened to him. But he's a gentle thing. Abused like you wouldn't believe, skinny and mangy and scarred when I got him out. Never bit or attacked, though. People mistake that for him being cowed and broken, but I dunno. I think that takes a different kind of strength. Most people he just ignores. Always feels worth noting when he doesn't.'

For a few minutes, they walked in silence.

'Jack and me grew up out here,' Julie said. 'We both had bastard parents so we kind of gravitated towards each other.' She glanced sideways at Maggie. 'He used to talk about wanting peace and quiet, wanting to settle down eventually. When he got this place, I thought he finally might. But some people can't keep themselves away from the fight. They see a situation going sour and they dive on in, consequences be damned. Maybe not because they want to but because they need to. Because maybe they think it'll fix some broken part of themselves.' She shrugged. 'Or maybe I'm talking out of my arse. I'm not a shrink. Anyway, that's why I help him out when he needs it. I don't wanna know the specifics; plausible deniability is the sweet spot when it comes to Jack Carlin. But I still trust that by and large, he's doing the right thing. And besides, Argos likes him.'

Maggie glanced up at the sky. Lazy clouds drifted around a high sun.

'Argos is a dog,' Maggie said. 'And a dog who's had a shit time of it. I'm not sure I'd swear by his judgement.'

'I'm not swearing by anything,' Julie said. 'I'm saying that dogs are a lot simpler than us. They know how to recognise what's inherently bad. They'll attack or stay away from the things that are more likely to hurt them.'

Argos padded over, a stick in his mouth. Julie threw it. They watched the dog go together.

'You ever get jealous of that?' Maggie asked.

Julie laughed. 'Oh shit, yeah. Might be why I like dogs so much. Some clichés are bullshit, but the one about animals being good judges of character isn't.'

'I don't find myself wanting to trust Jack.'

'That doesn't put you in a minority. I'm not pretending to know your story, but a girl your age doesn't collect that many scars without being involved in some deeply improper shit.'

It wasn't phrased as a question but Maggie took it as one. Eyes still on Argos's search for the stick, she nodded.

'Does Jack get much benefit from helping you?' Julie asked.

'Some.'

'But enough to justify the lengths he's gone to?'

'On the surface, probably not. But I'd be stupid if I only looked on the surface.'

They continued walking in silence. Argos returned with a different stick. Maggie threw it for him.

Maggie was lying on her bed, towards the end of her book, when she heard the door, followed by Carlin's distinctive loping steps. She listened as he moved around the kitchen, and as his steps passed again. The door creaked open, then clicked shut.

Maggie closed the book and looked at the ceiling, then the door. She got off the bed.

Carlin sat on the front steps, an open bottle of Scotch next to him. He was carving something from a chunk of wood, whistling tunelessly. Maggie looked at the sky. Grey clouds infused with a dull dusk purple that in some areas neared red. Beneath it the treetops looked ragged and black.

She sat next to Carlin. He didn't acknowledge her. His attention was on the wood in his hands, the knife hacking away thick chips.

'Have some, if you like.' He nodded towards the Scotch.

Maggie didn't take it.

'An old dead mate of my used to rave about that stuff,' he said. 'Loved to tell me he'd sold his soul for it. Not sure it's soul-worthy, but it's pretty good.'

'Got a lot of old dead mates?'

She caught the sideways edge of a wry grin. 'My age and way of life? More than a few. How about yourself?'

Maggie shrugged. 'I don't think I have any mates. Dead or alive.'

Carlin looked at her. He went to speak but didn't. He returned to his whittling. 'Either sad or wise. Not sure which.'

Maggie wasn't either. Since Ness, the only positive relationships she'd had were brief and built on deceit. Or else they were alliances of necessity, closer to comrades in the trenches than friends. Certainly not people she'd be dropping round to visit at any point. Another cost of the choices she'd made.

Carlin was focused once more on his carving. Maggie considered him, then asked, 'Were you and my dad friends?'

Carlin stopped mid cut. 'Yeah. At first.'

'What was he like? Back then?'

Carlin looked at her again. 'You really want to know?'

'Why wouldn't I?'

'Because there's no point to it. I tell you he was a scumbag; I'm just confirming what you already know. I tell you he was a saint; I'm complicating a perfectly accurate assessment. Either way, he did what he did and he was what he was.'

'But was he always?'

A heavy pause. 'No,' Carlin said. 'I mean, we're not talking a complete 180 here. There were signs. He had a temper. He was ruthless. But to a lot of people, those were the things that made him a good cop. There was this sort of unspoken theory that sometimes the worst traits a person has can be leveraged into something good, that they were essentially skills needing the right outlet. It was easy to believe that that might be the case with Eric, given the rest.'

'The rest?' Maggie said.

'He was resourceful. Driven. Strong sense of justice. Real skill for noticing the kinds of minor discrepancies that could break open a case. The fact that he was such a good cop is probably why people turned a blind eye to how bad he was getting.'

That was a scalding notion.

'For what it's worth,' Carlin said, 'I always thought that was bullshit. The moment even the best lawman in the world starts hurting the innocent, it doesn't matter what he's done before. But in the end the police force is made up of people, and people, as a rule, tend to do what's easiest.'

He started whittling again. It looked like he was trying to make some kind of animal but it was impossible to tell which. After a few more minutes, he hefted the misshapen creature with an expression of distaste and threw it. It disappeared somewhere at the edge of the tree line. The sky had darkened, the purples descending into a deepening blue, the trees little more than a mass of shadow.

The silence contracted. A breath held before something finally unleashed.

Maggie didn't look at Carlin. She waited.

And finally, he started to speak.

CHAPTER TWELVE

Taking the money had been Harrison's idea, but Jack would be lying if he tried to claim they'd put up much of a fight. Early in their careers, stuck doing boring shit with a pay cheque that meant you really had to believe in being a cop to stick it out, they were all looking for ways to make ends meet. And that night, moving through the slightly smoky, chemical-stinking halls of an abandoned drug den, they'd found it.

At that point, the bust was about the most exciting thing they'd ever been part of, or at least it had seemed to be until they'd arrived, guns drawn and blood hot, to find no-one was left. Even when the three rookies were sent to clear upstairs, it was hard to pretend they'd find any real surprises. Until Harrison, floppy-haired and wide-eyed, had stuck his head out of a room and beckoned the others in.

'Fucking hell,' he'd said, nodding to the bagged-up stacks of cash sitting at the bottom of an old wardrobe. 'Anybody would think drug dealers made good money or something.'

After going through the academy with Harrison, Jack was used to his little funnies. But there was something different about this. Something clenched in his voice.

Eric knelt and picked up one of the bundles from the open bag. His angular, handsome face was almost always set in an expression of focused seriousness, but at that moment Jack could have sworn there was a hint of wistfulness in his eyes. 'Gotta be twenty grand here. At least.'

A burst of rough laughter from downstairs. They hadn't found anything either. Hearts were slowing with a mix of relief and disappointment. Jack, for his part, wasn't sure which he felt.

Harrison glanced at the door, then back to the cash. Jack watched him. Harrison met his gaze. Lifted an eyebrow. A silent question.

'Are you an idiot?' Jack asked.

Eric glanced up at them. Saw the look on Harrison's face. 'It's evidence.' He was trying to sound firm. He looked at the money again.

'You kidding me?' Harrison said. 'This whole *house* is fucking evidence. You think this cash is gonna be the difference between closing the case and not? Nah. If somebody else doesn't pocket it, it'll be tested for the fingerprints that they've already found on every other surface in the place then stuck away in some evidence locker and forgotten about. And when rent rolls around again or that pretty lady of yours,' he nodded to Eric, 'starts pestering you about the biggest ring in the shop, you're gonna be kicking yourself that you didn't take a gift from the universe when it practically fell into your lap.'

'This is a gift from a pack of drug dealers,' Jack said.

Harrison shrugged. 'A gift all the same.'

A yell from downstairs, tinted with amusement. 'All clear up there, boys?'

'All clear!' Eric turned the bundle over in his hand.

'Come on.' Harrison gave him a shove. 'We could have been killed tonight. Live a little' He winked at Jack.

Jack looked over his shoulder but nobody was coming up the stairs. He knew this was one of those moments the old cops always spoke about, the ones that would make or break the kind of lawman you wanted to be. But Harrison had a point. Money was tight. And twenty grand split three ways was hardly a fucking heist. In the grand scheme of things, it was the bonus they never received from their actual employers.

'Magnus,' Eric said.

'Huh?' Harrison looked impatient.

Eric lifted the side of the bag. The name was written across it in black marker. 'Who's Magnus?'

'Right now,' Harrison said, 'he's my best mate. Now, we doing this or not?'

The older cops downstairs didn't notice their slightly thicker pockets. A couple of them, bored, had already headed outside and lit their smokes, complaining about wasted time and unnecessary paperwork. Jack had been jumpy, feeling the heat of a non-existent spotlight. He was sure they'd missed something glaring and obvious, something that would give them away. But nobody even brought up the idea that money might have been left behind. Everyone knew that even in a hurry, fleeing dealers wouldn't leave without it.

It didn't occur to Jack that the fact that they had was strange. Not straight away. Not soon enough.

The end of the week meant hitting the pub. Jack got there a bit late, stuck behind writing up some domestic disturbance. By the time he got there, most everyone was already pissed, the air thick with smoke. He saw Harrison in the centre of the room, regaling a bunch of the other guys with a story about a dickhead junkie who'd thought he was a knight. Harrison was laughing and miming the attempted use of a plunger as a sword and his own exaggerated dodging as he tried to get the cuffs on. The whole clump of them were erupting in bursts of raucous laughter.

He found Eric over at the bar, nursing a pot of beer as he watched Harrison. Jack joined him without a word and lit a smoke. Eric raised his glass but didn't drink. He didn't look at Jack as he asked, 'Thoughts?'

Jack didn't bother to play dumb. Nobody was listening to them. 'I reckon somebody should get Harry's wallet before he fucking tells everyone.'

'He's already bought a round for the sergeants. Little suck-up.'

Harrison Cooper liked being liked. And he was good at it, too. Jack, for his part, had never had that talent. He'd also never cared.

'Reckon we were right?' Eric asked.

He wasn't asking to assuage some internal uncertainty. Eric wasn't uncertain about very much; once a decision was made, it was made. He genuinely wanted to know Jack's opinion.

'I reckon,' Jack said slowly, 'that there isn't a man in this room who wouldn't have done the same thing, given the chance.'

Eric smiled. 'Doesn't answer my question, mate.'

Jack took a drag of his smoke. 'Ask me in ten years.'

As it turned out, they didn't have to wait that long. That night all three of them individually arrived home to find a letter addressed to them. Each had the same message. A time, a place, and the word *Magnus*.

That they had to go to the meeting was clear. In stolen moments between shifts they would talk, not wanting to discuss anything on the phone.

'Someone fucking saw us,' Harrison, pacing, said.

'Like who?' The only hint that anything was bothering Eric was a slightly deeper furrow to his brow. 'Everyone else was downstairs and there were no windows in that room.'

Jack, for his part, immediately concluded that the money had been planted. Nothing else made sense. But by who, and why?

As the days crept towards the demanded meeting, he found it harder to sleep. His palms were sweaty, his heart rate high. The fear became anger that he wanted to direct at Harrison, but in the end, he'd had a chance to refuse and hadn't taken it. He even considered going to the boss and explaining everything, but given that whoever they were meeting had not only known that somebody had taken the money but known *who*, he couldn't be sure who else might be watching.

The address should have been a giveaway. The Pit: a bikie bar on the outskirts of the city, sitting squat and square in the middle of a concrete lot, providing a 360-degree view of anyone undesirable approaching. Early on they'd heard stories from cops that if anybody wanted to cripple half of crime in Melbourne, all they'd have to do was burn down The Pit. Which made Jack wonder at times why nobody ever had.

When he arrived at the bar, it was immediately evident that arson might have been the best thing for it. The floor was sticky, a stench of beer and petrol hung in the air, and only half of the dangling lightbulbs were working. Harrison and Eric were already in a corner booth, pretending to talk but scanning the room intermittently. The bar was otherwise unoccupied – but then it was 10 am. Jack, glad of the gun in the back of his jeans, joined them but didn't speak. He couldn't muster much more than a nod.

Right on time, the door opened and a man strode in. He was tall but thin. His black hair hung around a long face that looked accustomed to smiling. He wore the leather cut of the Scorpions bikie gang, and on his chest a patch bore the word *President*.

'Rook,' Eric had muttered.

None of them had met him before, but they knew him by reputation. He was charismatic, well liked, and recently elected after the death of their previous president. Also, much to a lot of cops' irritation, clever enough to avoid getting caught out on anything actionable. If it wasn't for the fact that they obviously weren't, Rook Gately might have been able to convince the world that the Scorpions were a legitimate organisation of motorbike enthusiasts.

'Gentlemen.' Rook met them all with a round of handshakes. His voice was deep. 'Drinks are on me. What are we having?'

None of them replied. Rook called for a bottle of vodka and a glass for everyone. He sat next to Harrison, across from Jack, and asked them how they were finding the job as the bottle arrived. Harrison was the only one to reply.

'Now, boys.' Rook poured out a double shot in each of the glasses and slid them around. 'I'm not going to waste anyone's time here. You got my gift.'

'Your gift?' Eric's voice was low, tight.

'I've got a friend in admin at the station,' Rook said. 'He passed along the crime-scene report. I know it was you three who were sent to cover the upstairs and I know the money disappeared. Now, to put your minds at rest, I'm not about to report on anyone. There's no blackmail or any of that awful shit going on here. And I'm not after getting the money back. It was a gift, and in the interests of good faith, I'd like you to keep it even if you tell me to go fuck myself after my proposition.'

Fear was giving way to a dull, simmering unease that was somehow worse.

'You're young, but you're not stupid,' Rook said. 'Case in point, you know not to throw away good cash. This tells me you also know that sometimes situations aren't as straightforward as our Sunday School teachers would have had us believe. Take my boys, for example. That the

Scorpions exist on the wrong side of the law is true. But there are plenty of players in this scene who are far, far worse than us. And we don't go near those players. The opposite: we actively work *against* them. In the meantime, we make our money running protection for some carefully chosen operators, moving some firearms around the place. I mean, we're essentially couriers and bodyguards. Fairly harmless, really.'

'Unless you get shot with one of those illegal firearms,' Eric said.

'Because nobody's ever been killed by a legal one,' Rook replied. 'The point is we're connected but not culpable for the worst you go up against. But in our position, there will always be those on the force who want to take us down, fairly or not. What I need are some friends among the boys in blue. Friends on the ground, not in admin. Friends who can let me know when the tide turns against my men.'

Eric went to speak, but Rook raised a hand.

'In return,' he said, 'I can feed you information nobody else can. The movements of the biggest syndicates. Where to look to find the evidence that can put them away. I can give you a direct line to the criminal underworld. And I can pay. A lot. It's an arrangement of mutual benefit, although to be frank the benefit is weighted far more towards you than me.'

'You're asking us to work for a criminal organisation,' Eric said.

'I'm asking you to work *with* a criminal organisation,' Rook said. 'No obligations, no strings. The moment you want out, you are out, no questions asked. The very fact that you worked with me provides a pretty solid insurance policy against you turning informant. But listen, I don't believe in forcing anyone into anything. You stop working, you stop getting paid and you stop getting information. We part ways and that's that.'

The music, if that's what anyone could have called it, was louder now. Jack lifted his glass but didn't drink. Harrison poured another vodka. Eric was watching Rook.

The bikie smiled. 'Any questions?'

They'd argued, of course. Each taking turns as devil's advocate, going back and forth on where they stood. Jack was surprised to find that even with the anxiety of the days before the meeting, he wasn't completely certain that telling Rook to get fucked was the right move. The money was one thing, but the chance for a line of information nobody else had, that was a career-maker.

'It goes without saying,' Eric had said, leaning against the wall at Jack's cramped, peeling apartment, 'but I'll put it out there anyway. This is an all or none deal. It's the only way to protect ourselves. If one of us refuses, we all do.'

'Is it really that bad?' Harrison asked. 'I mean, I know on paper it is, but it's a compromise that could save lives.'

And turn your wallet fatter than you'd ever imagined, Jack thought, but didn't say. He couldn't judge Harrison when the same temptation was weighing on him. Badly. The idea of getting out of this shithole, living somewhere nice, maybe somewhere with a yard and trees. He didn't believe Rook's claims that it would be a simple or clean arrangement, but that was a given. There would be challenges to this, but in the end Harrison *was* right. They could save lives.

And that, he had told himself for a long time, was his main reason for finally saying yes.

For the first few months, the certainty that they had done the wrong thing lingered. Every knock at the door, every ring of the phone, every tap on the shoulder – there was always the lurch in the gut that said *you've been found out; it's over.*

But it wasn't, and as time went on the needling discomfort faded away. The monthly payments in exchange for updates that rarely had anything of substance kept coming in. To be fair, what came from Rook was usually just as innocuous, but every now and then he would live up to his word and give them gold.

And so they rose through the ranks. Their superiors were impressed with the information they found, and the genius deductions that might bring down a drug dealer or standover man. Before long they were given their pick of where they wanted to advance to.

Eric quickly landed on a murder squad. Jack almost rolled his eyes when he heard. Of course Eric would go for the showiest, most impressive-sounding job. But then he was good at it and he had the right steely constitution to walk through those kicked-in doors and face nightmares. Jack was almost willing to set his watch by the growth of Eric's legend, and sure enough he was soon the star of the department, something helped in no small part by his brand of intense charisma and chiselled good looks.

'They're exaggerating,' Eric told Jack and Harrison over drinks one night. 'My solve rate isn't any better than anyone else's. Honestly, half the time cops are like little kids who just want a hero.'

Murder detectives could be like that: despite what they dealt with, there was something more black-and-white in their way of thinking, a lack of moral ambiguity when you were trying to track down the perpetrators of horrors you saw first-hand.

Jack had half-expected Harrison to tail Eric, but maybe he was sick of being overshadowed. Instead, he joined the drug squad, which, Jack initially thought, had done wonders for his disposition. In the academy days and afterwards, Harrison had been like an overgrown child, never taking much very seriously. And while the smiles and the jokes returned in the pub after a few drinks, whenever Jack saw him around the station, he seemed to be ageing at double speed. That perception wasn't only due to the new lines on his face or the way his hair got shorter and neater by the week, but the way he held himself. Once, Harrison had stumbled along, wide-eyed and grinning, always with the slight impression of a kid struggling to fit in among the grown-ups. Not so anymore. He would stride at the head of his pack, serious and direct and with that slight weariness to everything he said and did. Jack understood. The drug squad was tough. For every bad guy who went down, you'd have to lean on some poor teenager or struggling parent who had turned to a little gear to keep their head above water. Whatever Eric said about heroes,

Jack – and Harrison – knew that there were none in the drug squad.

Jack had been uncertain about what would suit him, but a few drinks with McDonagh, a grizzled and gruff older cop who hated everyone but seemed to hate Jack marginally less, led him to undercover. At first Jack had been unsure about it but soon found that whether he liked it or not, he was too good at it to waste his talents. The qualities that made people uncomfortable around Jack were perfectly suited to looking and acting like your average criminal piece of shit, and so that was what he did. He could think on his feet and, when he needed to, talk fast and sound convincing. And for the most part his job was observation. It wasn't easy but Jack couldn't deny that there was *something* to that fear of being caught – so similar to his initial worries after the deal with Rook – but when you were unquestionably on the right side of it, it became almost intoxicating. A rush that left you trembling and grinning and ready to go again.

Over time, buried in their work and the individual complexities of it, Jack, Harrison and Eric drifted apart. Every now and then came a polite dinner, but there was an unspoken sense that it was best for all of them if they didn't appear too close, if they lived their lives and did what they had to do and never strayed too far into each other's orbit. When Jack's daughter was born – an accident after a slightly-too-long fling with a flighty local bartender – he only received a congratulatory phone call from Harrison and a card from Eric, which suited him just fine.

Like everyone, Jack heard the rumours that Eric had become obsessed with one case in particular, a string of murders that the department was divided on. Some thought the similarities in the locations they were dumped and the wounds connected them. Others thought the connections were tenuous at best. The idea of a serial killer seemed like wishful thinking on the part of a young detective in search of some excitement. Without knowing much about the case, Jack had fallen vaguely into the latter camp, which was why he was as surprised as anyone when Terrence Adams, a drug dealer he'd once met at some deadbeat's party, turned out to be the perp. There were some whispers about what exactly had gone down between Eric and the murdering prick, but in the end, nobody was mourning Adams, and Eric, once again, was the hero cop.

But at his celebration drinks, he didn't look like one. He was drawn, his cheeks pinched and his eyes ringed dark. He barely said anything when he was asked to give a speech. He gave a curt thanks and went back to join his wife, a slim, pretty woman nursing a baby. Jack didn't know either of their names. He didn't remember if he'd ever been told.

'It'll take him some time,' Harrison said, when Jack found him later.

'Has he had to drop someone before?' Jack asked.

Harrison nodded. 'But always clean. By the book. You know, body shot. Adams got his gun off him. Eric found a bottle.'

And Adams had died. Jack looked through the chatting crowd to where Eric sat. His wife was whispering to him, but he didn't seem to hear whatever she was saying. He was nodding but his eyes were empty.

Harrison and Jack had gone out for a smoke when they saw Eric and his family leaving. Eric had paused, then told his wife to go on to the car. Hands in pockets, breathing mist, he joined them. Jack passed him a cigarette and was surprised when Eric accepted it. He'd never smoked before.

The pleasant smell of tobacco filled the cold night air, along with the buzz of voices from inside. None of them spoke.

'Fucked-up world, isn't it?' Eric said.

He was slurring slightly, Jack noticed. He wasn't sure he'd ever seen Eric drunk before.

'But we do what we can,' Harrison replied.

Eric nodded. 'Yeah. Yeah, we do.'

A hollow smile, then he ground out his cigarette, shook their hands and walked into the night.

It was the last time they would all be together as friends.

The first time Jack had encountered members of the Scorpions while undercover, he'd been worried. Enough to go to Rook about it.

'They don't know you, mate,' Rook assured him. 'I'm the only one who does. Just treat them like you would any other crooks.'

But the Scorpions *weren't* any other crooks. Jack now realised that he would be put in a very tricky position if he saw one of them do something bad.

Luckily, for the most part the Scorpions just seemed to be *there*. Hired muscle to protect paranoid dealers at potentially dangerous meets. Their very presence seemed to be enough to dissuade attacks or ambushes, which was a good thing. If nobody gave them a reason to attack, Jack didn't have a reason to step in.

Jig Matthews, a small-time dealer who thought he was Escobar, liked using the Scorpions a lot. Jack even got to know the two regulars by name as they hung around Matthews like a couple of scowling sentinels – Mo and Rhys. When Matthews held court in his smoke-filled house, they'd stand on either side of him, probably loving having to do fuck-all for good money.

At the time, Jack was posing as one of Matthews' lackeys. He'd seen enough to get a conviction, but the department was pushing for something stronger. They knew Matthews had killed at least one person, and without spelling it out had suggested to Jack that they wanted to catch him in the act to make sure he never got out.

One night Tim Leighton, a weedy man pushing forty, arrived at the house. He was stumbling over excuses, but Jig, sitting in his armchair, his mostly bald head slick with sweat and his chins wobbling with every fake laugh, wasn't having it.

'My gear is my gear,' he said, somewhat pointlessly. 'You lose my gear, you replace my gear, or you replace what it's worth, with interest.'

'It wasn't me who lost it!' Tim said. 'I told Nils not to bring it round, I told him my girl wasn't having it, and he—'

'You blaming your missus now?'

'No!' Tim said. 'No, it was Nils, it was—'

'Blaming Nils, then?'

This went on for a while. Jack half-listened but wanted to get home. He'd come up with an excuse to be away for a few days starting tomorrow – a few days in which he had custody of his daughter.

Finally, they seemed to reach an accord. Matthews told Tim to get out. Jack was about to ask if he could take off, when he noticed the slight nod Matthews gave to the bikies. As one, they slipped out of the house.

It was just a nod. It could have meant anything. But covertly returning to the station that night, he'd checked Tim Leighton's record. A wife and two young kids.

He'd sat there in front of the wheezing computer, trying to think. He was off the clock. It was just a nod. He had nothing actionable. The Scorpions were protection, not killers.

But still he drove to Leighton's house. It was well past midnight when he arrived. The place was small, surrounded by a sagging fence and overgrown grass.

He walked through the weeds and scattered toys to the front door.

He stopped. It was already open.

They'd been thorough and efficient. There was no way to link the bullets dug out of the bodies to any known criminal. No fingerprints, no DNA, no witnesses. That the deaths of the Leighton family were linked to organised crime was a given, but before long they were just four more names on the endless list of gang violence casualties.

When Jack slept, the nod appeared unbidden in his dreams. Awake, he'd see it everywhere: between friends, customers and staff at bars, parents and children.

He considered turning himself in. Maybe that would end the guilt that tore apart his insides and turned his sleep fractured and full of nightmares. But there would be no point. He couldn't prove a nod meant murder any more than he could prove the Scorpions had been at the Leightons' that night. If he relayed the nod to his superiors, then at best they might secure a warrant to haul in Matthews for questioning. But that would blow Jack's cover, make him a target for Rook and likely go nowhere.

At one point, he tried to convince himself that he couldn't know for sure, that maybe the nod meant something else. But he knew it didn't. And even if he could pretend otherwise, that wouldn't have changed the weight in his stomach that grew by the day.

One time he picked up the phone to call Rook, to tell him. But the naivety of that move was obvious. Rook knew. The Scorpions would not have acted on Matthews' orders so immediately if murder wasn't part of their mandate.

The smart move would have been to pretend nothing was wrong and use his connections to come up with some way to bring the Scorpions down from the inside. But the smart move vanished from his mind every time he thought of those kids' bodies. Of the blood and the uncomprehending confusion on their dead faces.

He arranged a meeting with Rook. In the same booth at The Pit where he had first made the deal, he did his best to maintain his composure as he told Rook that he was calling it, that he was done.

Rook's expression was all concern. 'Why, mate?'

'You said no questions asked,' Jack reminded him. 'That if I ever wanted out, I could go without a problem.'

Rook leaned back. 'That's true. But I thought we'd got to know each other well enough to speak plainly.'

If only that was true.

Jack forced a shrug. 'It's a dangerous game, Rook. You know that and I know that. I've got a kid now. I can't be playing both sides.'

'Alright.' Rook smiled. 'Family comes first, of course.' He extended a hand. 'We'll miss you, Jack.'

He wanted to dive across the table. He wanted to tear that smile off Rook's face. He wanted to attack until he was bleeding out on the floor just like the Leighton children.

But he took his hand, shook once, and left.

The day after his meeting with Rook, Jack reached out to the others. He wasn't looking forward to this. Not just because of what he had to tell them, but because it was news around the station that the Terrence Adams case, as it was still called, was potentially being reopened after another body had been found with the same distinctive wounds. There was talk of Eric spending long hours in the bar, poring over photos and case files as he spent hundreds on whisky. Jack felt for him. He'd made his fair share of mistakes, but he'd never got the wrong guy. Let alone killed him.

They met in a rundown old warehouse in a largely forgotten industrial scrapyard. The inside had long since been hollowed out but for a few hunks of rusted machinery sitting among the weeds that grew from the partly caved-in floor. When Jack arrived with his duffle bag, Harrison and Eric were already there. Neither spoke. Harrison sat on what looked like it might have been a large old printer, eyes on his clasped hands.

Eric, for his part, was pacing. If Jack thought he had looked bad at the premature celebration of his closing the Adams case, that was nothing compared to now. His hair, once immaculate and gleaming, was greasy and hung in his face. His skin was waxy and he'd lost weight. He stopped moving when he saw Jack. Just looked at him with those unblinking, bloodshot eyes.

'I'm done,' Jack said. 'With Rook, the Scorpions, all of it.'

Silence for a moment. Harrison didn't look up.

Eric shook his head. 'No.'

'Sorry?'

'No. You're not done.'

There was a cold certainty to his voice that Jack didn't like at all. 'I think you'll find I've made that call for myself, mate.'

'I think you'll find, *mate*, that it's not that simple.' Eric's nostrils flared. His fists clenched so tightly Jack could see the white of his knucklebones. 'What did we say, back at the start? All of us or none of us.'

'Then it's none of us,' Jack replied. 'It's past time you both pulled the plug as well.'

'*NO!*' The sudden, explosive violence in Eric's voice almost made Jack step back, but he held his ground.

Eric moved towards him, slowly. 'You don't get to decide for us, Carlin. You should have called. Let us talk this through. Now you're gonna call Rook and you're gonna—'

'I'm gonna do fucking nothing.' Jack could hear the tremor of rage in his voice. How could Eric be so goddamn dense, so blind to what he was dealing with? 'They're killers. The Leighton family—'

'Shared your little theory with the force, have you?' Eric said.

Jack didn't reply.

'Nah. Nah, didn't fucking think so. It was never gonna be that easy, Carlin. Once you were in, you were in.'

'Now I'm out,' Jack said. 'And if you put down the bottle for five seconds, you might realise why that's the only move.'

A terrible stillness from Eric. 'Want to say that again?'

'Eric,' Harrison said.

'I said it once,' Jack said. 'You heard it once. I don't need to retract or repeat.'

'But you should,' Eric said. 'You really fucking should.'

Harrison stood.

Jack was done with this. All of it. 'How about I clarify. You're a stinking, drunken wreck and I don't give a fuck what you say.'

Eric lunged for him. Harrison tried to grab him but he was shoved hard out of the way. Spitting and seething, Eric came at Jack, only for the full, heavy bag to take him in the head. He hit the ground.

'Enough,' Jack said. He dropped the duffle bag next to Eric. 'That's all the money I have left from Rook. Keep it if you want. I'm out.'

He turned and walked away.

'Try to take us down, you'll be right there with us!' Eric, trying to stand, called after him.

Jack kept walking out into the cold grey.

In years to come, Jack would wonder if Eric's fury was because he was finally starting to understand that the case he was buried in was linked to that choice the three of them had made so long ago. If, like Jack, he knew without being able to prove it that they had sanctioned the reign of monsters.

Jack avoided Eric after that, but signs of the other man were everywhere. Anonymous complaints about Jack's conduct. Rumours of affairs with CIs, of planted evidence and violence towards potential witnesses. A constant stream of untraceable attempts to tank his career.

Nothing ever held enough water to be followed through, but it was a relief for Jack when he finally got the inevitable call that it was time for him to move on from undercover. Cops in that department had a use-by date; the ones who didn't burn out were found out. There was a lot of debate over which was worse.

Over the years even the wounds that couldn't truly heal hurt less. There was never a day that Jack didn't think about the Leightons, but there were a few where he could think about them without the breath going out of him, without the feeling of barbed wire being dragged through his insides. He threw himself into his work, but chafed against the structures of every new department he spent time in. He missed undercover. He missed being part of the underworld knowing he was above it.

So it was a relief when he learned that Eric had been kicked off the force and his daughter taken away from him. He considered calling Harrison and asking for details, but on reflection realised he didn't care. Eric being gone was enough.

He wondered at times if Harrison ever regretted their choice the way he did. Outside of the force, Harrison kept to himself, focusing on raising the son Jack had never met. By all accounts, he was the picture of propriety and responsibility. Not somebody you'd ever think might take payouts from a bikie gang.

Time passed.

Jack wasn't sure what to expect when he received an email out of nowhere from Olivia Dean. He knew her by reputation only; she was relatively young, had made detective fast and had a reputation for fastidiousness and drive. By this point he had bounced around so many departments that he knew some of the younger cops called him 'Pinball Jack'. Behind his back.

Dean's smile was warm and her handshake firm when they met in a café. A glance at her gave him the wistful feeling of how old he was getting. She was in her late thirties, not *that* much younger than Jack in the grand scheme of things, but whatever Dean had seen and done, nothing about her looked worn or weathered. Her blonde hair was tied back, her suit worn with care, her movements natural but, he suspected, calibrated.

They made pointless small talk. She laughed at Jack's wry cracks about various older cops, something that surprised him, given her evident professionalism. But the longer they spoke, the clearer it became that Dean wasn't there for any sort of friendly getting-to-know-you session.

Finally, the point came out.

'I heard from Eric recently,' she said.

Jack didn't react. His mind was moving fast, trying to work out pre-emptive replies to anything Dean could be about to drop on him.

'He wanted information. Some old files. Played up the whole "I mentored you" thing. Naturally, I said no. But what he asked for … I mean, look, I know what he was like towards the end. And I could hear it on the phone. He was clearly wasted. But it sounds a lot like he's trying to get us to reopen the Adams case.'

Fucking typical. At least it had nothing to do with Rook. Jack relaxed slightly. 'Maybe I'm being harsh,' he said. 'But the way I see it, a heart attack would be Eric's best friend right about now. He's an abusive, delusional drunk. I'd ignore him.'

'Except he seems to think that the real killer was a member of the Scorpions,' Dean said. 'And he thinks he might know where to look to find evidence.'

Jack went to speak. Didn't. He sat back. 'Okay.'

Dean placed both hands flat on the table. 'Look, whatever you say about him, I know. Of course I do. But if he's right. If there's a way to *prove* that a member of the gang was a killer, that could be grounds for—'

'Whatever the Australian equivalent of RICO is,' Jack said.

Dean nodded. 'We don't have one, exactly, but there are things the Crime Commission can do that will be as good as, provided we can give them reason. I asked Eric what files he wanted but of course I didn't say I'd give them to him. He figured out the wilful omission pretty fast. Now, I know that you and Harrison Cooper were close to him back in the day. Cooper didn't want to tell me anything, pretty much brushed the whole thing off. But if you have any idea where to look, or if, I don't know, you could speak to Eric, get the information from him somehow.' There was an electric gleam in Dean's wide eyes. 'Imagine it. Bringing the Scorpions down.'

Jack could imagine it. Had been doing so for years.

It was dangerous, of course. If any hint reached Rook that he was involved, the bombshell that was his one-time involvement with them would go off and then some.

'Let me see what I can do,' he said.

He still had contacts from his undercover days. Many of whom, even knowing now that he was a cop, remained on relatively good terms with him. Of course, they were the ones he had strategically decided not to put away. So he hit the streets and started asking questions. Questions only those who had been a part of the scene back then would know the answers to. Had the Scorpions sheltered a serial killer?

He knew Eric would tell him nothing. He also knew that Dean – having spoken to Harrison Cooper – had set off dangerous tripwires. If Harrison was still involved with Rook, then he would be working overtime to ensure that any information Eric had did not see the light of day.

Of course, he knew Eric could be full of shit. It was possible that his belief of the Scorpions being involved was some alcohol-induced manifestation of his own long-buried guilt. But if there was even a chance it wasn't, if Jack could find some sliver of proof that the Scorpions were directly linked to several murders, then everything changed. He could leave the force having realised some kind of justice for the Leightons, even if all he did was pass the relevant information on to Dean.

Then the call came from the commissioner.

Commissioner Walsh had never liked him. This was fair enough, given the feeling was mutual. Walsh was tough, almost entirely humourless, and a big advocate for cleaning out the last cops left over from the days where the rules were largely seen as guidelines. Jack had been careful to never give her any reason to kick him out on his arse, but as it turned out somebody else had handed her that on a silver platter.

It was the kind of minor thing that he had almost forgotten about. The kind of thing that Eric had spent years failing to turn into anything solid. But now somebody had. A fight with a crook from years ago, one that ended with the prick in hospital, brain-damaged. It had been written off as self-defence, except now some non-existent witness had come out of the woodwork and claimed aggravated assault. Jack had always seen Walsh as joyless, but damned if she didn't take evident pleasure in telling him that he could not continue to serve on the force with such a stain on his record.

That simple, in the end. The 'victim' had long since died of an overdose and wasn't about to testify, so Jack avoided jail but was off the force. Twenty-five years of service gone in minutes.

He didn't want a big final bash or the shaken hands or heads or the pity or lack thereof. He cleared out his desk late at night, then walked into the cold. He stood in the glow of a streetlight as the wind blew feeble rain across the city. As he lit a cigarette he remembered, briefly, doing the same so long ago with Harrison and Eric.

Something made him look back. There, in the shadows of the overhang that fronted the sliding doors to the station that had been his home for so long, was Harrison Cooper.

The other man didn't nod. Didn't smile. Just watched. And Jack watched back and knew.

He didn't say anything, didn't accuse or attack. He just stood in the rain until he finished his cigarette. Then he walked to his car.

He had work to do.

Maggie didn't speak as Carlin finished his story. Wasn't sure what she could add.

Carlin seemed to feel the same. His eyes were on the night. Maggie wondered if he had ever told all that to anyone before. If anyone else understood what he had been through and done to end up here. It was possible he was lying but Maggie didn't think so. A liar would try to make themselves look better.

'All of those things my father started as,' Maggie said, 'could he have stayed that way, do you think?'

'He didn't,' Carlin said flatly. 'So obviously not.'

'So you think he was doomed to become what he did.'

'I think he made small concessions that became big concessions. I think the moment he took Rook Gately's money, yeah, he was doomed.'

'But you did as well.'

Even in the dim light she could tell Carlin's smile didn't reach his eyes. 'Never said I wasn't doomed, girl. But we're all different, so it stands to reason that bad choices can lead us each down different roads. 'Course, it can take time to know *how* different. And that's the danger.'

He slid Maggie the bottle. Out in the night a bird sang something low and mournful that died away into silence. Maggie picked up the bottle and drank.

CHAPTER THIRTEEN

It was late. Maggie sat in the kitchen, a cup of tea in hand, staring at the plain wall. She was out of reading material and there wasn't much else to do after nearly ten days here. She checked the clock. Close to two in the morning. This relative peace was creating its own peculiar form of restlessness, a perpetual sense that these were stolen moments she couldn't afford.

Carlin's story had been reverberating through her head all day. In some ways he had been right when he told her it didn't matter. It didn't change her predicament. But looked at slightly differently, it changed everything.

She knew better than to absolve her father. His choices were his own. But hearing the way that Carlin spoke about the man he used to be, about that serious, driven, hero cop, turned her thoughts to Rook Gately. To the bikie president who was still out there, still alive and in power, still pulling strings and turning things to his own benefit. The fact that Cooper could willingly work with a man like that, even knowing what he was capable of, bothered her more than she liked.

But, she reminded herself, Cooper didn't matter anymore. Whatever she had thought he was, whatever she had *wanted* him to be, that delusion was gone. Her childhood fantasies had been proven definitively incorrect. And in the end, of the three young policeman who had taken Rook Gately's deal, only one had chosen to walk away from it, for which he had lost everything.

Simmering underneath her attempts to understand Carlin's story was a more pressing question: whether or not she should tell him what she suspected about the hard drive. But she knew now which way the scales were tipping. She needed the information on there, but for her to take it and run would also mean the Scorpions continued to get away with everything they had done. There would have to be a compromise of some sort. A deal with Carlin that she could take what she needed to from it and let him have the rest.

But for now she knew: Carlin had to be told.

The phone rang. She looked over; it sat on the kitchen bench, beside the kettle, and while she had noticed it before she'd soon put it out of her thoughts. There was no-one she could call even if she had wanted to. But now, for the first time since she had been here, it was ringing.

There was no reason to answer. She didn't. She waited until it rang out.

It started again.

She walked over, picked the phone up and put it to her ear.

'Girl.' Carlin's voice. 'Tell me that's you.'

A spike of cold fear. Maggie looked out the window. Just darkness. 'Yeah.'

'I'm on my way back but I just got word from one of my informants – there are men coming there right now.'

Maggie's hand tightened on the phone. 'What men?'

'Len Townsend's fucking men. Six of them. My guy got the offer a few hours ago – good pay, immediate work. I have no clue how the hell Townsend found out where I live, but they're coming and they're looking for you. They don't know for sure you're there, but—'

'Townsend didn't send six men to suss out a hunch.'

'No, he sent six men because he saw what you did to the last two.'

'What makes him think I'd be here?'

She could hear Carlin's frustration. 'Probably some prick with information to sell, some prick who heard I was looking into the hard drive and had reason to shelter you. Some prick I'm going to find and kill. Listen, above my bed is the entry to the attic.'

'They'll check the attic.'

'You'll find a toolbox up there. There are things you can use. All the knives and everything; I stuck them away after you arrived, just in case, you know.'

Fair enough, Maggie thought.

'You can try to get clear but my bet is they'll be coming through the trees, dressed in black, spread out and closing fast. I don't know how long you've got, but I wouldn't be fucking around. I'm coming as fast as I can but I'm gonna need you to find somewhere to hide and stay there until they've left. Maggie, you—'

Maggie hung up. She listened. There were no sounds from outside. But then, there wouldn't be. She scanned the kitchen. *What did she have?*

She gave herself a moment. Just a moment to breathe, to let her heart slow and her head clear.

She turned on the kettle. Then she went quickly back down the central hall of the house. There were two main doors at either end, the front door and the one in the kitchen, facing each other directly down the hall. The other rooms were on the sides. She turned left into Carlin's room. She hadn't been in there before. It was messy and cluttered with files and papers but she ignored them. She looked at the roof; the outline of the trapdoor into the attic sat directly over his bed. Wincing, she clambered up and pulled it downwards. She smelled dust. With some difficulty, she lifted herself up into it.

There were boxes everywhere. It didn't take her long to locate the drawer of knives and a faded red toolbox. The contents were not inspiring. A hammer, a couple of chisels and spanners, some string. She took the hammer and stuck in through her belt. She grabbed a handful of steak knives and lowered herself back through the trapdoor. She left it open.

The kettle was boiled. She tapped it, checking the heat. She glanced out the window. Still nothing.

She pulled the back door slightly ajar. A chill crept into the room. Maggie opened the kettle and placed it on top of the door, leaning slightly against the frame. She stepped back. The kettle stayed put, but it was precarious.

She hurried to the front door. She had three serrated steak knives. Kneeling, she pressed the blades one by one against the floorboards until they all snapped free of the hilts. Then she stuck the jagged, broken bottom of the first blade between the floorboards, about a metre from the front door. It was a tight fit, but it worked. She planted the other two the same way nearby then stood and backed away. She turned off the hall light and the house was plunged into darkness. She moved sideways into her room and crouched beside the bed. She found her money, now bundled into an envelope, and stuffed it into her pocket. She listened.

She had been waiting less than a minute when she heard the creak of the front porch. Her heart rate increased. She took the hammer from her belt. She moved just beside the door, pressing herself up against it.

She heard the front door handle turn and open, slowly.

Then the shoved open back door, followed by a thud, a clatter of metal on wood and screams, screams of stunned pain as boiling water soaked the man who had just come through.

'Vic!' A yell from the front, heavy footsteps, then a gasp and a cry of pain, which got louder as he pulled himself forward and staggered past Maggie's door, a silhouette in the dark.

Maggie moved through the doorway, saw his crumpling figure from behind, saw the back of his head and brought the hammer down hard on it. A crack and he was down.

She glimpsed flailing on the ground near the back door but ignored it; she bolted straight through into Carlin's room as the first gunshot sounded.

The renewed pain in her back and leg didn't matter. She was up on the bed and clambering through the trapdoor as she heard more yells and pounding feet. She pulled it closed; a moment later, from below, she heard somebody enter the room. She slid away from the door and her eyes landed on the drawer of knives.

A gunshot burst through the wood below and missed her by half a metre. She didn't move. Silence.

She reached out and, taking care not to make a sound, took one large knife from the drawer. She placed it on the trapdoor, near the hinge, pointing towards the handle. Then another, a bit further across.

Splintering wood and a deafening shot. No closer. Maggie didn't move. She counted to five then placed the next knife. And the next. She moved away. The trapdoor shifted. It creaked and Maggie stood. It was pulled down, hard and fast. The knives fell. A yelp.

Maggie picked up the toolbox and flung hard it through the hole. A crashing rattle of metal and body hitting the ground and then silence.

She didn't wait. She moved, slow enough to not make any more sound than necessary, to the dust-coated window. She slid it open – it was louder and heavier than she'd hoped, but she figured attention down below would be elsewhere. Cool night air filled the musty attic. She heard voices, low, scared, angry. She climbed through the window, out onto the gentle slope of the roof, into the deepening cold of a cloudy, starless night. She moved to the side, clear of the attic window. The wind picked up. She listened.

It was brief, so brief she might have missed it. A snatch of heavy breathing from below. A guard. She counted in her head. *Six men. One scalded, one stepped on the knives and got the hammer, one taken out by the toolbox.* That left three unharmed. At least two would have stood guard but maybe the swift dispatching of the men inside attracted at least one of them. The other, it seemed, had kept his post.

She slid down the roof. She heard no sound from the attic, not yet; hopefully, whoever was in the house assumed she was still hiding in there. She reached the edge and listened. There it was again. Fast, shallow. She stuck her head over the edge and looked. A shadow, on the porch, looking at the front door, hands forward, holding a gun. Maggie pulled back. She moved into a crouch. Pre-emptively she winced. However she handled this, her leg would not thank her. She slid forward again, legs over the edge, and dropped.

She hit the porch, pain bit down. She tottered, heard the gasp and the half-formed yell and she swung, bringing the hammer to where she knew his face was. For a moment she saw his eyes, wide, scared, young – then the hammer hit, his eyes rolled back and she snatched his pistol from his limp grip as he fell. A shape appeared in the door and she fired twice. A bullet scorched her ear and Maggie pulled the trigger again.

A thump.

One left.

She moved.

She knew he'd be coming, whether from the doorway or behind the house. She knew and she zigzagged, erratic and low to the ground. She could see the road up ahead, a gaping maw in the midnight trees. She hit the tree line, swung behind a trunk, leaned out and pointed her gun at the low, dark shape of the house.

No movement. Just a groan from within, whether the toolbox man, the kettle or both, she didn't know. An incapacitated opponent was not an inactive one. She focused on the front door.

It was the cracking twig that made her fling herself forward; she tasted dirt just as the gunshot went off and the bullet hissed over her head. She spun, saw the approaching figure moving down the road from the opposite direction to the house. She lifted her gun knowing it was all too late, then the sound of an engine, a movement of racing darkness and the rip of tyres in dirt and the man was flying forward, slammed by the speeding van and thrown through the air until he hit the ground less than a metre from Maggie.

He was face down and squirming, whimpering something as he tried to push himself up. He was black-clad and looked fit. Another professional.

Maggie stood as the car door opened. Jack Carlin approached from the shadows. There was no laughter on his face as he looked at the downed man. Just cold, terrible, anger, anger that made Maggie want to attack because she recognised it so very well. With one boot, Carlin rolled the man over. His eyes, glazed and unfocused, stared at the sky.

Carlin shot him in the head.

The sound echoed through the clearing around the house and up the road, thinning to a ghostly remnant by the trees. Maggie wasn't sure she had ever before experienced the depth of silence that followed.

'Let's not fuck around here,' Carlin said. 'Because any tolerance I had for games is gone. The bastard found my house. A house that is not registered under my name. The information is out there, which means it's only a matter of time before the Scorpions know it too. So if there's anything you can tell me. Anything you know—'

A sound from behind them. Maggie turned just as the figure veering from the house fired his gun. She felt the heat from the bullet but it flew past her – and slammed into Jack Carlin's chest.

He hadn't even fallen before the next two hit him, sending him flying like a ragdoll into the shadows.

Maggie was crouched low and firing. The approaching figure didn't slow. Dirt exploded around her. Maggie squeezed the trigger and the gun clicked. She glanced towards Carlin's still form. Another bullet hit centimetres from her feet.

Maggie ran. She hit the side of the van, wrenched open the door and clambered in. The engine was still running. More gunshots. Maggie reversed. The van careened backwards. Ahead through the windscreen, the last assassin was swallowed by night and then there were only the trees and the dark.

CHAPTER FOURTEEN

Maggie's knuckles were white, her grip stone.

Carlin was dead.

In some faraway, disconnected part of her brain, the impact of that seemed outsized. A man who had threatened her, placed her in danger, taken away the closest thing she had to a birthright. But also a man who had protected her, patched her up and done more than what he needed to keep her safe. A man who, somewhere in the strange amorphous mass of time that had been the past days, she had come to respect, even like.

It seemed wrong, that his wry quips and wolfish grin had been wiped out by the bullets of some nameless assassin, an assassin Maggie had failed to kill.

She tried to force away those thoughts. None of them was helpful. But still they bit and tugged and gnawed at her as she drove through the night and tried to keep from falling apart.

Dimly, the notion that she could escape came into her mind. Townsend might already know that she had avoided his men yet again, but it would take time for the bikies or the police to figure that out. For the first time since arriving in Melbourne, she had an advantage. All it would take was her hitting the highway and continuing on her way, driving for days on end until Melbourne was a distant memory again, this time never to be revisited.

But the idea that had occurred to her in Jack Carlin's kitchen, the notion of where the hard drive – and with it, the chance to finally come face to face with her mother and ask her why – might be hidden, wouldn't leave her alone. And now might be her only chance to find it.

When she saw the lights of an open café, she stopped the van. She leaned back in the seat. Her stomach was growling and despite it all she could feel tiredness eating at her. She wanted to arrive at her location to plan her next move, but now that the adrenaline had worn off, she needed energy.

The café was small and unassuming, tucked between a mechanic and a plumbing supplies store, both closed. The kind of place tradies or truck drivers went for an early feed. She stepped inside to be met by the strong smell of bacon and coffee. An old doo-wop song crackled from a single speaker. Washed-out posters for brands that she was pretty sure no longer existed covered the yellowing walls. The booths that lined the smudged windows were covered in laminated menus that looked sticky.

A middle-aged woman in an apron emerged from the kitchen area behind the counter and stopped upon seeing Maggie. 'You right there, love?'

An honest answer was probably a bad idea. She nodded. 'Just after a coffee and something to eat. Bacon sandwich maybe. No egg.'

'Was just fixing one for myself,' the woman said. 'Grab a seat.'

Maggie did. She could hear the woman singing along to the song in the kitchen, her scratchy voice punctuated by crackles from the cooking bacon. Maggie closed her eyes.

Maybe she fell asleep because a moment later she was jerking in her seat as a plate was put down in front of her.

'Dead on your feet there,' the woman said, placing a steaming mug of coffee next to the plate. 'These'll give you a kick up the arse.'

She smiled and returned to the kitchen. Maggie picked up the sandwich but found she couldn't bring herself to take that first bite. Her limbs felt seized up. Her chest was contracting. She needed air. She went to stand then—

The squeak of the door and a low, guttural laugh. She sat back.

Two men had entered the café, deep in conversation. One was hulking but stooped, bald with heavy features. The other was relatively thin with a pinched face and darting eyes.

Both wore the distinctive black cut of the Scorpions.

Maggie didn't move. The smaller bikie glanced at her but there was no recognition. They reached the counter and the bigger one pounded it once.

The woman emerged. There was a brief exchange and, looking miffed, she went back to the kitchen. The bikies slid into the next booth along.

'I'm telling ya, this shipment better be worth it,' the smaller one was saying. 'Early fucken' starts will be the death of me.'

They hadn't been following her, then. Maggie looked at her sandwich, then the door. She couldn't eat anyway. She should just slip out now.

'Reckon they'll be a bit nicer to us this time?' the bigger one said.

'If they know what's good for 'em. Remember how that little bitch carried on? Anybody would have thought he was attached to those toes or something.'

More laughter. Maggie sipped her coffee.

'His fault, really,' the smaller one went on. 'Shouldn't've let that pretty girl help him with the flat tyre. That didn't work out well for anyone, did it, genius?'

'She *was* pretty too,' the big one said. 'Fucken' shame.'

'Ya could have left her face.'

A gurgle of laughter. 'Could have. Didn't.'

'We getting some food or what?' the smaller one hollered at the kitchen. 'Jesus Christ, put down the fucken' needle for a sec, you dried-up old cow.'

Maggie stood. Both bikies glanced at her. Watched as she passed them and walked to the counter. She saw a pen, left there by the woman. She picked it up.

The bikies started talking again.

The woman, looking harried, emerged from the kitchen. 'Something wrong, love?'

'Reckon you should duck out the back for a smoke,' Maggie said quietly.

'I quit the darts.'

'Then duck out for something else.'

The woman considered Maggie, then nodded and walked back through. Maggie listened – one of the bikies was in the middle of what sounded like a rambling joke. Maggie rounded the counter and followed the woman.

The back screen door had just swung shut. There was a frying pan sitting on the stove, a thin layer of oil across the bottom. Maggie turned up the heat.

She could hear the joke, still going.

The oil on the pan spat and crackled.

The joke stopped.

Maggie hovered her hand over the pan. She could feel the heat emanating from it.

The bikies were talking again, but quieter now. She could hear rustling, then heavy footfalls. She took the pan off the stove and, holding it level, walked back out into the main area.

The two bikies, approaching the counter, stopped upon seeing her. The big one looked at the pan.

Maggie flung the oil into his face.

He screamed, falling back. The smaller one swore and reached into his jacket but Maggie dived across the counter, swinging the pan as she did. It collided with his face – the sound of sizzling, another scream and Maggie hit the ground. She jumped to her feet; the smaller bikie was clawing at his face as he fell back into one of the booths. The bigger one lumbered for her.

Maggie rammed the pen into his eye. He yelled, grabbed at it, tripped backwards and hit the ground, writhing violently.

Maggie turned to where the smaller bikie was trying to climb out of the booth. Half his face was an angry red. His eyes bulged. Maggie hit him with the pan, then again.

Movement on the ground. She turned. The bigger bikie, the bloody pen still sticking out of his eye, had managed to get his gun clear and was fumbling with it.

Maggie stomped on the pen. He spasmed and went still. She picked up his gun and pointed it at the other bikie, still in the seat of the booth.

Through the pain and confusion and rage, a hint of realisation crossed his face.

'You're her,' he managed.

'Yeah,' Maggie said. 'I am.'

She pulled the trigger.

Silence but for the jaunty bounce of the doo-wop music. Maggie returned to her booth. She downed her coffee. Her appetite had returned. She picked up the sandwich and left.

CHAPTER FIFTEEN

She arrived in Williamstown as the sun rose. She parked down a back road near a few factories and, after checking the van for anything she could use and finding nothing, lay down on the mattress in the back and closed her eyes. She didn't want to sleep but knew she had to at least try. After maybe an hour of fitful, fractured rest, she didn't try to force herself back into it.

She was inside a Kmart the moment it opened, buying cheap clothes with notes she'd already removed from the rest. A pair of jeans, a couple of T-shirts and dark jumpers, a black fake-leather jacket and a beanie. In the van, she changed out of Carlin's oversized gear and tried to ignore the ache of seeing his old clothes discarded in the corner.

She shouldn't have killed the bikies. She knew that. She could easily have slipped out and not risked the extra attention. But knowing that, in the moment, hadn't been enough. Still wasn't. The thought of their cruel cockiness slipping into knowing fear even made her smile as she walked from the car into town.

She was aware that she likely had a small window of time here, but she needed the cover of night to properly search. In summer, Williamstown bustled with tourists, but winter wasn't as different as she would have liked. The suburb was as beachy as anywhere in Melbourne got. Despite being close to plenty of industrial areas, its streets were lined with fashionable bars and restaurants, across the road from vast stretches of perfectly maintained grass that reached down almost to the water, dotted with statues and monuments. Across the bay, grey and flat but still bobbing with boats, you could see the towers of the city.

It was hard to pinpoint how she felt, being back here. She almost wanted to identify this strangely cloying feeling as nostalgia, but that would be absurd. As a child she had loved Williamstown because being here meant something different and rare and, to her young self, special. But that beauty had come at the discretion of a man who spent the rest of his time ensuring that she understood just how ugly the world could be.

She didn't want to return to the van, so she walked through parks and down backstreets. She had a crumbling pie for lunch, then sat under a tree and waited for the sun to slowly vanish, then waited some more before she made her way towards the boat sheds near the beach.

She passed the area a couple of times before she was reasonably confident there was nobody else lurking around here. Not that she was especially surprised by that. Her father's paranoia extended to a lot of things being done either through cash-in-hand deals or under fake names. The shed, she had surmised, would not be any different.

As such, she knew that the unsettled chill in her chest as she walked along the darkened pavement towards her father's shed was not to do with the potential of being found here, but rather with something harder to define. Something she hadn't even felt back at her childhood home.

The shed was padlocked, as it had always been the times her father had taken her here. The lock was old and heavy, almost certainly unchanged in years. She took a piece of aluminium foil from her pocket, folded it, then with a quick glance over her shoulder, wrapped it around one of the now-burnished bars of the lock. She worked it down into the dull gold body, moving it back and forth until the lock came free. She removed it and pulled up the roller door.

The smell immediately told her nobody had been here since her father had died, and likely not for a long time beforehand. The air was thick with disuse and decay. Cobwebs hung low from the ceiling and coated the tools scattered across the benches.

The long boat lay tilted on the concrete ground, spared by neither the dust nor the spiders. Maggie had once braved asking her father why he kept it here instead of at the jetty. She had braced for the attack but he had given a gruff laugh and told her that this was both cheaper and harder to steal. Besides which, the relatively small boat would have looked a bit pathetic next to the far bigger, more impressive ones. Eric did so very much hate looking pathetic.

It felt like invading a tomb. But Maggie wasn't here to be reverent. Quickly she got to work, moving things around, checking in the stiff drawers of the bench. Finding nothing, she clambered into the boat.

She closed her eyes. For just a second she had smelt the sea and felt the warm wind and the fragile, fearful laugh that had risen as she watched her father, hair blown back and face for once not furrowed and furious, standing at the prow, the city shining and brilliant against the clear blue sky above the bay. Once or twice a year, he would knock on her door and tell her to get in the car. She always knew what it meant and while she would never risk showing too much obvious joy, it had risen powerful and breathtaking inside her.

For years she had hated the fact. That she could ever feel such gratitude towards her father. She had despised her younger self's stupid, easily manipulated wretchedness. Now, that terrible, illogical joy just seemed deeply sad to her. Yet it remained so ingrained and elemental that even now she could still taste its lingering vestiges.

Tucked under the stern of the boat, she found a small tin box. She pried it open.

The hard drive sat there, silver and small enough to fit in her pocket, a short USB cord sticking out of it. She lifted it to the minimal light creeping in through the door and turned it over.

It was so innocuous, no different to millions of others sitting on desks all over the world. Held on this, allegedly, were the answers to the case that had broken her father.

And, potentially, answers that mattered a whole lot more to Maggie.

She stepped out of the boat but found she couldn't leave. She told herself that she had to be out of Melbourne. That she was in danger. She had to move. She looked back around the dim shadows of the shed, then leaned against the bench.

She had never felt any real need to understand her father. The impact of what he did had always outweighed the ultimately irrelevant question of why. Maybe the same should apply to her mother but in her almost lifelong absence, save for vague and warped old memories, there still remained the potential, however slim, for something more than monstrous, something that could even make sense. Until Maggie knew otherwise it was as possible as anything else.

But now, sitting in the dark of the one place she had known where for whatever reason her father wouldn't hurt her, she wished with a keen and painful yearning that she could just once have seen inside his mind. To know what it was that twisted him to the point where he could turn his fists on the child he was supposed to love. And more to the point, how that violence could somehow coexist in the same man who took his daughter on impromptu sailing trips. Every time that small and rare human side of him came out, Maggie had wanted to cling to it and beg it to stay and love her, to forgive him for everything he had done as long as he could just be this way forever.

She closed her eyes. It went beyond her father. How could her mother have read her stories and fallen asleep holding her yet still abandon her? How could Jack Carlin put a gun to her head then hours later bandage her wounds? How could Harrison Cooper eat burgers and talk about the future with her all the while knowing that he was betraying her? And how could Maggie, who knew better than anyone just how evil the world was, find herself hoping for a different outcome time and time again?

She couldn't have named the last time she cried. It felt foreign to her and yet somehow too familiar, as though she had in this moment looped back around to the child she thought she had run away from. Maggie slid down the bench and sat in the dust and ruins of the one thing her father had loved and sobbed. For Jack Carlin, for Harrison Cooper, for her father and for herself. For all the ifs that had never happened and, in never happening, led her to this.

She pulled the door of the shed closed and locked it again behind her. She stepped back and looked it over. No sign anyone had been here. Eventually somebody would realise that this shed had sat ignored for years and try to work out who owned it. By then, the cobwebs and the dust would have covered over any evidence that its forgotten rest had been disturbed.

Maggie reached out a hand to touch the roller door but didn't. For a moment her hand hovered, then dropped.

'Maggie.'

She turned.

Harrison Cooper stood in the shadows behind her.

CHAPTER SIXTEEN

It was like Cairns all over again. Together Maggie and Cooper approached the bustling, up-market pub – all porthole windows and maritime imagery. Maggie didn't look at him as they went.

She couldn't say why she hadn't run. Maybe it was the fact that he wasn't holding a gun. Or else the look on his face: one of absolute, bone-deep weariness.

So she had agreed to talk, but on the proviso that they went somewhere public, somewhere Cooper couldn't easily shed that worn-out, almost benevolent guise. But as they sat together at the most isolated circular table in the dimly lit room, a table uncleared of the wine glasses from its last group and just a few metres from what seemed like a raucous staff party, the sense of being all too exposed grew.

'How did you know?' Maggie asked.

'I knew Eric had a boat shed down here,' Cooper said. 'He brought me here once, so I ran surveillance until I saw you.' He laid his hands on the table and looked at them, as if a script was written on the backs. Maggie, for her part, kept her gaze on him.

'I'm sorry,' Cooper said finally. 'For everything.'

Maggie didn't reply.

Cooper looked up at her. His eyes were red-rimmed, his cheeks hollow. He almost certainly hadn't slept for days. 'I owe you an explanation.'

'You don't owe me anything,' Maggie said. 'I never should have listened to you.'

'But you did, and for that I think I need to clear up at least a couple of things. It won't … it won't excuse anything. But maybe it can explain it, a bit.'

'I know you're taking money from the Scorpions,' she said. Then, with an unexpected pang, 'Jack Carlin told me.'

A flustered waitress was delivering more drinks to the staff party table, prompting a round of catcalls and cheers.

Cooper blinked, looking surprised even in the low light. 'Jack?'

'He found me after Darch's office,' she said. 'He's dead now. Townsend.'

Cooper stared at her, then looked away. It was hard to read the expression on his face. It wasn't quite pain, but it wasn't quite not either. 'I always thought Jack Carlin was invincible,' he said quietly.

'You don't need to explain, Harrison,' Maggie said.

Cooper shook his head, wildly. 'Jack didn't know all of it.' There was something new in Cooper's expression, some desperation, as if he needed Maggie to understand. 'Yeah, I sold out to the Scorpions. I cut ties eventually. But before I did' – a deep breath – 'they told me to feed Eric evidence that Terrence Adams was the killer he was looking for.'

Somebody at the staff party table cheered. Maggie stared at Cooper.

He closed his eyes. 'I did it. God help me, I did it. I did it because if the Scorpions went down, so did we. Jack had cut things off with the gang by then and I didn't think Eric would stop digging if he realised the killer he was looking for was a gang member. Back then he was too ...' Cooper waved a hand, looking for the word. 'Too fucking noble. Or reckless or whatever. So when Rook promised me he would deal with it, I figured Adams was the perfect solution. But then Eric killed him and the murders kept happening and ...' He rested his head in a trembling hand. 'So I told Rook. Deal with it or I would. Rook got rid of his man, whoever it was, and I was out. Eric fell apart. And I never told him. Never told him it was me who ...' He swallowed. 'Maybe I would have, eventually. But at that point I told myself the lie was better. Then Jack started digging.'

'And you planted evidence. Again.'

Cooper's laugh was ragged. 'Hardly. I just pointed the police towards shit that was already there. Jack was no saint. But by then the dominoes had started to fall. Olivia Dean picked up the slack. And Rook got back in touch.'

There were tears in Cooper's eyes now.

'My son, Aaron, has a problem.' His voice was thick. 'Drugs. Not uncommon, among cop's kids. Jack's daughter ...' He faltered. 'He was in deep. Owed money to a really nasty figure. The Scorpions got wind of this and bought his debt.

Suddenly, he's in their pocket. And for a long time, they did nothing about it. Until they found out Dean was trying to get the case reopened. Then they called. They'd heard that Eric had evidence on a hard drive. They said they'd consider the debt paid if I found it for them. I had no idea where to look. And then I saw the footage of you.'

'Seems to me that all this was your son's problem to deal with,' Maggie said.

Cooper's smile was sad. 'It's not that simple. Not when it's your kid. Not when you'd do anything to keep them safe.'

Something inside Maggie wrenched. From the nearby table came a wave of laughter.

'I tried to pay Rook off, but he wasn't interested,' Cooper said. 'I tried to reason with him, but that had been off the table the moment I told him I was out. So it was simple. I had to do whatever I could to stop Dean's investigation, or Aaron …' He let out a deep breath. 'But now things have changed. Maggie, if you have the hard drive, I need you to give it to me. I know there might be some information on there but—'

A shadow fell over them as another seat was pulled out. Maggie went to rise but a hard hand on her shoulder forced her down as somebody sat.

It took Maggie a moment to place him, but even before she did the leather cut told her all she needed to know, as did the click under the table.

'No fast movements, you hear?' He was looking quickly between them, eyes wide and excited, straw-like hair hanging in his face.

'Nipper,' Maggie said, remembering him from Darch's office.

'Shut up, bitch,' he said.

'What the fuck are you doing?' Cooper said.

'Was tailing you, wasn't I?' Nipper said. 'What, you thought we were gonna let you fuck around after that shit at the lawyer's office?'

'And they sent a prospect to do the job?' Cooper replied.

'I won't be a prospect after this.' Nipper's grin was savage. 'Won't be called fucking Nipper no more neither. That fucking prick who joined up this year, got his patch straight away; he'll look fucking stupid once I've given Rook that hard drive.'

He had taken his hand off Maggie's shoulder, but not too soon for Maggie to feel the trembling.

'Neither of us have it,' Maggie said.

'Prove it.'

'How?'

Momentarily, Nipper looked confused.

'Rook didn't send you,' Cooper said. 'Neither did Byrne. This was your idea, wasn't it?'

'And it was a good fucking idea,' Nipper snarled. 'Wasn't it? Otherwise that bitch would have slipped away again. She's gotta answer for Brew going down.'

'From memory, you're the one who shot him,' Maggie said.

'Listen,' Cooper said. 'It's under control, okay? This isn't helping anyone. I'm doing what you want.'

Nipper's bulging eyes were on Cooper. Maggie slipped one of the empty wine glasses off the table.

'But if you make a scene here, you lose your chance,' Cooper said. 'The police will be on you in seconds.'

'This gun's silenced, dipshit,' Nipper said. 'With those pricks carrying on over there, I could kill you both now and nobody would notice.'

The staff party had all started singing something off-key and awful. Under the table, Maggie squeezed the stem of the wine glass and pressed the top with her thumb. It snapped off; she caught it before it shattered on the ground.

I don't think it'll be that simple,' Cooper said. 'You shoot me, you'd better hope you can do it before Maggie or I get to you. Then what? Even if you survive, the cops will be on you in minutes. You want to hand them the Scorpions on a silver platter?'

Nipper was shaking his head. 'Nah. Nah, that's not gonna happen. We got out of that lawyer's office shit.'

'You got out of that because Byrne knew when to drop the guns,' Cooper said. 'Think you're gonna do as well without him?'

'*Yes!*' Saliva flew from Nipper's mouth. 'Yes, I will, because I'm a fucking Scorpion and that's what we do. Nothing will ever bring us down.'

'Mate,' Cooper said gently. 'You're a prospect.'

Maggie knew it was a mistake before the words had fully left his mouth, before she heard the pop from under the table and Cooper jerked back in his seat.

Maggie slammed the broken stem of the wine glass hard into Nipper's windpipe.

A brief, choked gasp from Nipper. Under the table, Maggie snatched the still-hot pistol from his loose grip, spun it and shot him three times in the gut.

The other table was still singing. Nipper slumped in his seat, blood tricking from behind the embedded base of the wine glass.

Cooper's face was pale and pained. Maggie stood, sticking the gun down the back of her jeans as she did. She tilted Nipper's head forward – to a passing glance he'd look like a drunk sleeping it off – then moved fast to Cooper and got his arm over her shoulder. He tried to stand and staggered. His other hand was clenched at his stomach, blood running between his fingers. Maggie managed to get him up and together they shuffled past the bellowing table and through to the front door of the pub, Cooper's weight almost pulling her down as they went.

Nobody paid them any attention as they stepped out into the cool night and moved across the road. Maggie was aware of all the loud-talking, laughing drinkers clustered around tables out the front, of the people passing them by, of the way with every step Cooper's feet dragged more. They had maybe minutes before somebody noticed the dead prospect.

Back down towards the beach, into the dark between the sheds, Cooper heavier by the second, until finally Maggie guided him to the door of her father's boathouse. Again she got it open, pulling the roller door back up. Inside Cooper collapsed against the wall. Even in the dark Maggie could see how pale his face was, how his eyelids fluttered and his mouth feebly attempted to form words.

'Give me your phone,' Maggie said. 'I'll call an ambulance.' Her voice sounded high-pitched, childlike, scared. She didn't want to look at why that might be, at what she knew was building inside her every second she looked at the man she had so deeply wished to be her father, the man she still loved despite everything, the man who had failed her so many times.

Cooper shook his head. 'Too late.' His voice was barely a breath. 'Maggie, you need ... you...' His eyes briefly closed.

Maggie grabbed him by the arms, her fingers digging into flesh. 'Harrison, no. *No*. Please, let me call someone, let me ...'

'No.' His voice, briefly, was hard and strong. 'It's you now. It has to be you.'

He was lifting his phone in his loose fingers. Maggie took it, went to dial triple-0.

'No ambulance,' Cooper said. 'Too many ... too many questions. Just l-look. Look on there and you'll ...' A tear ran down his bone-white cheek. He recited a number, a passcode. His shirt was soaked in blood. 'Help him. Please.'

Cooper's hand dropped. His head fell to the side. His eyes were empty.

Maggie shook him. Gently at first, then harder. Cooper didn't move.

'Harrison, come on. Please. Wake up. Come on!'

But it was pointless.

Gently, she rested her head against his and closed her eyes.

CHAPTER SEVENTEEN

In the van she took hold of the wheel but didn't start the engine. She knew that she had to move. Knew that already police would be on their way, scouring the area. The black panel van was hardly going to absolve her of suspicion. And yet she couldn't move.

Both Cooper and Carlin were gone now. The two men who, along with her father, had made the choice that had set all of this in motion, the choice Maggie was now paying for so many years later. The fucked-up part was, for all that they had done, those two were the closest things to allies Maggie had had in all of this mess.

And Cooper. The one positive thing from her childhood; he'd been a complicated positive, sure, but the only one she had, as fucked-up as that was. Dead in seconds because some shithead thought he deserved more than he had.

She had to move. Whatever had happened, she had the hard drive and that was that. Her only goal now was to vanish from Melbourne before anyone managed to find her.

Be on the highway tonight and vanish somewhere random and untraceable, somewhere she could lie low, go through the contents of the drive and work out her next step. Part of her – a big part – wanted to search it tonight, to find a computer and go through everything on it. But it was too dangerous. Sooner or later somebody, probably Olivia Dean, would start joining dots. Maggie had to vanish before that happened.

She turned the key, but as the engine came to life below her she remembered Cooper's phone. Its weight in her pocket seemed suddenly pronounced. She took it out.

Just look. Look on there and you'll …

Cooper had fucked her over and let her down; if not for him she wouldn't even be here in the first place. She owed him nothing. Leaving had to be her only focus.

But she still held the phone.

She unlocked it, using the code he had given her. The background was a generic photo of a lake somewhere.

Look on there. She opened up the camera roll. There wasn't much. A few shots of pretty trees, a couple of sunsets, some photos of Cooper with a young man she guessed must be Aaron, with a sour face and dirty blonde hair.

She opened the web browser. The last site Cooper had visited had been about boating sheds in Williamstown. She checked for other tabs. There weren't any.

He didn't have any social media apps on here. So she went to text messages.

The first was from an unknown number. She opened it.

Immediately she saw a photo. It was grainy and dark, but it depicted somebody slumped in the corner of a filthy room.

His white shirt was bloody. His hands in his lap were bound. His fair hair was long and hung in his face.

Maggie lowered the phone. Her ears were ringing. Her mind stumbled as snatches of Cooper's final words fell into place around the photo.

Now things have changed.

I'm doing what you want.

Help him. Please.

The Scorpions had Cooper's son.

It had nothing to do with her. None of this was her fault or her choice. She hadn't wanted to be a part of any of it. Aaron had made his own choices. He had got himself into this mess. Maggie owed neither him nor his father a damn thing.

There was one other message from the same number.

Be at the BD joint with the hard drive or he dies. Bring anyone else, he dies. Tell the cops, he dies. Reply to this message, try to negotiate, he dies.

Following was a time and date.

Which gave Aaron something like twenty hours.

She could call the police. But Cooper had avoided doing just that. He hadn't even allowed Maggie to call an ambulance that might have saved his life. And Cooper, who had been involved with the Scorpions for years, clearly knew better than anyone just how ruthless and connected they were. What was to say that they hadn't replaced Cooper with another mole in the force? Somebody who would alert the bikies the moment the cops found out about Aaron?

The rest of Cooper's messages held very little that shed any light, apart from the fact that it didn't seem anybody else knew about this. So there was no-one else who could pick up the slack; no-one else to help Cooper's son. Either Maggie stepped in, or Aaron died.

She slammed the wheel. Again and again, Cooper dragged her into the fucked-up web he had created. Again and again, it was she who suffered for those stupid, long-ago decisions.

Except it wasn't just her. Aaron, too, had been forced to answer for the mistakes of his father. And unlike her, he didn't have a choice.

She leaned back in the front seat. Ringing in her mind now were different words, older words, words that came back to her often late at night and sometimes, unbidden, in the middle of the day. Words that reminded her of the last time she had ignored somebody in danger, the last time she had focused on what mattered to her over somebody else's very real fears.

She exhaled. All that rage had given way to something like grim acceptance. The knowledge that whatever she tried to tell herself, there was no choice. Not for her.

In the distance, she could hear sirens. She glanced at the hard drive, sitting on the passenger seat. At the phone, now resting on the dashboard. She pressed down the accelerator.

What did she have?

It took Maggie a while to find a payphone. She'd parked in a rough and rundown part of the suburb of Footscray, all washed-out shopfronts, cracked windows and uneven roads. Even the early-morning air had a faint tinge of urine and neglect. She had slept briefly and badly, knowing she'd need it, but hit the streets as soon as the sun began to rise. There was barely anyone else around; a couple of homeless people were slumped in corners, some straggling drunks. Nobody who'd notice or remember her.

She'd figured Footscray was the kind of place likely to still have a payphone somewhere and she was right; she found one, heavily graffitied, tucked away behind a supermarket. She moved under the slightly askew shelter and took out Cooper's phone. She checked the number again then gave herself just a moment to ask, one last time, if this was really how she wanted to play things.

She dialled the number.

Two rings before an answer. The woman's voice was low and expressionless, giving away nothing, not even whether she had been woken by the call. 'Hello.'

'Detective Olivia Dean,' Maggie said.

Silence on the other end.

'I want to make a deal,' Maggie said.

Silence, still. Maggie didn't push on. Just waited.

Finally, 'Maggie.'

It wasn't a question so Maggie didn't answer. 'I have Eric's hard drive.'

Maggie was ready for the feigned ignorance, but Dean apparently was smarter than that. 'And what do you plan on doing with it?'

'That depends,' Maggie said. 'There's information on it that I want. But I'd be willing to hand it over in exchange for something.'

Another silence, then, 'Are you aware that Len Townsend is in Melbourne looking for you?'

Just what she fucking needed. 'Isn't that the kind of thing that you'd usually arrest someone over?'

'Ever tried arresting someone based on hearsay? It never works out quite as well as you'd hope.'

'I'll keep it in mind. But the hard drive—'

There was still very little expression in Dean's voice. It wasn't monotone, exactly, but she was good at giving nothing away. 'Generally speaking, police don't make deals with wanted criminals.'

'Generally speaking, police want to close cases,' Maggie said. 'Or so I'm told. I don't know if what's on here can help you bring down the Scorpions, but based on how desperate everyone seems to be to secure it, I'm going to guess there aren't many other avenues available to you.'

Dean didn't confirm or deny. She seemed to be waiting for Maggie to name her price.

'I need a list of all potential Scorpion clubhouses,' Maggie said. 'More than that; any properties they're suspected to own. Even a tool shed.'

'What make you think we'd have a list like that handy?'

'The fact that you're working their case. You might not have a warrant, but you'll sure as hell have the addresses that you're planning to hit the moment you get one.' She glanced over her shoulder.

Dean didn't reply.

'So. Will you give them to me?'

'I don't think so.'

'This is a one-time offer.'

'How do I even know you have the drive? Or that you won't vanish the moment I give you what you want?'

'Well, I'll certainly vanish if you *don't* give me what I want, so you don't have much to lose there.'

'Only my job. You think the police customarily go around handing out private addresses to murderers?'

'You might want to consider it in this case.'

'If I consider it, I'll be lucky not to get kicked off the force.'

'Depends on how quiet you keep it. I'm not going to tell anyone.'

'Except for the bikies you're presumably going after.'

'I'm not going to be telling them much of anything.'

'So what will you be doing?'

With a twinge, Maggie remembered Julie's words about Carlin. 'Plausible deniability is the sweet spot here.'

Without seeing her face, Maggie could tell Dean was thinking. The detective was right to be sceptical. But in the end, Dean knew that the drive might be her only chance to put an end to the Scorpions, and Maggie was banking on that winning out over anything else.

'I need proof,' the other woman said. 'That there's anything on the hard drive worth my time.'

'How?'

'If my information is right, there's a mix of photos and videos. Send me a photo.'

'How will I know it's the right one?'

'If it clearly shows a Scorpion doing something incriminating, it's probably right.'

'If I send you that, you won't need the whole drive.'

'How many court cases do you think are won based on a single photo?'

Maggie checked the time. She had until that evening to find wherever Aaron was and save him. She didn't have time to fuck around. But she'd be completely aimless without those addresses.

'Give me an hour.' She checked Dean's contact listing on Cooper's phone again. 'I've got your email. But I need you to send me the list within five minutes of getting the photo. Otherwise the deal's off.'

'You want me to sit and hit refresh until you send something?'

'You want to bring down the Scorpions or not?'

'And how will you get me the drive?'

'I'll leave it somewhere. Somewhere I'll tell you about. Tomorrow.'

'Today.'

'No.' She might still need the drive as leverage. 'Tomorrow or nothing.'

Dean didn't reply.

Maggie tried to keep the desperation out of her voice. 'That's the best I can offer.'

'Why do I get the feeling you're fucked without this?'

'It's mutual benefit or mutual nothing,' Maggie said. 'You get the hard drive tomorrow. Give me an hour.'

Ten minutes from Footscray, Maggie parked in North Melbourne before heading fast to the public library. She slowed a little as she walked in, trying to look tired and a bit hungover. A student grudgingly completing an assignment.

She found long banks of public computers upstairs, adjacent to shelves thick with reference books. She took a seat and moved the mouse, waiting for the computer to come to life. She checked the stop of the stairs. Nobody else was coming up. The computer was still waking up. She reached into her jacket pocket and removed the hard drive.

It was more than just the key to destroying a dangerous criminal gang. It might also be the only chance Maggie had to find her mother. The only chance she had to finally face up to her and know *why*. She had already been through hell for that and had thought the need behind her, but she knew now that was only a matter of lost opportunity. Now that the chance for a real direction was so close, the prospect of giving it up was like driving a knife into her own chest.

But she could live without knowing the truth. It would hurt, but she would survive. Aaron did not have that luxury.

As the computer finally came to life, she plugged in the hard drive. At the top of the stairs a couple of actual students had arrived, a guy and a girl, mumbling at each other as they took seats at computers further along. On the screen, the hard drive had appeared. Maggie opened it.

There were three folders. Each was titled simply *S*, *A* and *M*.

She opened *S* first.

There was a lot on here. Many other photos, all with dates and names she didn't recognise. She opened the earliest-dated folder. As Dean had said, photos. She clicked. Black-and-white grainy shots from what looked to be the security camera of a service station, depicting a man rounding a corner past a fuel pump. She clicked through until she found one where his back was to the camera. The Scorpion insignia was blurry, but obvious.

A couple more people had come upstairs now. More students by the looks of things. One girl sat only a single computer away from her.

Quickly, Maggie created a new email address, typed in Dean's and hit send. For a few seconds, the screen just stayed on a 'loading' symbol. Maggie checked the stairs again.

The email was sent. Maggie made sure the people to each side were engrossed with their own computers, then navigated back to the hard drive. She clicked the *A* folder. Just photos here. She opened the first one.

The impact was almost physical.

Her mother, older, lined, but unmistakable, was on the screen in front of her. Dressed plainly in jeans and a shirt, mid-stride, unaware that she was being photographed.

She was alive.

Feet on the stairs. Maggie looked up. Caught a glimpse of a police hat. Instinct told her to move but she didn't. She returned to the email screen. Hit refresh. Nothing back from Dean.

The cop, a young man, had reached the top. He cast a lazy eye over everyone on the computers. Maggie tried to remain focused on the screen. She hit refresh again.

The cop was consulting a notebook. He started walking around the bank of desks, glancing at the people working.

Maggie slid further down into her seat. Her heart was pounding, every instinct shrieking at her to run. Refreshed again. Nothing. Again.

The empty inbox flickered and then there was an email from *Dean, Olivia*. Maggie opened it. A list of addresses. She didn't have time to print. She took out Cooper's phone and snapped a photo of the screen.

The cop was looking at her.

Maggie didn't look back. She unplugged the drive and pocketed it again. Deleted her account. Then logged off and stood.

The cop was still considering her.

If Dean had traced the call, then she could have guessed Maggie had to be headed to a public library or internet café, somewhere she could email the photo. Somewhere less than an hour from Footscray. Or else she was going off the location of Nipper's body. Or Cooper's.

Maggie started to move around the bank of computers.

The cop moved with her on the other side of the bank. His hand went to his gun.

Maggie bolted for the shelves.

Yells from behind her, yells of 'freeze' and 'police' – as if that much wasn't already obvious – followed by scattered cries from people in the library. Maggie lunged for the end of one of the shelves and swung around into the aisle. Seconds later, the cop appeared at the other end. He was young and his eyes were wide. He lifted his gun.

Maggie stayed where she was, rooted to the spot in apparent fear.

The cop moved towards her. 'Freeze,' he repeated, even though Maggie wasn't moving.

Until she did, going backwards fast then sideways into the next aisle.

The cop ran.

Maggie brought both hands hard into the heavy reference books at head height, just as the cop appeared through the shelves in the next aisle. A yelp as the books on the other side were forced through, clocking him in the head, one after another.

Maggie snatched a hefty hardcover off the shelf, swung back around into the first aisle, and as the dazed cop straightened up, brought the spine of the book crashing into his nose. A cry, a spurt of blood and Maggie was running past the bank of computers, past the terrified students, then—

Thunder on the stairs. His partner was coming. Maggie threw herself against the wall, looked to the students and yelled, 'That way!', pointing as she did. Like scared sheep, they looked the way Maggie pointed just as the cop burst onto the landing and did the same.

Maggie swung the book into his gut. He doubled over with a gasp as Maggie brought it down hard on top of his head, sending him crashing to the ground. She threw the book aside and ran, diving over the cop, hitting the stairs and tearing down them, feet colliding with the first floor then running past stunned faces and out onto the street again.

CHAPTER EIGHTEEN

Had Dean sent the police? It made more sense than the alternative: that two cops had either decided to check out a library first thing in the morning or had happened to see Maggie pass them, but whatever the case she had no way of being sure. Just like she had no way of being sure if the list Dean had sent was genuine.

But she was willing to bet that it was, just as she was willing to bet that Dean hadn't sent more cops to watch these addresses. If Dean was behind the near miss at the library, then it made more sense as an attempt to capture Maggie cleanly; something that would be impossible the moment they were trying to carry it out around a bikie clubhouse. If Maggie disappeared, Dean didn't get the hard drive. If the bikies got it first, then Dean's chances of destroying them vanished. It was safer for Dean to just let Maggie do her thing and expect that the deal still stood at the end.

Maggie hoped.

Hurting those cops definitely wouldn't have helped her case, but given she was already wanted for murder along with God knew what else after the past couple of weeks, there wasn't a lot she could do to endear herself to Dean anyway. She wasn't wholly comfortable with how things had played out in the library, but it wasn't as though she had had a world of choice in the moment. It was break noses or be arrested.

She hadn't taken the hard drive out of her jacket pocket, but she felt its weight as Melbourne slipped away behind her and the landscape out the window turned slowly to brown grass and rugged hills, to expanses of forest and harsh drop-offs into scrubby nothing. She knew where she was going, but the destination seemed unimportant given what she had seen on the drive. In the end, despite the alcoholism and the abuse, despite his descent into an incoherent mess of violence and delusion, the good detective in her father had come through, securing not only evidence about the Scorpions, but actual information about her mother. Somewhere on that drive, and the thought came with a terrified rush, was likely a location, somewhere Maggie could head for the moment this was over. She just had to make it through the night.

It was simple enough to work out where Aaron was being held. The message to Cooper implied it was a place he knew about, and for that to be the case it had to be somewhere the bikies had had for a while, back in the days when he was still involved with them. Anywhere they'd owned for that long would almost certainly be on a police radar. And when she'd checked Dean's list, several locations scattered across the country, one had jumped out.

Bonnie Doon. *BD*.

Less than three hours from Melbourne, it was a tiny town nestled on the edge of a vast, mostly dry lakebed that stretched and wound for kilometres between bush-heavy hills. She knew this from a search using Cooper's phone. The address, which the maps app on Cooper's phone told her was high up in the hills overlooking the lake, made perfect sense as a bikie hideout. Remote without being far-flung, hidden without being inaccessible.

She didn't know what to expect when she got there. Whether the bikies relied enough on the secrecy of the place and Cooper's compliance to only have a small group guarding Aaron, or whether they had the place surrounded by killers armed to the teeth. The former, apart from being Maggie's preference, seemed more likely. Less noticeable and, if Cooper *did* decide to bring the police down on them, less likely to result in a huge chunk of their number imprisoned or dead.

Either way, how she planned on getting close was key. The bikies would of course be on the lookout for a single person. But Cooper, willing to die rather than risk the bikies discovering he had told anyone about Aaron, would not have taken Maggie's approach. He would have driven straight up, slow and deliberate and doing everything in his power to appear non-threatening.

The deadline was ten o'clock that night. By eight it would be dark and that was when Maggie planned on making her approach. She would move slow and silent through the trees, dressed in black, and attempt to get a look at the place. She had Nipper's silenced pistol along with a length of rusted pipe, about the size of her forearm, that she had found in a carpark along the way. Both relatively quiet as weapons. If there weren't many guards, then hopefully she could take them out, then attempt to gain entry to the house.

The element of surprise would be her best friend here. The fact that there were only thirteen rounds left in the gun was the opposite.

Would tonight lead her to Rook Gately? Since the moment the Scorpions' involvement became clear, his name had lingered over everything; the bikie leader had set this in motion by making an offer to three young policemen. Now all of those cops were dead and still Rook endured, his gang continuing their reign of terror with impunity.

She partly *wanted* Rook to be there tonight. She wanted to come face to face with the man behind all of this and pull the trigger. The thought was intoxicating.

It was late afternoon by the time Maggie arrived in the tiny township of Bonnie Doon. From there it wasn't a long walk down to the lake. The houses dissipated, leaving brown grass, rough bushes and soon cracked red dirt peppered with jagged rocks. This continued down into the basin of what, when the rains were heavy enough, sometimes counted as a lake.

Today, however, it was just a dusty bowl of mounds that rose and fell around tilting dead trees that jutted, jagged and gnarled, from hardened clay. Maggie walked out onto the lakebed. On the far side, she could see the point where the water had once come up to, a harsh line across the steep hill faces, dividing the browns from the dull greens and yellows that were the undulating hills surrounding the lake. There was a strange, haunting beauty to it all, to the sprawl of the empty lake, the hills, the skeleton trees that Maggie now walked among as she neared the centre of the basin.

She looked up towards the nearest hill. Somewhere among those clumps of trees was the hideout. The day was cooling. She reached back under her jacket and felt the butt of the gun.

Darkness shrouded the hills and stars filled the night, spreading through the clear dark sky, their shine making the dead trees look ghostly, the shadows stark and unforgiving.

Nestled between a few bushes, dressed dark in her jacket, the pipe in her belt and Nipper's gun in her hand, Maggie began to move. She had taken the time to plot out her approach, placing herself on the other side of the bridges near the base of the hill on which the bikies' house was situated. This side was slightly thicker with trees, but between them remained clear patches a little too vast for Maggie's liking. But in the dark she would be as obscured as possible, plus she would be approaching far from the road, which was surely where the bikies would be watching most intently.

She reached the first lot of trees and stopped, listening. For breathing, cracking twigs, any sign of the bikies waiting here for anyone to do exactly what Maggie was doing. But there was nothing. Light, cool wind in the leaves. The plaintive cry of a faraway bird. A lone car trundling along the bridge.

She kept going. Reached the edge of the trees, scanned the first uphill clear stretch of grass. Watched for movement in the shadows on the next lot of trees. Nothing. She ran. Low and fast, feet light. She hit the next clump and repeated the process, but still there was no sign of movement.

The closer she got, the louder and faster her heart beat. But every step she took without encountering a bikie lent credence to her prevailing theory; that the Scorpions were operating with a skeleton crew. How many would remain to be seen, but her chances of coming out of this alive seemed to be rising.

Behind her the lakebed fell away. When she glanced back from between trees, it looked full of looming dark, even in the starlight. The sprawl of the landscape and the lack of any new sounds made her feel, despite the cover, exposed and alone, vulnerable. Her hand around the gun tightened.

The higher she went, the slower she moved. She paused longer in the trees, listening intently even for the particular vacuum of noise that was somebody holding their breath, determined not to make a sound. But there was nothing.

She was nearing the top of the hill. Her legs were burning from the bursts of uphill running and she was out of breath. The land ahead plateaued towards the trees she knew obscured the house. She walked, now, across to the edge of them. Still listening for sounds that never came. She reached the trees and through them saw a dim glow of electric light.

She stopped. But there were no voices, no flickers of moving shadow through the dark trunks. Still, she waited.

She wasn't going to charge forward in what could easily be a lull, a moment between changing guards.

Seconds passed, then minutes. Still, no sound outside the natural.

Maggie slipped forward through the dark. The trees parted ahead. She stopped intermittently as the house became clearer. It was a hut, really, low and squat, a dark green with a corrugated-iron roof. There was only one window that Maggie could see, situated above a pile of chopped firewood in overgrown grass. Without the light, it could have been an abandoned hunters' cabin.

Metres from the edge of the trees, Maggie listened again, watching her surrounds. Still, no sound or movement. She knew the road was on the other side of the hut from her, but it stood to reason that the bikies would at least have somebody watching the rear, just in case. But there was no sign of life outside the house.

Closer again. She stopped in the last bit of shadow coverage given by the trees. She could see the house clearly now, the scratched paint, the cracked window. She took a risk and closed her eyes, focusing only on sound. By now she would have expected to hear a low rumble of voices from inside, or else the shuffling of feet. Those walls couldn't be thick. But still, nothing.

It was around nine, now. An hour before Cooper's deadline. The lights being on indicated that somebody was here. Unless the Scorpions had caught wind of Cooper's death and killed Aaron already. The thought turned Maggie's stomach.

She lifted the gun. Moved forward in a crouch, into the open. Looked left then right. The trees were still. There was no shape of a watching bikie.

She darted forward. Tensed, ready for gunfire. None came. She was at the chopped wood. She turned and looked across the grass behind her, back to the trees. Swept it all with the gun. Still silence.

She needed to look inside. She could be quick, could glance through the window and be down again before anyone saw. Only the worst of luck would lead to somebody noticing, although Maggie knew not to count out the worst of luck.

But she had been expecting to come across at least a few guards out here. Without knowing what waited inside, she couldn't proceed. She could throw a rock, but while that might draw the bikies into the open, it could also have the opposite effect, leading them to hunker down, now on guard and ready for an attack. Catching them unawares, however doing so played out, was likely her only advantage.

She rose, still listening. Her head was now just below the window. She gave herself one last moment, then stood, looked and dropped.

The room was empty. She had glimpsed bottles, moth-eaten furniture, ashtrays – but no people.

What the fuck?

Had Dean given her false addresses? Surely not; the BD/Bonnie Doon link was far too clear. But if Aaron wasn't here, then where the fuck was he?

She went to turn, and as she did something closed around her throat.

CHAPTER NINETEEN

It was hard and biting, cutting off any air. The gun was gone from her hand. Maggie didn't even have time to gasp as whoever it was yanked her hard backwards and onto the ground. Her vision blurred and she grabbed at what she now realised was thick metal wire, but then her wrists were tugged together by the burn of rope. Her fingers still scrabbled uselessly at the noose but then with an awful constricting pain in her throat, she was moving, dragged by the wire around her neck across the hard ground. Grass and twigs scratched her face but it didn't matter, it was nothing compared to her throat closing, to the unrelenting tightness of the noose.

Lights, harsh and sourceless. The ground below her now flat. Dragged through bottles now. She was inside.

Then she was still. She managed to get her fingers under the wire and pull it slightly loose. It was still eye-watering, still too tight, but she could breathe.

She saw now the shape of her attacker, dressed in black and moving around her. He had been dragging her by a long stretch of wire that ended in the noose around her neck. The other end he was now binding to an old-fashioned wall-mounted heater. Maggie tried to stand. He kicked her in the stomach and she was down again. She felt the pipe tugged from her belt and heard it clatter on the floor metres away.

She blinked, trying to clear her vision. He had run to the door and slammed it shut. Items became solid and formed. Bottles. A table in front of the old couch. Lying on it a needle, spoon, lighter, ashtray.

Maggie looked up at him. Half his face was covered by a bandanna, the rest obscured by shoulder-length hair. He wore a leather jacket that, as he paced, she saw had the Scorpion insignia on the back. He was tall and lanky; something in his movements suggested youth.

He lingered near the door, muttered something behind the bandanna, then ran back to the table, picked up the gun and pointed it at Maggie.

'Where is Harrison Cooper?' He was struggling to hide the unsteadiness in his voice.

Maggie managed to sit upright. She looked at him. His blue eyes were wide. Terrified.

'Aaron,' she said.

She hadn't phrased it as a question, but the sudden rigidity to his stance answered it for her. He seemed uncertain as to how he should proceed. He tugged down the bandana.

He was unmistakably the young man from Cooper's photos, but his features were pinched and hollow. He had lost weight; his skin was flaky and his lips were chapped. His cut was too big for him.

Maggie tugged at the noose again. Aaron raised the gun but Maggie just looked at him until he lowered it.

'I need to breathe if I'm going to speak,' she said.

'Where is Harrison Cooper?' he repeated.

'Dead.'

A stricken look crossed Aaron's face. He tried to speak but couldn't. He lifted the gun again without looking sure of why. Then, shaking, he turned away.

'Fuck,' he said. 'Fuck, fuck, *fuck!*' With a scream, he slammed the gun into the wall.

Maggie's thoughts and feelings were grappling with each other as she tried to sift through not only the situation but the rising ice and fire in her gut, the mess of scalding emotion that built with every second she looked at Aaron Cooper.

The specifics eluded her but the truth was clear. The Scorpions had never kidnapped Aaron. Aaron was *one of them*. And Harrison Cooper, desperate to save his son, had charged blindly to his own death without ever realising that Aaron was part of the con.

Aaron, breathing heavily, was leaning against the wall. He was shaking badly. Whether because his plan had blown up in his face or because his father was dead, Maggie didn't know. And it didn't matter. She was stuck here with somebody clearly unstable, somebody who was not thinking straight and being far, far too cavalier with that gun. Her eyes swept over the room, looking for something within reach, something she could use as a weapon, something—

The young man spun to face Maggie, the gun up again. 'You,' he said. There were tears in his eyes. 'You killed him.'

Maggie shook her head. 'One of yours did that. Nipper.'

'*Fucker*,' Aaron's voice was high and pinched.

'What, you're angry?' Maggie could hear the note of fierce amusement in her voice. 'Even though your bullshit led him there?'

'His *own* bullshit led him there,' Aaron spat. 'I just ... I ...'

'What?' Maggie said. 'Faked your own kidnapping to lure him here? For what?'

The empty room. The lack of guards. The terror on Aaron's face.

'Rook doesn't know about this,' Maggie said.

Aaron didn't reply.

Maggie's voice was low, dangerous. She was keeping the fire at bay, but barely. 'What the fuck is this, Aaron?'

Realisation seemed to cut through whatever was going on in Aaron's head. He pointed the gun at her face. 'The hard drive. Where is it?'

'I don't have it,' Maggie said. 'Neither did Harrison.'

Aaron's face crumpled. He crossed to the couch and collapsed onto it, dropping the gun on the table as he put his head in his hands.

Pieces were falling into place but not fast enough. Maggie was trying to keep a clear head, to focus and connect the dots, to work out just what the fuck she had landed in the middle of, but with every second the fire built.

'Why don't you explain what you were going to do if your father *did* turn up?' Maggie asked.

'Explain yourself. Who the fuck are you?'

Maggie just looked at him.

A glimmer of clarity in his eyes. 'You're her. Eric's kid. Maggie.'

Maggie said nothing.

'So you should get it,' Aaron said. 'Byrne told us how my – how Harrison brought you back to Melbourne for the hard drive. Even though he knew you'd be arrested.'

'Because he thought you were in danger.'

Aaron's laugh was wild. 'What, you're fucking *defending him*? He would have sold you out in a second—'

'*For his son!*'

Aaron stopped, staring at Maggie.

Maggie looked away, trembling. 'For you. You know how much I would have killed for that? For a parent who loved me enough to put everything on the line for me? But instead you, you took advantage. Tried to lure him here, to what? Impress your cool bikie friends? Jesus Christ. You snivelling piece of shit. You know why I came here? To help you. Because it was the last thing your father said to me. *Help him.* But this ... you ...' Maggie didn't have the words. The scope of the betrayal, the scorching loathing she felt just looking at Aaron's dumbfounded expression, the fact that she could have just left with the hard drive if she hadn't been stupid enough to try to do the right thing, stupid enough to stumble into the exact same trap that had killed Cooper.

Aaron had fallen silent. Even the shaking and the tears had stopped. He looked at the bottle in his hand, as if considering something. He drank, then stood.

'He wasn't what you think he was,' Aaron said.

'You have no idea what I think he was.'

Aaron shrugged. 'Sure I do. The hero cop. The good guy. And he hung that over my head my whole childhood. Any time I got in trouble, any time I acted out. Oh man, the *disappointment*.' His laugh was bitter. 'Because Harrison Cooper would never behave that way. And oh the shame that his fuck-up son brought on him. You know, when I was eighteen he let me spend a night in a lock-up because I was caught with some weed? No, not only that. He *told* them to lock me up. With the drunks and the junkies and the rest. The cops were gonna let me go with a warning, but Cooper *told* them to make sure it was on my record. Said it would teach me.'

Maggie glanced at the needle.

'That wasn't the only time either,' Aaron said. 'I'd get into trouble, try to keep my dad out of it, then some well-meaning cop would think to call him and Harrison, in his infinite wisdom, would always advocate for the harshest possible punishment. That would beat it out of me, right?'

'What a shame you couldn't stop getting in trouble,' Maggie said flatly.

Aaron shook his head. 'You have no idea. You don't know anything about me. I might have acted like a dickhead, but that was only ever because of *him*. My whole life he told me what to do, who to be. What subjects to do at school, what career I should be pursuing, and if I deviated from that for even a second ...' He exhaled. 'First came the guilt. *I haven't spent my life upholding the law for you to throw it back in my face*. And whenever he could make it worse, make me suffer, believe me he took that chance and then some.' He leaned against the wall, eyes unfocused and distant. 'You know, for a long time, I thought that was what parenthood was. That being a father was just this uncompromising, fucking drill-sergeant way of approaching things. But none of my friends' dads were like that. And eventually I realised I wasn't his fucking son, I was a project. Something to be fixed and shaped in his image. God forbid I wanted to be anything else.'

He drank.

'I owed money,' he said. 'Rook bought my debt. But he didn't hang it over my head. He told me he got it. Knew my old man, knew what he was like. He understood.' A flickering smile. 'I'd never ever seen anything like that before. That was a *father*. You know he said no when I asked if I could join the Scorpions? "Too dangerous." He actually cared. But I convinced him.' His eyes were alight with fervour. 'I showed him I deserved my patch.'

Nipper's words rang in Maggie's ears. *That fucking prick who joined up this year, got his patch straight away.*

Jesus, Rook was clever. He had lured in Aaron the same way he lured in his father. Even rewarded him immediately with something the rest of the bikies had to work for. Convinced Aaron he was a special case, in the process securing the eternal loyalty of a wayward cop's son.

Aaron sat again. Now he had started he wasn't going to stop. He'd never had the chance to tell his story fully, all his childish resentments and false victories. And Maggie, bound here, was the perfect audience for his cavalcade of grievances.

'Try to imagine,' Aaron said. 'How I felt when I found out that after everything he had told me, Harrison Cooper was in the pocket of the bikie gang. That he fabricated evidence for them. Covered things up. Took their money and kept his mouth shut. The fucking *hypocrisy*. How dare he tell me how to live my life. How *dare* he punish me for dumb shit that paled in comparison to what he had done? No. No. Fuck that and fuck him. He was a criminal, and maybe it's time people knew.'

'You were going to frame him,' Maggie said. 'For the killings.'

Aaron nodded. 'I mean, it seems far-fetched, right? The serial-killer cop. But fuck, Harrison didn't do himself any favours. He tampered with evidence, sent your father on a wild goose chase, even brought you back to Melbourne to try to get the hard drive before the cops did. Rook wants to destroy the drive and leave it at that, but it'll never be enough. I was going to give him someone to blame.'

'What now?' Maggie said. 'You'll give him me instead?'

A moment of silence. Aaron leaned back, watching Maggie. His eyes weren't unfocused anymore. He went to speak, then stopped. He looked towards the door, then down at the gun. His mouth twitched in the beginnings of a smile. He nodded, apparently in response to some internal suggestion.

'Yeah,' he whispered. 'Yeah. That could work.'

'What could?' Maggie said.

Aaron flinched, as if he'd forgotten she was there. But his smile was growing, turning exhilarated with some wild new possibility. 'The plan. Actually, you're the perfect missing piece.' He shifted down from the couch, so that he was sitting across from her. 'Think about it. Your father finds evidence on this missing killer, tells Harrison, then goes down the stairs. The case gets reopened and Harrison brings you back to help him. What if the truth was fudged a bit? What if, for example, he brought you down here at gunpoint? Made you try to get the keys from that lawyer, but you escaped? You could testify. Tell the cops all of that. Get yourself off the hook and pin the lot on Harrison. We plant a couple of incriminating things to back up our story; the police get their culprit and they drop the investigation into the Scorpions and the hard drive, end of. *Harrison* was the murderer Eric was trying to find. Which is why Harrison killed him. He was responsible for all of this.' There was something chilling about the hopeful, almost innocent expression on Aaron's face. 'Think about it, Maggie. It makes perfect sense, right? A few white lies and you don't have to run anymore. You get a normal life.'

She wanted to tell him to get fucked, to explode and give this petulant little shit what he deserved. But.

Cooper was dead. He would never know. It wouldn't really matter, in the end. She could take this chance now to side with the Scorpions and her time as a fugitive could be over. They didn't even need to know she had the hard drive. She could take off and find her mother. Even the scrap with the police in the library could be explained away as self-defence driven by fear. She could claim to Dean she had lost the hard drive, make up some story that implicated somebody else outside the Scorpions. And with their help, bring this all to an end that worked out for everyone. No more bloodshed.

She closed her eyes. Tried to imagine it. Tried to imagine a world without that constant, needling fear of her past finally catching up with her. A future where her past belonged to somebody else, somebody no longer here to claim otherwise.

Help him. Please ...

Cooper's last words. And she would be helping Aaron, after a fashion. She would be diverting attention away from the Scorpions and, in turn, Aaron. Cooper had been willing to die for his son; was the posthumous destruction of his reputation really any worse? And in the end, didn't he owe her? For the blind eyes he turned, the ignorance of the kind of man Eric was, his own betrayal in bringing her back to Melbourne.

Even if she *didn't* take the offer, she could play along. Tell Aaron she would, and use that to her advantage. The lucid part of her brain was screaming that possibility at her, telling her to play the part and escape.

But.

Maggie looked at Aaron, at the expectant expression on his face. 'Once you lured Cooper here, then what? You'd catch him the way you did me, and then?'

Aaron said nothing.

'You'd kill him,' Maggie said. 'Your own father.'

Aaron just watched her.

Something in Maggie's chest tightened. 'That's different.'

'How?' Aaron asked.

Maggie didn't reply. She was thinking of Cooper's face,

at the end. Of his desperate, painful desire to help his son. Of the love that was evident even through the pain, the love that stung so badly because Maggie had wanted it so much for so long. And Aaron, who had had it all along – and had done this with it.

Aaron drank, then fixed Maggie with a bleary smile. 'They fuck you up, parents. You know that old poem? It's true, isn't it? But we're supposed to respect them, look up to them, learn from them, *be like them*. Where does that get you?' He gestured around himself. 'I know you hated your father. But you don't have the monopoly on that. Just because Harrison Cooper seemed great to you doesn't mean he was to his own kid.'

'Except,' Maggie said, feeling now as though her whole body was vibrating with something too powerful and terrible to name, something that obliterated rationality, 'my father beat the shit out of me. Hurt me. Made me suffer for no reason. My father was a selfish monster who just needed to put his hate and rage and self-loathing *somewhere*, so he aimed it all at me. But you ...' She shook her head. 'What, he was tough on you? Tried to teach you a lesson but didn't do it well? Tried to make you sure you were better than he was? *That's* behind all of this?'

'It's more than—' Aaron began, but Maggie wasn't finished.

'Your father loved you,' she said. 'Whether he did it well only counts for so much. *He loved you*. He was human and he fucked up, but he loved you. And you want to throw that back in his face. Tell me, Aaron, did it ever occur to you that

235

getting involved with the Scorpions was his biggest regret? That you doing the same, in the end, was only repeating his mistakes? That no matter how hard you've tried to distance yourself from your father, you've only succeeded in becoming *exactly like him*? That you—'

Aaron smashed the bottle across her face.

Pain exploded, a blinding glare of light behind her eyes. She tried to breathe and inhaled fire. She was on her side on the ground but didn't remember hitting it. She blinked and saw red. She touched her face. Her hand came away wet and hot. Waves of agony. She blinked again. Aaron's boots stepped into her vision.

A kick in the gut. She couldn't breathe. She tried to move. All she could see were the boots and the blood.

Aaron knelt. Fumbled for her jacket. Absurdly, muttered an apology as he brushed her chest. Then found her pocket and tugged clear the hard drive. He stood.

'You lying bitch,' he said.

The wire, resting across her.

He lifted his foot.

Maggie grabbed the wire trailing from her noose and wrapped it fast and hard around his raised ankle. She pulled. A cry from Aaron as he went over backwards and then Maggie lunged, snatching the broken bottle from his grasping fingers and bringing the broken end hard into his chest. Aaron screamed. Maggie dragged it. Felt the resistance of skin give, felt blood douse her hands, mingling with the blood pouring from her ruined face. Aaron was wailing but it wasn't enough, not nearly enough; she needed more, she needed him to—

Whether intentionally or instinctively, his knee jerked up and into Maggie's stomach. She hit the ground. Whimpering and spluttering, Aaron scrambled to his feet. Fell, then rose again. Through the blood and the darkening and the edge of her vision, through the pain that built and built and didn't stop, Maggie saw him pick up the gun from the table. He put a hand to his chest; it came away drenched in blood. Swaying, he turned to Maggie.

From outside, the thrum of engines.

Cars, by the sounds of it. Several. Not here yet but getting closer by the second.

Aaron looked towards the door.

'What did you do?' Maggie rasped. Blood trickled into her mouth.

Aaron was crying now. He shook his head and ran for the front door. It slammed behind him and Maggie was alone on the ground.

The engines were louder.

Maggie found the broken bottle. With some difficulty, she brought it around so that the jagged glass was working at the bonds around her wrists. She couldn't see properly. She wasn't sure it was working. She felt glass cut her hands but it didn't matter.

The bonds broke. She grabbed the noose and pulled. It gave a little, then a little more, then she pulled it over her head. She tried to stand. Couldn't. Managed on the second attempt.

Light under the door.

She staggered for a cabinet to the side. More booze and a couple of old books. There was one closed door that turned out to be a bathroom. Over a grimy sink, a cracked mirror opened and Maggie found a first-aid kit. She needed to be out of here but that would be pointless if she bled to death. Her jacket and shirt were soaked with blood. With the back of her hand, she wiped her eyes and made herself look.

Three gashes, left side of her face. One long, stretching from just above the temple to halfway across her forehead. The second, below the temple, stopping just under her eye. The third running under her cheek bone, stopping a centimetre from her nose. They were deep. They would scar. From outside, the engines were still going.

She worked fast and sloppy, wrapping one bandage around her head, covering her nose and the two lower wounds. Another bandage higher up, across her forehead. Then one diagonal down her face. The knot was loose and in moments the bandages were soaked red. The pain hadn't ebbed. Her hair, jutting between the bandages, was already matted thick and dark.

The floor was mostly blood now. Out of the bathroom she found the pipe near the couch. It felt good in her hand. Like the rounders bat so long ago. She put it back into her belt. She looked to the small, single window. No light through it. Back to the door. Nobody had come in yet.

Who?

Weak, fearful, jittery Aaron Cooper was never going to kill his father. Nor were the Scorpions.

'Well?' the voice of Len Townsend called from outside. 'You got something for me or what?'

CHAPTER TWENTY

Maggie closed her eyes. It was almost funny. Of course Aaron had known about Townsend's hit, and that the gangster would come for Maggie if he was tipped off that she was here. Aaron needed somebody reckless, somebody who would arrive and, not finding the person he wanted, massacre whoever was left here – even a cop. Except Aaron's plan had gone awry and, as a result, Townsend was about to get exactly what he wanted.

'I'm warning you,' Townsend called again. 'If you're not out here in the next minute with the girl, we're gonna break the door down. Let's handle this nice and gentle.'

Maggie looked to the window again. It didn't have a latch, didn't open. The moment she smashed it Townsend's men would hear.

'I'm really fucking hoping you haven't wasted my time,' Townsend said.

What did she have?

'Ten seconds,' Townsend said.

Maggie ran for the cabinet.

'Nine.'

She found a bottle of absinthe. Opened it as she stumbled for the old couch, snatching the lighter from the table as she went.

'Eight.'

The couch wasn't heavy but trying to lift it sent the pain in her face surging. Didn't matter.

'Seven.'

She had the couch up now, lifting from one side. It was as tall as she, as tall as the door.

'Six.'

Trying not to be too loud, she shuffled the couch towards the door.

'Five.'

She doused the top cushion in absinthe. She held the top of the couch and the lighter in her right hand; in her left she had the bottle.

'Four.'

Maggie sparked the lighter, placed it to the cushion and as she did screamed, 'Help! Please, help me!'

The men outside didn't think. The door cracked as someone slammed against it. Heat from the igniting couch cushion licked Maggie's hand but she didn't let go.

The door shattered inwards. Maggie caught a glimpse of a man in black holding a gun, then she shoved the couch onto him. As she did, she brought the bottle up hard, splashing absinthe all over him, absinthe that caught fire the moment it doused his shirt.

The man screamed.

Maggie ran. She pulled the pipe from her belt and brought it hard into the window. In the doorway, the man still grappled with the burning couch as his own shirt went up. The window glass was gone. Maggie swept the bottom of the sill with the pipe then hefted herself up and through. The cries from behind her continued. She fell through into cold night air, landing hard on the pile of wood. She rolled off, hit the ground and struggled to her feet, taking a couple of steps forward as she tried to regain her balance, then—

A man came around the corner of the house. He saw her, went to shoot but she swung the pipe up hard. It caught his chin and his head snapped back. Maggie spun, checked for Nipper's gun left on the ground but there was no sign of it and then she was running, into the trees, running through the agony, away from the screams now mingling with yells of fury and confusion as Townsend tried to work out what the fuck had happened.

She burst from the trees surrounding the house. She tripped and fell onto grass. Ahead, streaks of blood, black in the moonlight. Aaron had gone this way.

On her feet again and charging. The pain was far away now. Townsend would catch up to her, her face was ruined, and she never should have come here, but all of that receded – she knew what she had to do. She would get the drive back and she would make Aaron hurt. For herself, for Cooper, for all of this.

She wasn't steady on her feet. She was moving in stumbles, hitting the ground then getting to her feet again, colliding with trees and slipping in dirt. Her vision warped. Dark trunks then white grass then the endless stars and the looming moon and the desolate stretch of rugged ruin that was the empty lakebed.

And finally, emerging from the last of the trees, Aaron.

He was a lone figure, skinny and small among it all, tripping across the lakebed.

She kept going.

Grass gave way to rocks that cascaded under her feet down the last of the slope, and then to spreading cracks in dirt and dry mud that was once underwater. The ground below her levelled. The dead trees grew and stretched for her. And ahead, Aaron grew closer.

She kept going.

Maggie could hear him now, sobbing and wheezing, speaking to himself in fractured mutters. He fell hard. Rose with difficulty. His movements were loping, lurching. There was blood on the ground in front of Maggie.

She kept going.

The pipe was in her hand now, fitting like it had always been there, like an extension of her. She *tasted* the thought of it caving in his skull, the thought of those cries stopping, the thought of him knowing too late that he had fucked up, that he had crossed the very last person he ever should have.

Aaron turned. Saw Maggie.

She kept going.

'S-stop!' he managed.

She kept going.

242

Aaron raised the gun in an unsteady hand. 'No further!'

She kept going.

Aaron fired. The ground a good metre from her feet exploded.

She kept going.

More gunshots. More bursts of dirt.

She kept going.

Aaron was begging now, crying out something desperate and strangled even as he fired again and the bullet missed and Maggie was on him. The pipe collided with the side of his neck and Aaron was down. He was soaked in blood but that didn't matter. Maggie brought the pipe down again and again, hitting his chest, stomach, his kneecap, and all the while the screams, louder now, loud and wild because he knew this was it, *because he knew and he deserved it and she was going to fucking kill him.*

Aaron stirred weakly on the ground. Maggie stepped back. Smelt the air. Only copper. Her blood or his or both; there was enough of it. Looked at the stars. At the pipe. Lifted it. Just like she had all those years ago with Elliot, before she'd been interrupted, before somebody had stopped her giving the prick exactly what he deserved. But this time there was no-one to stop her. This time she would be righteous and vengeful and would walk away from here with one more parasite of the world dead in the dust behind her.

Aaron was curled up on the ground, eyes tightly shut, shaking with feeble sobs.

'Look at me,' Maggie said.

He didn't.

'Fucking *look at me!*' The words tore from her and then she had him by the shirt, pulling him up to look at her face, at what he'd done, at the nightmare she now knew she was with the bloodied bandages and the wild eyes and the raised pipe. The last thing this fucker would ever see.

Aaron looked at her.

There was no understanding or realisation in his face. No lesson learned. No regret. Just terror. Absolute, all-consuming, insurmountable terror.

Terror she knew all too well.

She dropped the pipe. Fell back into the dirt. Aaron's eyes were closed again. He didn't even try to reach for the dropped gun.

A gust of cold wind. Maggie closed her eyes. Tried to breathe. The pain pulsed through her face, her hands, everywhere. How much blood had she lost? She could feel the icy crawl of tiredness spreading through her, her body protesting at the expended energy and the damage.

She picked up the pipe and stood. Considered Aaron just a moment. Went to go through his pockets, to get the drive.

And as she did, the lakebed came alive with bright light.

Fast across the dirt they came; three hulking black SUVs, silhouettes behind the glare of their headlights, bouncing over the rough landscape as they closed in on Maggie and Aaron. One came straight for them; the other two peeled away, ready to encircle them.

Instinct told her to bolt just as logic told her it was pointless. They would only run her down. So she stood, pipe in hand, as the three cars closed in around them.

Aaron was trying to get up. 'P-please.' He was slurring. 'Please.'

Maggie just waited.

The cars came to a halt. The sound of an opening door, then another. Shapes behind the white light.

Maggie said nothing.

Len Townsend stepped forward, a gun in hand. He looked just the same as he had in Queensland, dressed in his dark blue suit without a tie, the shirt open far too low. There was still amusement in those far-set eyes, but it didn't offset the fury, nor the vicious delight in having caught his quarry at last.

'Well,' he said. 'You've been a right fucking headache.' He looked her up and down. Took in the pipe with a sneer. 'Gonna beat us all to death, are you, sweetheart?'

His lackeys had joined him in the circle of light. Only three others, all with guns. No sign of the men she'd burnt and bludgeoned.

Townsend turned to one of the men. 'She used to be pretty, believe it or not. Looks like somebody else wanted to give the little cunt what she deserved.' Townsend stepped up close. Leered at Maggie. Grabbed her by the chin. 'Not so fucking pretty now, eh?'

Maggie bit down hard between his thumb and forefinger. Townsend yelled out. Maggie sunk her teeth in harder, then he was hitting her with the gun, each blow like a hammer, sending waves through her head. She let go. The ground tilted.

Somewhere nearby, Townsend was breathing heavily. 'Fuck. Jesus fucking Christ. Like a fucking animal.'

He punched her. Maggie saw it coming but didn't feel it. She was on the ground now, on her side. She could see Aaron, eyes still closed, mouth moving silently.

Townsend had moved back to the front of one of the cars, inspecting his hand. He nodded to one of his men. 'Get her up.'

The man had Maggie by the hair, pulling her to her knees.

'Now,' Townsend said. 'We're gonna kill you. We're gonna make it hurt. And we're gonna make sure you know just how big a mistake you made fucking with my business.'

Aaron's terrified face, briefly, flashed in front of her.

'Sam,' Townsend said to the man holding Maggie's hair. 'Cut something off.'

Sam's laugh was low and stupid. He drew a knife. Maggie looked up at him, didn't blink. His broad face contorted in something resembling glee. He lifted the knife.

The top of his head exploded.

Townsend flinched. The other men had their guns up, looking around.

The ragged, splintered remains of Sam's head, still including one eye, looked almost confused as he dropped.

There was no sign of another shooter. Even knowing it wasn't him, Maggie looked at Aaron but he hadn't moved; his gun still lay in the dirt.

Townsend was now hunched low in front of the car, looking around wildly as he spoke into a radio.

'Cal,' he said, 'there's a shooter out there. Have you got visual? Cal?'

Static.

'Fuck!' Townsend yelled. He tried again. 'Come on, Cal. Ned. Fucking *anyone*. Tell me you guys stuck to your stations? There's some prick with a sniper rifle!'

Silence.

Then—

'Speaking as the prick with the rifle,' Jack Carlin said through the radio, 'I'd say you're well and truly fucked.'

CHAPTER TWENTY-ONE

Maggie burst out laughing. Townsend, still hunkered down in front of the car, moved for her but another gunshot blasted off the driver's side mirror. He fell back.

Carlin was alive.

Maggie didn't know how, didn't know what she could have missed at the house, but that paled in the face of the beautiful reality. Carlin was alive and he was here. She wasn't in this alone.

'Do you know who I fucking am?' Townsend barked into the radio. 'You're making a big fucking mistake.'

'Let me tell you what a big mistake is,' Carlin replied. 'A big mistake would be sending your fucking goons to my house. A bigger mistake would be said goons not checking to see if I was wearing a vest after they emptied a few rounds at me. 'Course, the goons in question won't be making that mistake again so chances are it's a moot point, but it's a lesson you can stand to learn, Len.'

Townsend's brow furrowed. 'Carlin? Jack Carlin?'

Aaron glanced up.

'Aye, aye,' Carlin said. 'You know my address. You invaded my property. And that means you have to die. I'd apologise, but all told, I reckon I'll be getting more thanks than admonishments for finishing you off.'

Townsend was shaking his head. 'Don't be stupid. My men will come for you. They'll—'

'Your men will immediately go to work for whatever gutter rat replaces you in the scene.' Carlin sounded bored. 'You've got no leverage, Townsend.'

'Wait,' Aaron said, sitting up. 'Jack … Jack Carlin. I know who he is.'

'Congratu-fucking-lations,' Townsend growled. 'Who the fuck are you?'

Aaron was fumbling at his pocket. 'I have something he wants.'

'Don't,' Maggie said.

But Aaron was ignoring her. He lifted the hard drive. 'This is what he's been looking for.'

'What the fuck is that?' Townsend asked.

'Aaron,' Maggie said.

'Evidence,' Aaron said. 'On the Scorpions. Carlin's been after it for years. Rook told me. It's l-leverage.'

Townsend looked from Aaron to the drive. He nodded to one of his men, who crawled over to Aaron and took the drive. Aaron didn't resist; he just shrank back, staring bug-eyed at Townsend, waiting.

Townsend lifted the radio again and pressed the button. 'Carlin?'

'At your service.'

'We can make a deal.'

'I highly doubt that.'

'A hard drive. We've got a hard drive. Something about the Scorpions. Mean anything to you?'

Silence on the other end.

Townsend's smile was one of savage relief. 'You let us walk clear. You let us—'

'Jack, don't!' Maggie yelled.

'Shut up!' Townsend spat. 'You hear that, Carlin? Let us walk, let us take the girl, and we'll leave the drive right here. All yours to do whatever you want with.'

Still nothing from the other end.

Maggie looked up towards the vague outlines of the hills surrounding the lake. Carlin was out there somewhere. Hearing Townsend's offer, thinking it through. The thrill she'd felt just moments ago had given way to something sour and sinking. Whatever she had come to feel about Carlin during those days at his house, he had always been clear about his intentions. He wanted the drive. He wanted to destroy the Scorpions. Everything else was secondary.

'Answer me!' Townsend's voice had turned high-pitched, scared.

'Proof,' Carlin said.

'Then hold your fucking fire.' A look from Townsend to the man with the drive. Apprehensive, he stood. No shots. He lifted the drive up, high, where Carlin could see it through his scope.

For a long moment, silence. Maggie's fingernails were digging into her palm.

Townsend was sweating now. 'Well?' He croaked into the radio.

The man holding the drive screamed as a bullet tore through his wrist with an eruption of blood and bone. The hard drive hit the ground, still clasped in his severed hand. Clutching his stump, the man fell. The other guards were up, firing into the dark.

Townsend looked to Maggie. His grasp tightened around his gun—

Just as she swung the pipe hard into his jaw.

A terrible, loud crack. Townsend's jaw jerked sideways. He let out a strangled, pained cry as he went down.

Then Aaron was on his feet, snatching up the hand with the drive and bolting past the firing guards, past the cars, into the night.

Another burst of blood and another of Townsend's men dropped. The gangster was still writhing in the dirt.

Maggie ran after Aaron.

She was half-prepared to be taken out by a bullet, but none came. Suddenly the glaring headlights were gone and she was plunged into a darkness her eyes were unadjusted to. There were only shapes in the shadow, shapes that could have been anything, but only one of them was moving.

The pain had dissipated but she could feel the wetness of the bandages as they slipped down her blood-slick face. She knew that if she slowed now, she would drop. She was hurt badly and could barely fight. But she had to get to Aaron. Had to get the drive.

And she was gaining on him. Already he was faltering, hunched and unsteady, then he was right in front of her and she collided with him. They hit the dirt together. She grabbed for the drive, tried to wrest it from his grip. Aaron kicked and writhed. They rolled through the dirt. Maggie felt the impact of fists and knees but she had gone past the point where any more pain would matter.

Then Aaron grabbed her face.

His fingers dug into her gashes and under her skin. Maggie convulsed, her grip released, then Aaron was pulling away from her and on to his feet. Maggie saw blinding white. Her head was spinning and she wasn't sure where she was.

But still she stood.

Metres from her, Aaron had dropped the hard drive. He had Nipper's gun in his hand, pointed directly at it.

'Enough,' he wheezed. 'Okay? Enough. No more.'

Maggie didn't move.

'Please.' His voice was cracking. 'Please just walk away. Just leave me alone. Otherwise I'll shoot it.'

'And then what?' Maggie asked.

'Then you,' he said. 'Then I'll kill you.'

'No, you won't.'

Aaron's breathing was a pained struggle. 'You don't know … you don't know anything. Just stop, okay? Please. *Please*. Let me go home.'

'Give me the hard drive,' Maggie said. 'And you can walk away.'

A shape moved in the dark behind Aaron. Tall, slow-moving, holding something long that glinted in the moonlight. Carlin lifted the rifle, aiming it at Aaron's head. His vantage point must have been closer than Maggie realised.

She tried to keep her focus on Cooper's son. 'Aaron, please. Just give me the drive. Give me the drive and we can all walk away from this.'

Aaron was shaking his head. 'No. I'm a *Scorpion*.' The words sounded desperate and pathetic.

'If you could kill me, you would have,' Maggie said. 'You're not a murderer, Aaron. You need help.'

'Fuck you!' he cried.

'Leave it,' Maggie said. 'Please.'

She could see his finger tightening on the trigger now. His slack, scared face hardening. Carlin was getting closer; Maggie could almost make out his features in the dark.

Then movement behind Carlin, fast and sudden. One of the SUVs, the lights off, gunning for him.

Aaron's finger tighter still, ready to fire at a flinch.

In that moment Maggie saw it all. The terrified boy in over his head. The old rogue cop. The vicious gangster bearing down on them. That small metal rectangle that could hold all the answers Maggie had given up everything for.

And her. In the middle of it all. Daughter of a broken monster. Forged by hate and fury. Standing here on the precipice of what had long since been laid out for her.

Or.

'Jack!' Maggie roared.

Aaron pulled the trigger. The hard drive burst into jagged pieces.

Carlin turned, saw the car bearing down on him and dived out of its way.

For just a second, Maggie held Aaron's gaze. She saw the churning guilt and panic and confusion that had led him here. The final understanding of just how deeply he had fucked up.

Then the car slammed into him.

Aaron spun into the air. Maggie scurried back. The SUV screeched to a halt.

Aaron hit the ground.

Her vision shook. The night was fracturing. All she could see was the still, smoking car.

Maggie ran for it. Pulled the driver's side door open.

Jaw hanging bloody and loose, Len Townsend looked at her.

Maggie grabbed him by the jaw and dragged him from the car.

He squealed as he hit the ground. Maggie didn't let go. She could feel the shattered bones, feel them pulling loose, feel the skin tearing. She didn't care. Maggie smashed the pipe into his face.

The squealing stopped. Maggie brought it down again and again. Felt bone cave in. Saw Townsend twitch and squirm and stop, and still she hit him until his face was a red pulp spreading blood into the long-dry dirt, and still Maggie brought the pipe down until strong hands took it from her.

She struggled but then Jack Carlin was holding her close, hugging her to him and saying, 'It's over, girl. It's over.'

She tried to break free. Tried to get back to Townsend. But Carlin didn't let go and finally she gave in and stopped and sank into his arms as the pain and tiredness swept over her and the weight of it all tried to drag her down, but Carlin never let go.

'It's done,' he said.

CHAPTER TWENTY-TWO

The sky above the thick trees was heavily overcast and darkening by the second with the threat of rain. Alone on the porch of Carlin's house, nursing a beer, Maggie watched the clouds. She sipped and tried to ignore the aching itch from her face. The painkillers were doing their job, but wounds like this were hard to ignore.

She had been here several days now, but soon she'd have to be gone. Where, she wasn't yet sure. She got the sense that Carlin liked the company. Besides which, she didn't want to leave. Her time here had given her the chance to finally breathe and try to sort through everything that had happened. Not that she was getting very far with any of that. Every time she managed to reach some kind of internal accord with one part of the puzzle, there was another that kept her awake.

But if any evidence connecting Carlin to the lakebed massacre led the police here, then Maggie's presence would cause even more trouble for the man who had, once again, come through for her.

Leaving Townsend's body, Maggie had gone after Aaron, Carlin close behind. Not that there was any point. Not that Maggie knew what she would have done had he still been alive.

Harrison Cooper's son, for whom he had given up everything, lay twisted and broken near the SUV. His eyes were closed. A trickle of blood ran from his mouth. He would have looked almost peaceful if it wasn't for the rest of him.

Maggie had stood there for what felt like a long time, looking at the boy she had come here to save, continuing what Cooper had so desperately tried to do.

She didn't know what to feel about Aaron now. If she should feel anything. Her thoughts returned to when she was a kid, to asking his father endless questions about him, to the times she had imagined having a brother, imagined growing up with him. Had that happened, had Cooper taken her in, would she have ended up any different?

Yes, because unlike Aaron, she had the context of something far worse than a strict, hypocritical parent. But that didn't change the fact that the old fantasy of Cooper the saviour had gone.

Maybe Aaron had been right to hate his father. Maybe his scattershot plan did have a vein of righteousness. Maggie would never truly understand what had gone through his head. But from where she was standing, he looked only like a confused, angry, weak kid in desperate need of guidance, who had found it in the worst place possible.

Behind her, Carlin had rested a hand on her shoulder. 'We need to go.' His voice wasn't quite gentle, but as close to as it got.

'Should we ...' Maggie wasn't sure how to finish that sentence.

'Wanna go digging graves in your condition?' Cooper said. 'You need stitches and a sleep. Besides which, some local will have heard something. Police will be on the scene very fucking soon, and I don't know about you, but I don't want to be here when that happens.'

Maybe she was imagining it, but it was almost as though there was a question in that.

She shook her head. 'No. I don't either.'

Carlin had filled her in on what happened after she'd escaped his house. As he'd told Townsend on the radio, he had been wearing a vest, something he'd 'always done after some fucker dragged a knife down me'. Like Maggie, the would-be assassin had assumed he was dead and returned to the house to check if anyone else had survived Maggie's improvised traps. Carlin, momentarily stunned, had been on the shooter moments later.

'After which,' Carlin had explained, 'I was more than a little pissed off. I mean, for one, you stole my car.'

'Thought you were dead,' Maggie had said. It wasn't as though she'd had time to check.

'Ah well, I got my own back there.' It turned out Carlin had made his way to Maggie's own car where she'd left it near her father's place. From there, he had set to work tracking down Len Townsend.

'Don't get me wrong, I was keeping an ear out for you,' he had said. 'But I had no fucking idea where you'd gone. And given Townsend knew my address, and therefore that I'd been sheltering you, he knew way too much for comfort. He had to go. So I twisted a few arms and made a few threats until I found out he'd come to Melbourne after his hit squad got royally fucked on. Typically, he wasn't much for secrecy, so it didn't take long to work out where he was headed and follow him until I got a clear shot. Would have liked to kill him myself, but you looked like you had some feelings to get off your chest there, so I figured I'd let you have it.'

Most of the drive back, Maggie had slipped in and out of consciousness. Carlin had given her fresh bandages, but the bleeding was bad and soon they were soaked red as well. They had returned in Maggie's car, with Carlin promising he had a 'local mate who can swing the van back to me'. She wasn't sure if that was true or if there was any benefit to Carlin taking them both in a car that wasn't his, but she was grateful to him. Once she was relatively healed, she'd be able to leave again.

Julie had arrived first thing the next morning, and Argos had hurried over for a scratch.

'We need to stop meeting like this,' Julie had growled as she inspected the cuts.

She had worked steadily to stitch them all up, but her grim expression told Maggie that she didn't like what she saw.

For her part, Maggie hadn't known what to feel when she finally looked in a mirror. The stitching likely made them look worse, but even healed they'd be obvious, long and knotted, one over her eye, two under it. She thought back to the boy in Port Douglas, whose name she'd clean forgotten now. She'd been so worried that the scars she hid would be a marker that would make her forever memorable. She'd never have to think twice about that again. Her days of slipping easily into a crowd were gone. Not only were the scars obvious, they were unique. They said she had been through some shit.

She'd been told over the course of her life that she was pretty. No stunning beauty, but pretty. It wasn't something she had thought a lot about or had any time for, really. Just an accepted fact of her being. But whatever those people had meant when they said pretty, it wasn't what Maggie was now. In isolation, she didn't mind the scars. She'd never cared too much how she looked. But from a practical standpoint, they were a danger she'd have to factor into her future forever.

'Not gonna ask how you're feeling,' Julie had said a couple of days later, when she returned to check up on Maggie. 'Those would hurt like a motherfucker. And I can't imagine you're much thrilled about the location. But they're not your first, and the way you're going, they won't be the last.'

'You don't sound approving of that,' Maggie said.

'Not my job to approve,' Julie replied. 'My job to fix. Unless shit gets broken, I don't have a job. Still, seeing as nobody else seems to be telling you this, I'd suggest staying away from machetes and broken bottles.'

'They seem to have a way of finding me.'

'Maybe,' Julie said. 'But maybe that finding is mutual. And maybe it's worth asking yourself why that is.'

Maggie had thought losing the hard drive would hurt more. After everything she had gone through to get her hands on it, she would have at least thought she'd be angry. And while there was a dull sense of frustration, the whole ordeal had left her burnt-out. Still, when she considered the hard drive, she didn't think she'd feel much worse when she finally came back to herself.

It took her a while to work out why that was. Part of it, she thought, was Aaron. He had positioned himself so starkly in opposition to his father that it had destroyed him. Maggie, for her part, had long felt caught between what her father had done and what her mother had failed to do. Between an aggressive presence and an absence that retained the potential to be filled by anything. That potential, in Maggie's mind, had grown into something towering and unrealistic, the belief that she could be solved if she could only meet her mother. That the woman who had left her in a cage with a beast could provide her with a semblance of peace, with answers to questions Maggie wasn't even entirely sure of anymore.

But her mother was alive, or at least had been around a year ago. The briefly glimpsed image in that photo had burned itself into her thoughts. While she didn't yet know what her next move was, she found it hard to believe that she could forget what she knew. Or ignore another opportunity to find her mother, should it arise.

Maggie wasn't the only one to whom the hard drive had mattered. Carlin kept her updated with whatever information he managed to get through his various contacts. Unsurprisingly, Olivia Dean hadn't told anyone about their deal; she had, however, been behind the library raids, claiming she was responding to an anonymous tip. Carlin, who seemed less bothered by the loss of the hard drive than Maggie might have expected, suggested that Dean would privately be furious about the seeming double-cross, but Maggie didn't see a huge amount of point in trying to get in touch and explain, given she'd fully intended to double-cross Dean anyway.

The Scorpions, meanwhile, were keeping quiet. The discovery of Cooper's body had been linked to Nipper and with that came a whole new investigation into whether a bikie had murdered a policeman, so however annoyed she might be, Dean had her hands full for the time being. Carlin, for his part, didn't seem especially optimistic. Nipper's missing gun, found in Bonnie Doon, had created questions about whether it had in fact been Aaron who had killed Harrison Cooper – still a Scorpion, but one acting on his own out of some violent grudge rather than anything the gang had directed him to do. Not nothing, but not as much of a slam dunk as proof that the gang had been covering for a murderer operating in their midst, a murderer who lacked provable motive and therefore could more easily be presented to a judge as cause for the kind of warrant Dean needed.

'The hard drive was always a bit of a long shot,' Carlin had told Maggie. 'I doubt anything on there would really have been enough to bring the gang down. But that's the thing about ideas. Hang on to one long enough, it can grow into something big and false and dangerous. Lot of people did a lot of hanging and figured they were on the hunt for a game-changer. Either way, we'll never know now.'

'And the Scorpions get away with everything,' Maggie had said.

Carlin's smile was bitter. 'Welcome to the game, girl.'

One day, as Carlin set out to get a better sense of where everything stood, Maggie had asked him if he could do her a favour. He'd bullshitted and said predictable things about having done enough for her, but in the end agreed to check in on Ness.

The memories that had come flooding back upon her return to Melbourne had lingered for a while now. Memories of that brief post-school attempt at a normal life, of the moment in that alley with the rounders bat, the moment that had reappeared at the forefront of her mind standing over Aaron in the lakebed. With Elliot, she had been interrupted. With Aaron she had chosen not to finish him, although given Aaron was dead now anyway, that seemed essentially pointless.

When Carlin returned, it was with the news that Ness had married Elliot and was pregnant with his child. After that, whatever was left of Maggie's idea of a normal life quietly slipped away.

* * *

All of which left her ... where?

As she sat on that front porch with her almost-finished beer, the questions of where she had been turned fast to where she would go next. And there was no satisfactory answer to be found. Nowhere that made sense, no purpose to fulfil.

If she had hoped the swaying trees and billowing clouds might spark some inspiration, she was to be disappointed. The wind was rising now; what had started as small gusts was picking up, rocking the forest and threatening to become a gale. Still, Maggie didn't move. She liked the blasts of cold. Liked the feeling that each one was taking something away with it.

Movement behind her. She finished her beer as Carlin sat and handed her another. Cracking his own, he leaned against one of the posts beside the stairs and watched the angry sky.

'Cooper mentioned your daughter.' Maggie didn't look at Carlin.

For a moment, he said nothing. When he did, his voice was level. 'And what did he say about my daughter?'

'Not much. He implied she was troubled.'

'Troubled how?'

'Drugs, I guessed. Like Aaron.'

Carlin snorted. 'Drugs are the least of it.'

Maggie glanced sideways. Carlin's expression as he looked to the sky was somewhere between annoyed and deeply sad. 'In the end, I think Morgan's biggest problem is herself.'

'What does that mean?'

'Probably hard to explain without you meeting her. And if you asked Morgan, she'd lay a lot at my feet. Some of it valid. But at a certain point, parenthood becomes the cruellest type of punishment. You put everything into trying to do right by the person you created, or at least, right as far as you can see it. But in the end, they're not there to be shaped by you. They're going to make their own choices. And eventually you have to realise there's only so much you can do to influence them.'

Maggie's eyes had returned to the trees but she could feel Jack's gaze on her.

'Which, by the way, goes for being a cop as well,' he said. 'You can try to help people, but if they don't want to help themselves, then you have to ask yourself if it's really something you can keep doing. 'Course, asking that of yourself doesn't mean you have a choice. Some things are ingrained.'

'Like?' Maggie asked.

'I guess I'd point to Aaron Cooper. When you told me he was in with the Scorpions, I wasn't surprised at all. Harrison Cooper wasn't a bad guy, not really. But he was weak. He wanted the easy way out. His heart was never really in being a cop, not enough to do the hard yards. Rook Gately offers Aaron something he wants, something that probably looks too good to be true; he was always gonna take it. He was his father's son.'

'And Morgan?' Maggie asked. 'Is she her father's daughter?'

'Through and through.' A note of something strained and hard-to-read had entered Carlin's voice. 'And maybe that's the problem.'

'Or maybe what our parents give us, we don't have to keep.'

Carlin didn't reply. They both drank. In the distance a flash of lightning lit the sky and was gone. The rain hadn't started yet.

'Will you still try to bring down Rook?' Maggie asked.

'If I see an opportunity, I'll take it,' Carlin said. 'But in the end, I'm one person. The hard drive might have helped. A little. But without it, I'm not sure.'

A rumble of faraway thunder.

'And if you had help?' Maggie asked.

Carlin laughed. 'Two isn't much better than one, especially when one of the two is a fugitive and the other not far off that. The Scorpions have been careful for years. They might have made a couple of mistakes recently, like the lawyer's office and letting that Nipper fuckwit join up, but with all the heat now they're going to be making sure they don't give any potential enemies anything to grab onto.'

'Depends on the enemy. And on what they're looking to grab onto.'

'Well, that's a bit fucking cryptic. But ultimately useless. Look at me.'

Maggie did.

Carlin smiled. 'I like you, girl. But believe me when I say that sometimes you need to turn away before that thing you're eyeing becomes an obsession. What I'm saying is I've fucked up enough times to know when a cause is lost. I'm hoping you're smart enough not to arrive at the same conclusion from the same mistakes.'

Maggie said nothing. Carlin stood, considered the sky for one more moment, then turned and went inside.

Maggie stayed where she was as the rain started.

In Queensland she had sought peace and quiet. Briefly she had found it and, in doing so, the old fantasy of normality had crept back. But she knew now that it *was* just a fantasy, and not a particularly worthwhile one.

She could never escape her childhood. Not really. There were wounds that would always hurt, things about her that would forever be different and dangerous. Things that, to some, would look abhorrent. But being shaped by where she had come from didn't mean she was defined by it. Maybe there was a way to take the jagged, broken edges and turn them into something with purpose. Something that, in some small way, could do good.

She stood, still watching the rain. There was an idea turning over in her mind, an idea that grew bigger and more powerful by the moment. And as it grew, so did Maggie's grin.

EPILOGUE

He needed time to process it all. Time and quiet. But the music was loud and The Pit was packed. The low lights might have hidden the grime, as if any of them cared, but they also made it difficult to make out expressions in the mass of people. He'd wanted to hold the wakes at the clubhouse, but they'd had too many of those recently and the boys wanted a change of scenery. And they wanted to bring their girls.

The smell of sweat and petrol was heavy in the air. Not an uncommon aroma among bikies, but tonight it was giving Rook a headache.

Then somebody was yelling something and the bar went quiet, except for Ryan's sobs. Even the music was turned right down. Eyes were turning to him.

Silence in the bar. *The speech.*

Rook stood. Cleared his throat. Looked down into his drink. 'It hasn't been the smoothest run for us lately. But this is the life we've chosen, boys. Even freedom comes at a cost. And the hunt for freedom is what we embrace and what we are. The open road, the wind in our hair, the fact that the laws of a piss-weak government mean nothing to us.' As he spoke, he thought of twisted, bullet-riddled bodies, of years in jail, of the constant simmering fear of your door being kicked in or the bursts of gunfire that could come from anywhere. That and the fact that they wore helmets and very rarely felt the wind in their hair.

'Those young blokes knew that,' Rook went on. 'They knew it and they loved it. That doesn't make what happened to them okay. They should have had long lives as part of our brotherhood. Nipper should have got his patch.' And, Rook knew, Aaron shouldn't have. In fact, he was avoiding bringing up the cop's son because he was sure that that particular mistake was the one being most muttered about by his men. He couldn't blame them. Letting Aaron effectively skip being a prospect had been pure strategy, a way to get the kid onside and ensure his loyalty. What it had actually done was foster in him a dangerous combination of arrogance and insecurity. Aaron had known the men resented his quick rise but had told himself that he had earned it. That left him believing both that he had to prove himself *and* that he was smart enough, special enough, to strike out on his own and wow everyone else with his genius.

Aaron's botched plan itself, in essence, had merit. Rook had never considered the idea of framing Cooper, but when he heard later that Aaron had spoken about it among his mates, Rook had to admit there were parts of it that made perfect sense. That it could and maybe *would* be the answer they needed to throw Olivia Dean off their scent. But Aaron had gone about it all wrong, so desperate was he to impress. Consequently, here they were.

'Anyway,' Rook said. 'We're all still standing. And we're gonna stay that way, you hear?'

A rumble of assent. Rook had hoped for a cheer. Once he had known exactly what to say in any situation, had excelled at speeches that got his boys revved up and bloodthirsty. But now he was tired. He was sick of the smell, of the floor wet with spilled beer, of this garbage music.

'So drink up.' He lifted his glass. 'Drink up and remember them. Nipper and Aaron.'

Low voices and raised glasses. 'Nipper and Aaron.'

The music returned. Rook sat again. He lifted his drink just as somebody slid into the chair across from him.

She was young, dressed in a leather jacket. Her hair was dark. For maybe a second Rook assumed she was somebody's girl, but the gashes, one above the left eye, two below, curving and swollen and only recently stitched, said otherwise. Even if one of the men had got a bit shitty with his missus, he certainly wouldn't bring her here looking like this. Not least because they all knew how Rook felt about raising a fist to women.

'Rook Gately,' the girl said.

Maybe she was a hooker thinking she could make some cash with the sad old bloke. If so, she was shit out of luck. He'd never cheat on Wendy. 'Look, love, it's been a long day and I'm sure there's someone more fun to chat to.'

The girl said nothing.

And then Rook realised. The sharp cheekbones. The thin mouth. The simmer of something dangerous in those eyes. He'd seen those all before, years ago, in a different face.

'Maggie,' he said.

A single nod.

He should have had his gun out straight away. She had killed several of his men. But he also knew that they had tried to kill her, and beyond that, she was Eric's daughter. And after what he had done to Eric, part of him felt he owed her.

So, simply and directly, he said, 'I think you'd better get out of here.'

'First we're going to talk.'

'About what?'

'Everything. Aaron. Cooper. My father.'

'I don't think you understand,' Rook said. 'Every person in this room would kill you if they figured out who you are.'

'No, they won't.'

There was such certainty to the statement that Rook felt a crawl of worry in his gut.

'My father drove himself mad trying to find a killer you covered for,' Maggie said. 'Who was it?'

Instinct told Rook to deny. Common sense told him there was no point. This girl was more of a wanted fugitive than he was. Besides which, she clearly knew too much to be put off by lies. And Rook was sick of lying.

'He was a kid. Mal. Young. But troubled. His dad was bad news. His mum had been on the receiving end of it for too long. Nobody ever stood up for him, until us. But ...'

Rook shrugged. 'Sometimes the damage goes too deep. Sometimes you're too broken for anything to put you back together. And sometimes when you've been hurt too bad, the only thing you know is hurting. So he did.'

'And you protected him,' Maggie said.

A rise of defensive heat in his chest. Rook knew he had fucked up there. Knew it because even now, years later, the ripples of his choice continued to spread. 'When you join the gang, you become family. I don't give up on family. I tried to help Mal. It worked for a while, then it didn't.'

'Then Cooper told you to deal with him.'

Harrison Cooper. The most malleable of the three cops he'd bought. Until he wasn't. Until Rook understood the extent of his mistake.

'So you killed Mal,' Maggie said.

Cut brakes. A late-night ride together. A sharp swerve and a tree.

'Yeah,' Rook said. 'Yeah, I did.'

The pounding music seemed almost faint now. But the smell of petrol was worse than ever. Rook's head swam. He raised his drink but his hand was shaking. He put it down again.

'Why not earlier?' Maggie said. 'Why not the moment you realised what he was?'

'Like I said. You don't give up on family.'

Maybe he'd put too much emphasis on the last word. Too much for just another gang member.

'His mother,' Maggie leaned back. 'You were seeing his mother?'

Wendy. Back home now. She never came out anymore. Barely had since that night. Barely did much of anything.

Rook drank despite the shakes. Talking about this, finally, was like a long-avoided release.

'I think that there's a part of every man that's desperate to be a father. I never had my own kids. Couldn't.' Once, he'd been ashamed of the fact. Now it seemed irrelevant. He couldn't help what he was. Nobody could. 'But, see, that didn't mean the instinct wasn't there. And when you get the chance. To guide someone, to shape them, to be there for them ...'

'You end up with this.' Maggie's expression had turned faintly disgusted as she looked around the room.

'Some of the boys here were on bad paths before they found us.'

'And you put them on a better one?'

'Yes.' The girl's incredulous expression was pissing him off. 'Just because you don't understand—'

'Harrison Cooper, dead,' Maggie said. 'My father, abusive, drunk and dead. Aaron, Nipper – how many others? On balance, how many of your "boys" have seen their lives demonstrably improved by joining you?'

Rook's drink was finished. His jaw clenched. He was sick of this conversation. He looked over towards the bar. Byrne was still there, talking to a couple of the others. If Rook caught his eye, he could have this girl dragged off and dead in minutes.

'I think you've heard what you came for,' Rook said. 'And I think it's time you left.'

'Aaron Cooper,' Maggie said. 'You bought his debt. Won him over. Manipulated him into hating his own father.'

'Harrison did that himself,' Rook said.

'And you capitalised on it. Just like now you're planning to capitalise on Aaron's idea.'

Barely any change to her expression. The sounds of the bar had become unbearable, just like the petrol smell and this stupid bitch sitting across from him, needling. Under the table, Rook reached for his gun.

'I think you've been clever, Rook,' Maggie said. 'Moving in the shadows, preying on people's need for leadership and parenthood. Ensuring loyalty by pretending to provide what the wayward are looking for. But it's smoke and mirrors, really.'

'You don't know what you're talking about,' Rook said.

'Yes.' Maggie nodded. 'Yes, I do. I'm not blaming you for my father's choices. Or mine. But I *am* blaming you for targeting weaknesses and then making them worse. I am blaming you for letting murderers operate with impunity. And I'm blaming you for doing it all in the name of some twisted, bullshit conception of family.'

'ENOUGH!' Rook roared.

The voices stopped. All eyes were on them. Maggie didn't even react as from the bar, Byrne yelled, '*Her!*'

Rook and Maggie didn't look away from each other, but he was aware of hands all around them flying to weapons, of barrels levelled at Maggie as his brothers, his family, took up arms and prepared to drop the last threat standing against them.

Rook smiled. 'I gave you a chance. I told you to walk out of this. For your father's sake, I was going to let it slide. But you had to stay. You had to push. And now you know too much.'

'Sure,' Maggie said. 'But you're not going to do anything about it.'

'I think you'll find you're surrounded by blokes who are more than willing to *do something about it*.'

'Yeah. But they won't.'

Maggie lifted a lit zippo lighter.

A smattering of laughter. It looked pathetic. But …

Rook caught Byrne's eye. Realisation struck them both at the same time.

The petrol smell, heavier by the second. The wet floor. The cold fury in Maggie's eyes.

'Now,' she said, 'I'd say it's in your best interests if everyone puts the guns down.'

Rook shook his head. 'You'd burn with us. You won't drop that lighter.'

'Try me.' Her voice was hard and dangerous and absolute.

For the first time in years, Rook's heart had started to race. Because as he looked at this girl, he knew that there was no way to predict what she might do. Anything was possible. In all his years, he had been up against plenty of enemies whom he could anticipate or reason with, enemies who wanted the obvious and whose want could be used against them. But that wasn't the case here.

Rook gave a nod. The guns went down.

'Now,' Maggie said. 'You're going to send the women out of here. And the bartenders.'

'The prospects too.'

'No. They signed up for it.'

The fire danced from the lighter. Rook wondered if he could reach it. But the risk was too great.

'Send them out,' he said.

A rush for the door. He saw Ryan heading for it and nodded to Byrne, who caught the young bloke by the arm and pulled him back. The door swung shut as the last girl left. The bar was now maybe half as full as it had been. Even in the low light, Rook had a clear sightline to the petrol can over near the door, to the puddle spreading from it. She must have punctured the bottom then let the moving feet of the party do the rest, spreading it across the bar, the smell building by the second but nobody noticing because it was too commonplace for them. She must have slipped in and placed it while everyone drank and talked and paid her absolutely no attention.

'What now?' Rook said.

Maggie stood. A series of flinches, of hands twitching towards guns.

'Now, ' she said. 'I'm going to leave. And you're all going to stay put for ... let's say twenty minutes.'

'You can't stop us coming for you,' Byrne said.

'No.' Maggie nodded to Rook. 'But he can. And he should. If he's smart.'

Maggie went to turn.

'Wait,' Rook said.

She hadn't come in here just to hear confirmation of a name or of things she already knew.

'We can make a deal,' he said.

'I already made one.' Maggie took the phone from her pocket. 'Cooper's phone. Not only does it have this recorded conversation, but proof of Aaron's fake kidnapping. Proof that everything Cooper did was for his son. His legacy will be what it is, not what you make it.'

'We can give you money,' Rook said, 'help you disappear.'

'I've disappeared before.'

'Dean will still hunt you.'

Maggie smiled and walked towards the door. Bikies shrank back from the flickering lighter.

Rook stood. 'We'll come for you. You won't be able to hide. We have chapters everywhere. There won't be a single Scorpion who doesn't know your name. Maggie. *Think*. You don't want us as your enemies.'

Maggie paused. She looked back. 'Honestly, Rook, I'd say you've earned it.'

She pulled open the door and was gone.

Maggie's heart was racing, but not with fear. The girls and the staff were moving off in clumps, confused, wondering if they should stay or go. She closed the door then immediately turned and knelt. The trailing string lay where she'd left it, the end tied in a loop. She hooked it tightly over the door handle then stepped back.

Nobody had noticed what she was doing. Too caught up in the drinking and commiserating. But she had given

Rook a chance. More than he deserved, really, but then she knew he wouldn't take it. Which made what happened next entirely on him.

Even from out here she could smell the petrol. She backed away from the bar, into the dark. Her whole body pulsed with her heart.

She was ready.

Silence over the bar. Rook stared after her. His mind was moving fast, trying to work it out, trying to piece together what he should do next, what he *could* do next.

The girl was alone. Even if she had a gun, even if she managed to take one or two of the Scorpions down, there were too many of them. They could have her back in their clutches tonight, have the phone off her before it got to Dean.

All eyes were on him.

He nodded.

Byrne led the charge, rushing for the door, splashing through the petrol as the others ran after him. Rook went to follow.

He can. And he should. If he's smart. Rook stopped. Looked at the can of petrol. Then above it, to the high-set window, open slightly. To the small kerosene lamp placed there. To the string tied loosely around the base and trailing out the window.

To Byrne, grabbing the door handle.

'Wait!' Rook screamed.

Byrne pulled the door open.

The string tugged. The lamp tipped.

For a moment, one desperate moment, Rook hoped it would go out.

But that moment was all he had before it hit the petrol and shattered.

The room erupted. Screams as bikies were consumed by flames. The heat rushed up and then there were flames in his eyes and on his clothes. He saw the fire before he felt it, and then he felt it, and then pain, just pain, crashed into him like tidal waves, drowning out the screaming and the heat and everything.

He couldn't see his boys. He couldn't see anything but he ran. Shapes in the fire around him and still the pain, everything in his body protesting against the terrible evil being done to it, but even that shrank away in the face of having to be out, having to be away from the pain and the fire, having to be—

He smashed through the door and out into the night. He hit the ground and rolled, over and over. The fire was still on him and then it wasn't but the pain remained. Gasping, smelling his own burnt skin, he looked up across the concrete. Others were out here, bikies crying and writhing and, still, some burning. From inside the screams continued. On the air, sirens.

His vision pulsated. He managed to stand. The pain was slipping away but that wasn't good – he needed the pain, needed to feel it, needed to be alive to help his boys and get Maggie and ...

There she was. Standing in the light of the flames, watching him.

He moved for her but his vision swam and his muscles went loose. He hit the ground. The figure of the girl shimmered. He reached for her, tried to crawl.

Boots, then, stepping into his wavering vision. One of his boys, it had to be …

'She's right there,' he rasped. 'Get her, she's …'

The reply was ice through the heat. 'Nah. Nah, I don't think I will.'

He tried to look up. His body wasn't responding. He could see only rough shadows.

'Carlin.'

And then that face in his, thin and aged but alive with malice. The shadows arranged into a shape he held in Rook Gately's failing vision.

'Got myself a pretty little bundle of goodies here, Rooky. Problem is I dunno if you can be alive to see just how pretty they are.'

Rook swiped for the phone. A barrel in his face, gleaming silver.

Didn't matter. Carlin didn't matter, the phone didn't matter. It was the girl. He had to reach the girl, had to make her pay. He tried to move but the end of the barrel pressed hard into his forehead and he got one last glimpse of the burning bar but there was no-one there.

The girl was gone.

ACKNOWLEDGEMENTS

Some stories are easy to write. Others are *The Inheritance*.

I knew before I finished *The Hunted* that I wanted to continue Maggie's story. It was clear to me that there was so much still to discover about who she was and where she came from, what had shaped her into the force of nature we'd met in the previous book and what her path forward could possibly look like. Unfortunately, as exciting as those ideas were, the process of making a cogent story out of them proved the exact opposite of straightforward. The early pages of this book flowed with deceptive ease, but I quickly got lost in the reeds.

Luckily, I had the support of the brilliant Catherine Milne, who was kind enough to not only be honest about the book but also to help me find a path that worked, that naturally expanded on what I wanted to say and helped me learn far more about Maggie than I ever had before. I can't stress enough that writing a book is a deeply collaborative process: this book would never have worked without the help of a wonderful team who cared about Maggie as much as I did and wanted to make sure that the next story told about her was the right one. Once again, it was a pleasure to work with Scott Forbes and Samantha Sainsbury on the edit – the amount of times your notes made me slap myself on the head and wonder how I could possibly have missed what you were pointing out really does indicate how little authors know about anything. Julian Welch's careful proofreading ensured the discovery of many discrepancies that would have been highly embarrassing had they been left in the book. Tom Saras and Jordan Weaver-Keeney had big shoes to fill handling the campaign and publicity for this book, but said shoes proved a more than comfortable fit. The entire HarperCollins Australia team killed it; thank you all for having my back. Likewise to Angus Cargill and the team at Faber in the

UK: thank you for giving Maggie and myself another home and for getting behind a couple of books that must have looked like the biggest risks imaginable when they came across your desks.

To my agent Tara Wynne at Curtis Brown, thank you for being the best advocate I could ever ask for through this strange and wonderful journey we're on. Thanks to Caitlan Cooper-Trent for being one of the first people to see the potential in Maggie, and to Jerry Kalajian for making me look good to the major players of Los Angeles while always being able to quietly tell me when an idea I've brought to the table is outright dumb.

Throughout the development of this book *a lot* of people read it and gave feedback, at all different stages. And while in the interests of brevity I can't list every name, I hope you all know how immensely grateful I am for providing me with the perspectives needed to guide me towards a version of the story that worked. That said, there are a few key people that I have to include here. Jesse Farrell, whose hilarious notes pointed out some bad habits that I'd fallen into. Kate Murfett, with whom I have spent countless hours at our local bar agonising over Maggie and Jack's choices and directions. Tony Cavanaugh, who as usual identified some major shortcomings while providing me with the quote I wish we could have used on the cover: 'This book roars like a motherfucker.' Thank you all.

Thanks to my parents, Kim and Christian Bergmoser, and my brothers, Tristan and Mischa, for their willingness to bring me back down to earth while never being less than totally supportive. To the teams at Bitten By Productions and Melbourne Young Writers' Studios, my two creative homes, for your unyielding support and love. To Molly McPhie for all of the above and more – predominantly, patience.

I don't think there's any such thing as a smooth creative journey, and *The Inheritance* has been one of the rockiest ever. But in the end it has resulted in a book that I am so proud of. Thank you to all who helped make it possible. I owe you everything.